D0842564

CALGARY PUBLIC LIBRARY

NOV   2015

TRAFFICK

Also by Ellen Hopkins

TRAFFICK

Ellen Hopkins

Margaret K. McElderry Books
NEW YORK LONDON TORONTO SYDNEY NEW DELHI

MARGARET K. McELDERRY BOOKS • An imprint of Simon & Schuster Children's Publishing Division • 1230 Avenue of the Americas, New York, New York 10020 • This book is a work of fiction. Any references to historical events, real people, or real places are used fictitiously. Other names, characters, places, and events are products of the author's imagination, and any resemblance to actual events or places or persons, living or dead, is entirely coincidental. • Text copyright © 2015 by Ellen Hopkins • Jacket design and illustration copyright © 2015 by Sammy Yuen Jr. • All rights reserved, including the right of reproduction in whole or in part in any form. • Margaret K. McElderry Books is a trademark of Simon & Schuster, Inc. • For information about special discounts for bulk purchases, please contact Simon & Schuster Special Sales at 1-866-506-1949 or business@simonandschuster.com. • The Simon & Schuster Speakers Bureau can bring authors to your live event. For more information or to book an event, contact the Simon & Schuster Speakers Bureau at 1-866-248-3049 or visit our website at www.simonspeakers.com. • Book design by Mike Rosamilia • Book edited by Emma D. Dryden • The text for this book is set in Trade Gothic Condensed 18. • Manufactured in the United States of America • 1 2 3 4 5 6 7 8 9 10 • Library of Congress Cataloging-in-Publication Data • Hopkins, Ellen. • Traffick / Ellen Hopkins. • p. cm. • Sequel to: Tricks. • Summary: Five teenagers struggle to find their way out of prostitution. • ISBN 978-1-4424-8287-6 (hardback) • ISBN 978-1-4424-8289-0 (eBook) • [1. Novels in verse. 2. Prostitution—Fiction.] I. Title. • PZ7.5.H67Tp 2015 • [Fic]—dc23 • 2015000095

FIRST

EDITION

This book is dedicated to all those committed to helping victims of trafficking—child or adult, sex or labor—become survivors.

Acknowledgments

Special thanks to those who shared their stories with me, opening up so freely about painful situations. You've chosen to remain anonymous, and I've pledged to respect your privacy. Here's to your future as survivors. Walk forward proudly.

TRAFFICK

A Poem by Cody Bennett

Can't Find

The courage to leap
the brink, free-fall
beyond the precipice,
hurtle toward

                    the abyss,

end the pain. Mine.
Mom's. Oh, she'd feel
the initial sting, cry
for a day or two, but it

                    would be

short-lived, a quick
stab of grief. Finite.
A satin-lined coffin
and cool, deep hole are

                    preferable to

walking a treadmill
over a carpet of coals,
enduring the blistering,
skin-cracking flames of

                    this living hell.

Cody
Awake

A slow swim toward the light, breaking
the surface to crawl back onto the beach,
here in the land of the living. It seems

like a worthy goal. So why do I wish
I'd died instead? Should that be the first
thought to pop into my head?

I open my eyes. Snap them shut again.
I've been treading dark water for . . .
I have no idea how long. I test the light

again, and the fluorescent glare against
white walls makes me bury my head
in the pillow. Bleach stink assaults me

immediately, fights the antiseptic smell
that confirms I'm in a hospital. Hospital, yes.
That information sinks through the fog

licking inside my head, syncs with
the onslaught of noises. Monitors
beeping. Ventilators whooshing. And

somewhere, there's a game show on
TV. Tubes jut from my arms, and some
sort of brace wraps my midsection, limiting

movement, but I manage to swivel my head
toward the rhythmic snore marking time
very near my right elbow. Mom's dozing

on a gray plastic chair beside the bed.
Her voice floats from memory. *Come back
to me, Cody boy. Don't you dare leave me too.*

And I remember her hands, oh God,
soft as rose petals, and fragranced
the same way, as she stroked my face

over and over, urging, *Please, son.
We'll make it through this. We always
make it through. But I can't do it alone.*

I want to help her make it through.
I want to go back to sleep. Except
I've finally accomplished what she's been

waiting for—resurrection. "Mo-mom?"
I have to force the word through
a thick soup of phlegm and it exits

my mouth a hoarse whisper. She doesn't
stir until I clear my throat. *Cody . . . ,*
she mumbles, and her eyes stutter open

to find my own staring at her. *Cody?
Are you really here?* She jerks upright.
Oh my God! She jumps to her feet,

rushes bedside, and grabs my hand.
Too hard. A wicked buzz, like a static
shock, zaps the base of my skull.

A Low Moan

Almost a growl, leaks from my lips.
Mom drops my hand like she's the one
getting shocked, backs away like maybe

> I'm contagious. *I'm sorry. I'm sorry.*
> *Did I hurt you? Hold on. I'll get*
> *a nurse.* She pounds the call button.

"It's okay. I'm okay." Except I'm not
sure I am. A shimmer of pain, muted
but present, radiates from my neck.

It spreads across my shoulders,
down into my chest, swelling to fill
the space defined by my rib cage,

finally settling in my belly. It stops
there, having traveled pretty much
everywhere. Everywhere, except . . .

Anywhere below my waist. Weird.
What the hell? I see Mom watching,
assessing me in some alien way.

With great effort, I reach down,
poke my right leg. Nothing. Left?
Numb. "What's wrong with me, Mom?"

My voice slurs. My brain is slow.
I'm drugged, yeah, that's it. A phrase
comes to mind: morphine cocktail.

I'll have another, please, bartender.
That cracks me up, and I laugh like
a madman. Mom looks terrified.

"Don't worry, Mom. I'm just loaded,
you know? They gave me some pretty
good drugs." She nods agreement, but

   her expression argues there's more.
   Where's that nurse? I'll be right back.
   She hustles off, calling for someone

to come right away. Wonder how long
I've been here, hooked up to these
machines. A day? Two? A week?

Logic argues it's probably been
a few days at least, or Mom wouldn't
have been so worried that I wasn't going

to wake up again. And now, duh, it hits
me that must be a big part of the reason
my legs feel so weird. They're still asleep.

Try, try again. I pinch my right thigh.
Hard. Pinch my left thigh. Harder.
Zip. Nada. Man, this is excellent dope.

Bet old Vince would go for this shit.
Vince. Wait. There's something about Vince.
I need to remember. I close my eyes. . . .

Tumble Backward

in time to . . .
Vince's apartment.
A poker game.

I remember that and . . .
winning for once.
Did I win?

Yeah, that's right.
Six hundred . . . no,
six hundred and fifty bucks.

Played it smart.
Left the table still ahead,
like smart gamblers do.

Ronnie.
Oh, Ronnie, Jesus,
I'm sorry. I never meant

to hurt you.
That day, after work
(work?), I was going

to see Ronnie.
She wasn't mad.
I thought she'd be mad.

Quick stop at the bank.
Deposited the cash,
half in my account,

half in Mom's
before . . . my date?
I dated Ronnie.

It wasn't a date,
it was a three-way meet.
Oh shit, no. Misty . . .

The thought of her
makes me sad.
Sad? Why? Misty.

Sweet Jesus.
Ambulances. Stretchers.
Misty, but where is her face?

Under the sheet.
Dead.
Misty is dead.

Before that, what?
Misty in bed
with some squeaky guy

       with a teeny dick
       telling me to hurry.
       Time is money.

Time.
Tick.
Bam.

Noise at my back.
Splintering wood.
A fist against my kidneys.

Down I went.
Crack-crack-crack.
The report of a gun.

Small. Sharp. Deadly.
You fucking whore.
You promised no more.

Chris. Misty's boyfriend.
But she didn't answer.
And you . . .

Addressed to me,
right before
his boots found my ribs.

Boom. Boom.
He took out two
just like that.

And then, *snap!*
Electric. Brilliant
sizzling white heat.

A shattering
splintering of bone
in my back.

My back.
I felt it go.
He shot me in the spine.

Chris.
Shot.
Me.

He was at Vince's.
I taunted him.
He was crazy mean

and I knew that.
Why take chances?
My fault.

My fault Misty is dead.
My fault I'm lying here.
My fault that I can't feel . . .

No! Screw that!
I'm okay. I'm fine.
Just a little numb.

I'm just fucked up.
It's the killer dope.
Killer . . .

Spontaneously

Tears spill from my eyes, track
my face. Spontaneously, one word
falls from my mouth, in quick

repetition. "No. No. No. No. No."
I'm still babbling when Mom
returns with a nurse the approximate

> size of a large gorilla. *Take it easy,*
> she soothes. *I've sent for Dr. Harrison.*
> *She'll be here as soon as she can.*
>
> *I'm sure you have questions and*
> *she can answer them better than I.*
> *Meanwhile, how's the pain?*

I dissolve into hysterical laughter.
Both Mom and Nurse Gorilla look
ready to flee. "Can't feel a thing. Hey . . ."

I reach down to the approximate level
of my pecker. "Am I wearing a diaper
or what? How am I pissing?"

I pat, pat, pat. "Nope. No diaper. Do
I still have a dick? 'Cause I for sure
can't feel it if I do." Jesus. H. Christ.

> Laughter segues to sobs. Mom shifts
> into Mommy mode, rushes to my side.
> *It's going to be okay, Cody. I promise.*

She starts to reach for me. Remembers
what happened last time, withdraws
her hands. Her soft, rose-petal hands.

> Nursilla steers Mom back into the chair,
> and when she moves closer, her badge
> tells me her name is Barbara. *Listen.*
>
> *You have experienced major trauma.*
> *Do you remember what happened?*
> At my nod, she continues. *I'd prefer*
>
> *Dr. Harrison explain in more depth,*
> *but I can tell you that you have a spinal*
> *cord injury. The good news is it's in*
>
> *your lower thoracic region, which*
> *is why you've got the use of your upper*
> *extremities and can breathe on your own.*

Barbara lets that sink in. Spinal cord
injury. Lower thoracic region.
I have no clue what any of that means.

But, hey, I can breathe on my own,
and should that become difficult
I can still use my hands to pick my nose.

That's the Good News

I'm about to ask what the bad news
is when two people bustle into
the room. The nurse introduces us.

Dr. Harrison, apparently my neurosurgeon,
is a tall, pretty woman, with toffee-colored
skin and striking blue-green eyes

that seem determined to look anywhere
but straight at me. Not a good sign.
The dude, who's Hispanic, stands a good four

> inches shorter, but man, is he buff.
> *Federico will oversee your PT,* explains
> Barbara. When I look confused,

> Federico clarifies, *That's physical
> therapy.* He extends a hand. *Awesome
> to meet you, Cody. We've got work to do.*

PT. Also not good. I shake his hand
anyway, wait to hear the information
I need, but am absolutely sure I don't

> want to know. Dr. Harrison delivers
> it. *I must be perfectly honest with you.
> Your life has been irreparably altered.*

Great bedside manner, Doc. I swallow
hard. "What do you mean? I'm not
going to get better or what?"

*You will improve some as your body
heals, and we're not even sure
what the ultimate prognosis is.*

*We'll need to do some tests, now that
you're conscious. What I can tell you
is the most improvement you'll see*

*will be within the first six months.
That said, there are lots of promising
new treatments for spinal cord injury.*

*And SCI researchers are very close
to tremendous breakthroughs, for
quadriplegics as well as para—*

"Are you saying I'm paralyzed?"
No, goddamn it! It's just the drugs.
I can move, and I'll prove it. I try

as hard as I can, but no amount of
concentration makes my legs so much
as twitch. "No. You must be wrong."

*Finally, she looks directly into my eyes.
We can't tiptoe around the truth here,
Cody. Your spinal cord has been severed.*

*It's incomplete, so some function may
return. As I said, we'll have to run
more tests. But first, let me explain.*

Thirty Minutes Later

I know a lot more. Hell, I'm
a walking, talking SCI textbook.
Let's see. The spinal cord is a soft

bundle of nerves, traveling from
the base of the neck to the lower
back through the spinal canal—

a tunnel in a person's backbone.
Electrical signals ping from
the brain down that pathway,

reminding body parts how
to move, or telling them to feel
pain or pleasure or whatever.

But sever the cord, or even nick
it, the communication stops
beneath the site of the injury.

Now let's get technical. She sure
as hell did. The spine has thirty-three
vertebrae, divided into regions:

cervical (neck); thoracic (upper and
middle back); lumbar (lower back);
sacrum (pelvis); and coccyx (tailbone).

There are twelve thoracic vertebrae.
The bullet struck my lower spine,
sending bone chips on an upward

trajectory. One or more dinged
my spinal cord between T(horacic)11
and T12, but didn't cut through it

completely. Still, it silenced the flow
of energy between my brain and
the body parts beneath my middle back.

Oh, but wait. This is where it really
gets good. Not only are my legs
confused, but so are my bladder

and bowel. Far fucking out. I'll be
able to piss and shit with the aid
of "specialized equipment."

Meaning, (one) stick a tube in the end
of my penis several times a day.
And, (two) . . . well, that is just too

disgusting to think about right now.
So, yeah, once I get out of this hole,
where they've got waaaaay underpaid

orderlies to drain my dick and
massage my anus, it's giant Pampers
for me until I learn how to make

myself take a dump. Make. Myself.
Crap. I know I'm guilty of awful sins.
But do I really deserve this kind of hell?

The More

The good doctor talks, the more
I just want to fold up and die.
But since that won't happen

right away, there's something
she hasn't told me. I need to know.
"Will I ever walk again?"

>   *It's really too early to say. You might*
>   *be able to, aided by leg braces,*
>   *though you won't be running marathons.*
>
>   *It depends on how much feeling,*
>   *if any, returns. Meanwhile, your*
>   *wheelchair will be your best friend.*

Wheelchair. The word slams
into my gut like a brick. I will be
confined to a wheelchair, at the mercy

of a caregiver? Someone to tell me
where to go, when to go, if I can go?
"What about driving? Can I do that?"

>   *Absolutely, with a specially equipped*
>   *vehicle.* She smiles. *That's usually*
>   *the question I get* after *"What about sex?"*

Holy shit.

A Poem by Ginger Cordell

Will I Walk

Away from here, this dirty
city, where people come
in search of Lady Luck,
certain she'll guide them to
the fortune she owes them,

or

to shed their skins, reveal
the extraordinary creatures
beneath, aliens they struggle
to conceal from spouses,
ministers, their local PTA.

Will

I walk away from her?
My best friend turned lover
before our tumble from
enlightenment, if such a thing
ever belonged to me. Can

I

excise her from my heart
as easily as she deserted me?
If I opened my arms, begged
her to return, would she come
back, or would she turn and

run?

Ginger
How Can I Leave

Here without her—Alex, my sweet
Alex. At least, she was sweet until
Las Vegas claimed her, made her
its bitch. This city is a pimp, selling

fantasies. For a time, Alex and I
were a fantasy duet, working for
Have Ur Cake Escort Service,
despite being a couple of years

underage. "Eighteen" isn't necessary
to participate in a business that
props up the underbelly of Vegas.
It was not what I had in mind when

I ran away, but then again, I had no
plan, and sometimes it comes down
to survival. We survived, stripping
for pay in hotel rooms, mostly

working bachelor parties, two for
the price of one. I insisted on that,
refused to do more than take off
my clothes and dance. But Alex

couldn't care less about spreading
her legs and accepting foreign objects,
as long as the dudes were willing
to pay the going rate. Then she got

greedy, started working the streets
so she wouldn't have to kick back
Lydia's commission. I found her out
there, soliciting some guy wearing

ugly purple Bermuda shorts. That
pissed me off, but in hindsight,
looking for revenge by offering to let
him buy all he could eat, double-decker,

wasn't the smartest move. Turned
out, he was a cop on a trash run, prowling
for teen hookers. Vegas has issued
stern orders: get 'em off the sidewalks,

> bust their pimps and even their johns.
> Detective Bermuda Shorts was only
> doing his job. *Tell me who's sending
> you out, the court will go easy on you.*

Alex and I didn't roll on Lydia
or Have Ur Cake. Luckily, Judge
Kerry was sympathetic anyway,
an honest-to-goodness do-gooder.

> *Nevada considers trafficking
> children a serious offense.
> This is not a victimless crime,
> and you, young lady, are a victim.*

Nothing He Said

Made sense. How can a willing
participant be a victim? No one
tied us up at the end of the day
(although a few of our customers

offered). And we weren't trafficked,
as far as I knew then. No one kidnapped
us and smuggled us to the foreign
country of Las Vegas. Now, thanks

to my recent interaction with law
enforcement, the courts, and social
workers, I understand that three
things define trafficking: coercing

someone to turn tricks, transporting
them for that purpose, or in any
way threatening or encouraging
an underage person to sell their body.

Oh, and how good ol' Iris collected
money for allowing men to force
themselves on me? Uh, yeah. That,
too. Then, there's Have Ur Cake.

Since Alex and I haven't reached
the age of eighteen—that magic
birthday that supposedly makes
you an adult—Lydia was definitely

guilty of pandering minors for sex.
She arranged our "dates," and
collected a hefty fee for her trouble,
so technically she was our pimp,

though we asked for the work.
She never had to twist our arms.
But she totally knew how old
we were, and that we'd run away

with a minimal bankroll. Plus,
she did, in fact, put us in her debt
by letting us stay with her when
we first arrived in Vegas. When I

appeared before Judge Kerry, though,
I didn't understand all that. "I don't see
myself as a victim, Your Honor. I was just
trying to make enough money to survive."

> He looked at me with such sadness
> in his eyes. *I understand survival,*
> *but this is not a good way to earn*
> *money if you truly want to survive.*

I Guess I Was Lucky

I don't really know
what all Alex faced
when she did outcalls
solo. She refused to talk

to me about it. I only
did a few gigs alone,
and I never exactly felt
threatened. Together,

there were a few times
when I thought a client
might hurt us, and one guy
forced Alex to jerk him off.

More than once, we got
stiffed for payment, and
then we owed Lydia
anyway. She never really

bullied us. Convinced
is more accurate. She had
a way of doing that, although
she never could talk me into

stuffing condoms into my bag
and earning a hell of a lot more
money. I'm a dancer. A stripper.
But I'll never be a whore.

Now My Stripping Days

Are over, at least that's what Judge
Kerry said. After my advocate
determined Gram does want me
back in Barstow, they sent me

to stay in a group home until
Gram can arrange to come pick
me up. The law says I can only
be released to a "custodial adult."

Hey, at least I have one of those,
unlike Alex, who ended up in
a different group home—one that
accepts pregnant teens. Pregnant.

If she got that way, it means
she wasn't using protection, and
God forbid she picked up anything
else besides sperm. The father?

Some anonymous trick, and who
knows what color the baby will
be, or what defects it might inherit
from its paternal side? So sad.

Then again, everything about Alex
makes me sad—her childhood;
the things she's allowed herself to do;
the fact I might never see her again.

Our Goodbye Was Bittersweet

Bitter, because it *was* goodbye.
Sweet, because it meant she was
safely off the streets. I spent many
hours pacing our apartment,

pining for closeness and a return
to sweet adventures in bed,
wondering when she'd come home.
If she'd come home. She always

did eventually, but every time
another little piece of the Alex
I loved was missing. Tricking chews
you up from the inside out.

We had a few minutes together
while waiting to see the judge.
"Gram says she welcomes me
back, believe it or not."

> *I believe it. The one thing about*
> *you I've always been jealous of is*
> *how much your grandma loves you.*
> *No one's ever loved me like that.*

"What about me? I still love you,
Alex, don't want to live without
you. Please come with me. I'm
sure Gram will let you live—"

> No. Are you kidding me?
> She's got six kids to take care
> of, plus your mom. You expect
> her to add me and a baby?

"We can work out something.
Get jobs, our own place. I can
still help Gram with the kids,
and . . ." It sounded ridiculous.

> Aw, Gin. I want you to go back
> to school, get your diploma,
> head off to college. You can
> legit make it in the real world,

> and do it all on your own. You
> don't need me holding you back.
> She reached out, put one hand
> on my cheek. I directed it to my lips,

kissed each finger. "I don't know
what I'll do without you, and I'm
scared for you and the baby."
Her hand fell away, never there.

> Don't worry about us. We'll be
> just fine. Besides . . . She forced
> her voice cold. *I've been thinking
> and I've decided I prefer men after all.*

She Divorced Me

And though her remark was meant
to slice into me, sever the tie between
our hearts, I understand why she said
it so matter-of-factly. I don't believe

it, and the hurt she attempted hit
its mark square. I still have my cell,
and I've texted her dozens of times
in the two months I've been here

at House of Hope, where I'll stay
until Gram can get the guardianship
paperwork in order, take a day off,
plus find babysitting for the kids

and Iris, who is too sick to care for
herself, let alone her offspring.
Wonder if she'll let us call her "Mom"
now that men won't be coming around

and aging is the least of her worries.
She spent her youth on a slow death,
creeping closer for years, though
she was clueless until recently, when

a flu bug wouldn't go away. Tests revealed
advanced HIV-inspired lymphoma.
With her immune system compromised,
there will be no cure for her cancer.

House of Hope

Is a corny name, and I'm not sure
how much hope is actually here.
It's nice enough, and the food is good,
and the staff pretends like they care.

There are other sex workers here,
some younger than me, who happens
to be something of an anomaly because
my skin is white. The population is

largely divided by race, at least as far
as room assignments go. Hispanics and
black girls don't get along very well.
Their 'hoods are separate, and they stay

that way beyond those boundaries.
My roommate, Miranda, is Latina,
and pretty, though her plump face
makes her look younger than she is.

She says she'll be fourteen in two
weeks. She's thirteen, going on thirty.
Miranda was suspicious of me at
first, but after I told her my own

sob story, she decided to open up.
Right now, we're sitting on the lawn,
enjoying the mellow November sunshine.
After the god-awful heat of the past

few months, this feels like heaven.
The tale of horror Miranda's sharing
right now, however, is totally hellish,
and I have no doubt it's true.

> *My brother Ricardo runs dope*
> *for Los Sureños. He uses also,*
> *and too much on credit. He owed*
> *Papacito a lot of money.*

"Papacito," I interrupt. "That means
Daddy, yeah?" Lots of pimps insist
their stables refer to them as Daddy,
as if a father would sell them the same

> way. Truth is, I guess, some fathers
> do. *Sí,* she answers. *I don't know any*
> *other name, only he makes all the girls*
> *call him Papacito. One day after school,*

> *I'm talking with friends and a big car*
> *pulls up. Ricardo is inside with Papacito.*
> *He tells me to get in. I say goodbye*
> *to mis amigas, and we drive out of*

> *my 'hood, away from El Monte. I've never*
> *been so far from home. When we stop,*
> *I don't know where, Ricardo gets out.*
> *"Do what he says and you'll be safe."*

He closed the door, and I never see
my brother again, and not Mamá,
either. Papacito, he drive me all
the way to Las Vegas before we stop.

When we get here, he drives down
the strip. I never saw nothing like this
before. "Isn't it beautiful?" he asks.
"I know all the best places to show you."

He takes me to a house. It's nice
on the outside. Nice on the inside.
Except, what happens there is not
so nice. There are other girls, too.

This one, Belinda, she said she'd be
mi mamá now, she'll take good care
of me—buy me pretty clothes, teach me
makeup. Make me even prettier.

I say, "Mi mamá está en El Monte."
Papacito grab my arm and squeeze
real hard. "Your mamá, she doesn't
want you no more, so Ricardo give

you to me." I thought about that.
Mamá and I had a fight because
I told her about her man, how
he came into my room when

she wasn't home. How he touched
me. She said I was a liar. A puta.
But I didn't lie. . . . Her eyes water,
and it's the first time since I've been

here that I've seen real emotion in
the girl. "I believe you. It happened
to me, too." I don't add the part about
my own mother pimping me out.

Miranda nods. *It happens to many*
of us. Men are coyotes. I was eleven
the first time. Twelve when Ricardo
traded me for his debt. I found that

out later. But that day, I believed
it was Mamá's punishment. "But when
can I go home?" *I asked. Papacito*
tell me never, I'm his now. "Do exactly

as I say," he said, "and Belinda, too,
or I will hurt you so bad you'll wish
you were dead. But if you are a very
good girl, I will be your boyfriend.

¿Quieres un novio, no? Someone
who'll love you forever?" Every girl
wants a boyfriend, and I had no place
to go. The other girls seemed happy, so . . .

It isn't a unique story, but it *is* hers.
I think of my sister, Mary Ann, who's
about the same age, and pray it will
never happen to her. "Weren't you scared?"

She nods. *But not so scared then*
as later that night, when Papacito
come to my bedroom. "Such a pretty
little girl," he said. "Now I will make

you my woman." I knew what he meant
and tried to say no. He slapped my face
so hard I thought my head would snap off!
Then he grabbed my neck and squeezed.

I couldn't breathe. I begged him to stop
but he choked me until I almost blacked
out. I wore the marks from his fingers
for many days. I had no fight left then,

and he threw me on the bed, made me
his wife for real. When he finished,
he sent five friends to break me in
better. After that, what did it matter?

What came next, she says, is he pimped
her online or sent her out to work
truck stops, demanding a minimum
$800 per night. He kept every penny.

He Used Her

For almost two years, until a national
trafficking sting operation took
Papacito down good. Pandering
children under fourteen carries a life

sentence, if they can convict him,
which means they want Miranda
to testify against him, something
she's more than a little nervous about.

Men like that have a very long reach,
and his ties to Los Sureños make him
dangerous, even in prison. Miranda's
advocate has convinced her to do it, but

what will happen after that is anyone's
guess. Her mother's boyfriend says
she can't go back to El Monte. So, yeah,
I really am lucky. The court has freed

me, forgiven me, allowed me to go home.
Gram says her house will always be
my home, and she wants me there, safe
and sound. I guess, despite everything,

I'm mostly sound. But I wasn't safe
before, and I'm not sure there is such
a thing. All I know is, I'm happy to leave
Vegas. This city annihilates souls.

A Poem by Seth Parnell

My Soul

Has taken a vacation,
hitched a ride
somewhere cool and clean.
Maybe the mountains.

I

haven't seen it in months.
Perhaps it's deserted
me permanently.
I should feel bad, but I

can't

muster sympathy
for the boy-become-man
who is me. Man. Gay
man. Kept man. You'll

find

the ultimate meaning
of that term
in the eyes of every boy
forced by circumstance to

sacrifice

the truth of himself.
I keep digging
for truth
but can't seem to find it

in me.

Seth
I Swore

I'd never get used to living like this,
at the beck and call, and under almost

total control of another human being.
I say almost, because after Carl, my ex

sugar daddy when I moved in here
with David, I knew enough to find a way

to stash some cash in case I ever need
an escape plan. Carl, who brought me

with him from Louisville, a trophy
houseboy to decorate his Lake Las Vegas

luxury condo, allowed me no chance at
personal resources. He wanted ownership.

Slavery is alive and thriving in Sin City,
Nevada. Maybe that's why I gambled

on connecting with hot-stranger-in-the-gym
Jared—the growing need for rebellion,

or at least a taste of autonomy. Or maybe
it was simply because I'm only eighteen,

and still stashed inside is the belief
that love waits for me somewhere.

The Truth, However

If I'm to be perfectly honest with myself,
is that my attraction to Jared was totally

fed by lust. Well, lust and loneliness.
Carl may have provided well for me, but

he wasn't much for companionship.
Working out, lying by the pool, and

improving my culinary skills didn't exactly
tally satisfaction. Even the sex with Carl

(and sometimes an added friend of his)
didn't add much spice to our relationship.

So, yeah, I was pretty damn hungry when
Jared showed up in the gym, and that man

was something to look at. Ripped, not
an ounce of flab, and the chiseled face

of a god. I never suspected he was a ringer.
Carl baited the hook, and I bit. Hard.

When he reeled me in, I felt about like a trout
who knew that fly hadn't looked quite right,

but just couldn't help himself. And then,
Carl gutted me, threw me into the frying pan.

He Picked the Bones Clean

Disowned me completely, gave me
twenty-four hours to vacate his life,

not even a few dollars to help me
accomplish that goal. Luckily, I had

made a couple of friends online and
was able to convince one of them to pick

me up. Lake Las Vegas is quite a distance
from downtown, and the Mojave summer

temps are killer, sometimes literally.
I was ride-less. Homeless. Totally broke.

I did manage to stuff some very nice clothes
into a duffel bag. I figured I'd be the most

suave street person ever. But Jacques
was cool. He invited me to stay at his place

for a couple of days until I could find a more
suitable habitation, not that he didn't expect

a little *something* in return. I was happy
enough to oblige. Exchanging blowjobs

for room and board was nothing new.
There was one slight problem with that—

Jacques had a boyfriend. But I crossed
my heart that Morris would never find out.

As Far as I Know

He never has, which I'm happy about.
I like Morris. He's quirky and gentle,

and happens to be one of David's dancers.
In fact, it was Morris who introduced us

at one of David's infamous parties. My first,
but definitely not my last. It was a week after

I moved in with Jacques. Maybe Morris
felt a little threatened, and hoped I'd stumble

upon a different circumstance. I doubt
he expected what happened. It was late

      when he showed up at Jacques's. *Hey, boys.*
      There's a party at David's. Wanna go?

I had nothing better to do, and Jacques
goes along with anything Morris suggests,

especially when it's partying. "It's after
midnight. You sure it's still going on?"

      Don't you know this city never sleeps,
      especially not on a Saturday night?

      But even if it did, the crowd at David's
      wouldn't. Staying up all night is a hobby.

I Was Stunned

When we turned into the driveway
of David's amazing home in the Ridges,

a glitzy neighborhood, even by Vegas
standards. All lit up for the evening shebang,

the house looked like a five-star hotel.
Morris pulled his Prius right up in front,

where a hired valet took the keys. "You've got
to be kidding," I said, as I followed Morris

and Jacques up the marble stairs to the front
door. "How many people live here?"

> Morris laughed. *Officially, just David,*
> *although he keeps a steady supply of guests,*
>
> *plus a rather large staff. This place has,*
> *like, ten bedrooms or something. It takes*
>
> *three housekeepers just to keep it dusted*
> *and vacuumed. One day, Jacques darling . . .*

That house swarmed with men. Women.
Undetermined. Gay. Straight. Unspecified.

Everyone drinking. Everyone eating.
Everyone smoking. Snorting. Popping pills.

It was Sodom and Gomorrah under
a single roof. I was awed. Awkward.

Nervous. Bemused. Out of my element.
And also totally psyched to explore.

We maneuvered our way through
the house and out into the huge backyard.

Even at that time of the night, the air
was hot and still, and the Olympic-size

pool overflowed an assortment of noisy
guests, most of whom wore only their skin.

I trailed the boys to the bar, and no one
asked for ID when I ordered a mint julep.

I drew away from the tangle, to the edge
of the pavers, and lifted my glass. "Fond

memories, Carl," I whispered toward
the starlit sky. When I returned my focus

to the party, I noticed Morris and Jacques
had knotted into a small group listening

diligently to a compact man on the far
side of sixty, but decent-looking nonetheless.

Morris caught my eye, waved for me
to come join them. First, I took a big

swig of my mint julep, loving the burn
of exceptional bourbon. "Fuck you, Carl,"

I said out loud, before wandering over
to meet up with my friends. As I neared,

> the group's attention turned toward
> me. *Who's this?* asked David, although

I didn't know that's who he was until
Morris made the introduction that altered

> my life yet again. *Seth,* repeated David.
> *Wonderful name. Are you a dancer?*

"Not unless you count two-step, in
which case, I'm a hell of a dancer."

Everyone laughed, including David, but
his eyes were serious as they regarded

> me, his interest quite obviously piqued.
> *Well then, not a dancer. What do you do?*

I met his gaze square. "I am a top-flight
personal assistant. Currently unemployed."

The Crowd Began to Thin

As the earliest hours of morning
trickled toward dawn. David and I

hardly noticed, except the queue for
the bar grew shorter and shorter

and his personal entourage shrank
smaller and smaller. A few people

offered cocaine. At first I refused, but
David indulged and finally convinced

me to try it. *Oh, but you should. It
makes every bad thing better, and*

*everything good the experience of
a lifetime.* He winked. *Especially sex.*

I wasn't attracted to David, not in
the classic sense. But I was hypnotized

by the power of his wealth, and I knew
if I played the game intelligently the reward

could be well worth the effort. One snort
of what David said was damn fine coke,

I shed worry like rainwater. Two, conversing
came easier. Three, and the world righted itself.

At Some Point

Morris and Jacques wanted to leave.
I wasn't ready, but had no other ride.

> I must have looked anxious because
> David volunteered, *You two go on home.*
>
> *I'll take good care of Seth and my driver*
> *can drop him off when he's ready to go.*

The boys wandered off somewhere
close to two thirty. I can't say exactly

when because I was way too busy
mellowing the coke buzz with bourbon

and, conversely, fighting the alcohol
sluggishness with yet another line.

It's a great combination, one I've since
enjoyed fairly regularly, though David

doesn't keep a stash here at the house.
Most of it comes in with his guests.

That night we talked well into the morning
hours. Turns out, David was born in

Illinois, so we had neighboring home
states in common. I knew he was angling

for sex, of course. David doesn't try
to hide his attraction to pretty young men.

When he discovered I was still a teen,
though technically legal, he was intrigued

>   immediately. *So what's your story?*
>   *How did you get to Las Vegas from*
>
>   *Indiana? I take it you're on your own.*
>   *Do you still have a family back home?*

Without the cocaine stoking my mouth,
I would never have told him as much

as I did. "My mom died a long time ago,
but my dad still lives on the farm. When

I came out, he gave me twenty dollars
and told me to hit the road and stay gone

until I decided I wasn't gay. My boyfriend
was studying at the Louisville Seminary,

and I figured we'd just move in together.
But when I got to Loren's apartment, he told

me he was moving to New York to do
a field study with a congregation there.

> *Ah. And you weren't invited to go along.*
> *Queer rule number nine: avoid falling*
>
> *in love with members of the clergy.*
> *Even the best boyfriend can't trump God.*

"A very good rule. But what are numbers
one through eight? And is there a ten?"

> He smiled. *Maybe I'll fill you in one*
> *day. But you haven't finished your story.*

I didn't especially want to confide disgusting
details about Carl, so I gave an abbreviated

version. "I met an older guy in a club
and we hit it off. He was moving to Vegas,

asked me to come with him. When we broke
up last week, I had nowhere to go, so Jacques

let me move in with him temporarily. I need
a new living arrangement. If you have any

ideas . . ." At that point I was high enough
to be reckless. I looked him straight in the eye,

traced my upper lip with my tongue.
Needless to say, he didn't summon his driver.

I Wanted the Sex to Convince Him

To let me move in, so I offered anything
he wanted. Compared to Carl, who was all

about the kink, David's requests weren't
extraordinary. The thing is, he can have

whatever he wants with any of the cute
dancers in his stable who might be looking

to advance his career. But David doesn't want
easy sex, he wants affection. Okay, he wants

love, which isn't something I can give him,
though I profess to. I doubt it's possible

for someone my age to fall in love with
a man old enough to be his grandfather,

no matter how good that person is to him.
I want to experience real love again,

wrapped around sex and infusing lust
with meaning. But that won't happen here,

won't happen today, and I don't dare go
searching for it elsewhere right now.

It's enough that I can barter my body for
a lifestyle most people only dream of.

La Dolce Vita

That's what I'm living here with David—
the sweet life, and I can't discount that.

But neither can I count on it to last, as that
asshole Carl so aptly proved. So I'm bartering

my body on the side, via Have Ur Cake
Escorts. People travel to Vegas specifically

to create memories to leave here, and I'll stay
in Vegas with them. When Lydia interviewed

me, I was clear about the parameters—only
clients willing to pay premium rates for a top-

of-the-line barely adult. I won't risk losing
life with David for anything less than a grand—

five hundred in exchange for my company,
another five for invading it, condoms required.

Sometimes couples want three-ways, and that
costs a third more. For fifteen hundred,

I'll get it up for a woman, too. With limited
hours available plus a relatively high price

tag, I've had five dates, plenty to open a bank
account. That should multiply quickly.

I'm on My Way

To an outcall now, meeting the guy
at Picasso, one of the Bellagio's finest

restaurants. David's in L.A. for a couple
of days, so I don't have to fabricate

an excuse. I expect my client to be
older, but when the maître d' brings

me over to the table, the decent-looking
man who stands is in his early thirties.

> *I'm Joe,* he says, and that may or
> may not be the truth. *Thanks for*

> *joining me. Would you like a drink?*
> he asks, knowing I'm underage,

not that it matters. Carding is rare
in these situations, and should a waiter

get too nosy, I have a forged ID. I request
my favored mint julep, and Joe springs

for the prix fixe dinner. Four Five-Diamond-
Award courses, accompanied by wine.

I sit, staring at actual Picasso paintings,
while Joe tells me about himself.

I can't imagine he's lying. The details
are too specific. He's an art dealer, in

Vegas on business. His wife, three kids,
and two golden retrievers wait at home.

> You must be wondering why a married man
> would arrange to meet someone like you.

I shrug. "Everyone has fantasies or fetishes,
but few are brave enough to act on them."

> When I was a kid at summer camp,
> there was this teenage counselor, Rob.
>
> He wasn't exceptional, really. Still, I
> used to daydream about him holding me.
>
> Touching me. Using me. The first time
> I masturbated, I pretended it was Rob
>
> jerking me off. It's strange, because I'm
> really not gay. I love my wife, and having
>
> sex with her. But once in a while, this need
> rises up, and I want Rob to jerk me off.

After dessert, we go upstairs—Joe and Rob,
who does a whole lot more than jerk Joe off.

A Poem by Whitney Lang
Need Rises Up

From a bottomless well
of longing,
a whining so insistent

no

amount of willpower
can force
it silent. They say the

way

to be strong
when confronted with
the siren's song is

to shutter

your ears,
fight the darkness, reach
for the light, but

the windows

are draped
with memories
of ecstasy.

Whitney
A Chat

With the Grim Reaper
should be enough to scare
away any thought of relapse.
Wish it were that easy,
but not even days conversing
with death can disintegrate
the claws of addiction.

My memory banks
are foggy, misted by months
held fast in the arms of the Lady,
squeezed by need
you can't describe, can't relate
to unless you've experienced it.

I barely remember that last fix,
Mexican black tar instead
of my usual China white.
The Lady, she took me on
one hell of a ride
before we dove over the cliff,
falling, falling, falling.
Falling in slow motion.

Overdosing on Heroin

Is ugly business.
Well, the initial rush
is truly incredible. Similar,
I imagine, to a military jet taking
off, throwing you back in your seat
as you climb, almost perpendicular
to the ground. Yeah, close to that.

But then, the noise, a hurricane
inside your head, blowing.
Pounding. Exploding.

You try to fight the bad wind,
and everything slows.
Your breathing.
Your heart.
Slow.
Slower.
You
    can't
       find
          air
             as
                you
                    drift
                       toward
                                darkness.

Withdrawing from Heroin

Is a whole lot worse.
When you OD, you have no idea
you're tumbling toward death.
When you withdraw,
you have no doubt about it.

It's like being underwater,
and really, really needing to breathe.
You swim as hard as you can,
but you're too deep
and it's taking too long,
you won't break the surface
in time. If you inhale,
you'll drown, but there's no oxygen
left and your body's on fire
and your lungs ache with trying.

Then, there's projectile puking
and green water squirts.
Your joints throb and there's no relief
for three days because you can't sleep
without help from the poppy.
It's all you can think about.
Just one more rig to kill
the pain and rescue you
from the black depression,
knowing you're helpless,
smashed flat into the ground
beneath the feet of the Lady.

Unbelievably

The person helping me weather
those first few days
was the very woman I blame
for chasing me away from home
and into the arms of the man
who would become my pimp.

> I expected my mom's scorn,
> not her apology. *Oh, Whitney.*
> *Thank God you've come back*
> *to me. I'm so sorry. If I had*
> *lost you forever, I don't know*
> *what I would have done. Please,*
> *Whitney, whatever your reasons*
> *for leaving, for . . . for . . .*

She couldn't finish, could
not bring herself to put into
words the things the cops
must've told her, the awful
things their evidence showed—
that I'd been turning tricks
in a stinking apartment
in a disgusting neighborhood
in America's filthiest city.

I still don't feel even close
to dirt-free five weeks later,
despite the pristine living conditions
here at Clean Slate, a five-star rehab.

As Rehabs Go

I doubt you could find a better
one, or one with a higher
maintenance fee. That's what
they do here—maintain our sobriety.

You get what you pay for, yes
you do, and as the Clean Slate
brochure describes this place:
The buildings are sleek modern,
with big, open rooms flooded
with natural light gleaming
against polished ceramic tile
and walls painted in rich earth
tones. Client bedrooms are all
private, with windows that open
to invite the Pacific breezes inside.

Right. For a quote-unquote
lockdown rehab, the shackles
and bars are mostly invisible.

Clean Slate *is* close to the beach
near Santa Cruz, which used to be
where I lived. Those Pacific
breezes smell like home, and
the perfectly manicured grounds
remind me, too often, that I'll go
back there once they decide
I'm capable of reentering
mainstream teenager-hood.

My Day

Consists of group and
individual therapy.
Schoolwork to catch me
up to where I was when
I nose-dived into the bottomless pit.
Exercise, to keep my mind off
the ever-present craving
for the Lady. Exercise!
Man, after doing little but trolling
for johns for so long, my body
was slack. I chose yoga,
and have to admit it's helping
both muscle tone and relaxation.

Everyone on staff here, from
teachers to trainers to therapists,
looks like they stepped out
of a TV soap—cute, fit,
with pretty smiles they offer freely.

Most of the residents match
that description, too, minus
the smiles, which we're stingy
with. Of course, drugs of one kind
or another are largely responsible
for our collective willowy-ness,
which for many is exacerbated
by eating disorders.

Drug-free but fucked up—
that's the umbrella we share.

I'm Told

By rehab regulars that some
facilities encourage the use
of maintenance meds—
methadone or suboxone,
which allow substitute euphoria
without later withdrawal.

> But Clean Slate expects
> a total system scrub.
> As Guru Naomi says,
> *Relying on a substance*
> *to keep you off another*
> *substance won't make you*
> *self-reliant, and that's our*
> *goal. Weather the pain,*
> *the gain is greater.*

I am currently one-on-one
with so-cute-she-gags-me Naomi
who, if her looks accurately
represent her age, must be
right out of Therapist School.
Not the smartest woman, but
I think she thinks she cares.

> *Can we talk about why*
> *you first started using?*
> *Too much stress at home?*
> *Unrealistic expectations?*
> *Why your perceived need*
> *to escape reality?*

Perceived?

Escaping reality wasn't
a choice. It was necessity.
I've avoided opening
this box of memories,
but now that I can sleep
again, nightmares visit
regularly. Maybe talking
about it will help.

"I didn't use before I went
to Vegas. Well, a little weed
and alcohol, but everyone
I knew got high once in
a while. No big deal.
It was just having fun."

> But it became a big deal,
> and when it did, it almost
> killed you. Do you think
> you might've made better
> decisions had you avoided
> substances completely?

Ack. I hate when she asks
questions with obvious
answers. I know I shouldn't
respond, but my resident
interior smart-ass (RIS) has
a big mouth. "Do *you* avoid
substances completely?"

No, I don't, Whitney. But I'm
thirty, not fifteen, which is how
old you were when you embarked
on the journey to nowhere,
right? Fifteen years makes a huge
difference, as does experience.

Thirty? No way. Talk about
well-preserved! "What do you
want me to say? Of course I
would have made better decisions
had I not gotten high to begin with.
Or was that a trick question?"

Shut up, RIS. You aren't
being very helpful. "Look.
I wasn't hooked on weed
or booze. I don't even have
an addictive personality or
whatever. You can't *not* get
hooked on heroin, you know?"

Some people can use it once
or maybe even a couple of
times without developing
an addiction, but it's rare.
Obviously it didn't work like
that for you. Are you ready
to talk about Las Vegas now?

I Look at Her

All goofy-eyed and pertly
ponytailed. How can I admit
to *her* the raw things I've seen,
the slimy things I've done?
She only wants to obtain
my confession because it's her
job. Wonder if it will earn
her a bonus. Still, what have
I got to lose? It might even
be fun to freak her out.
"What do you want to know?"

> She looks surprised. *Everything.*
> *According to the police report,*
> *you were likely prostituting*
> *yourself. Is that accurate?* At
> my nod, she asks, *But why?*

"For love, at least at first."
I reward her with a shortened
version of how I met my former
pimp outside the Gap. How
he rescued me from a party where
my so-called boyfriend was groping
another girl. How he promised
to put me to work modeling,
convinced me to run away
to Vegas with him, set us
up in an apartment. How
modeling segued into sex
in front of a webcam, then . . .

I think I've heard this story.
He needed you to earn some
money so you could have
a nicer place. "Just once,
for me. Oh, and try a little
taste of heroin. That will make
everything easier." Before
you knew it, you were hooked,
and doing whatever you had
to do to keep supplied.

She *has* heard this story.
How many girls like me
there must be in the world!
And some of them leave it
in awful ways. At least
Bryn didn't hurt me, not
physically, the way some

pimps do. "That's pretty
much it," I admit. "Then I
found out he kept a whole
stable of 'models.' I was just
another one of his girls."

That stings to say. And while
he never beat me, he scarred
my heart. I doubt I'll ever be
able to trust a guy again.
As for love, what's the point?

I Don't Expect Sympathy

Okay, maybe a little. Instead,
Naomi's jaw stiffens like cement
setting up, and her eyes take
on a serious chill. Total

> transformation. *Let me ask*
> *you this. Why would you leave*
> *a cushy life in a nice home,*
> *with a family who supported*
> *you? Why would you let them*
> *worry for months that you might*
> *be dead? A little selfish, yes?*

Whoa. She can be downright
mean. Come on, RIS, think of
something to say. "You don't
know anything about my family.
All my mom cares about is her
country club and taking my sister,
Kyra, shopping. All my dad cares
about is work. They probably didn't
even notice I was gone for a week."
And Kyra no doubt threw a bon
voyage, good riddance party.

> *Sometimes there's a decent bit*
> *of distance between perception*
> *and fact, especially when it comes*
> *to teenagers and their parents.*
> *Did you ever stop to consider*
> *you might have been wrong?*

Not until Mom's barrage
of apologies in the hospital.
Of course, Dad showed up
all pissed and disgusted.
And Kyra, my loving sister?
All she cared about was
her reputation. *How could
you do this to me? What
happens if my friends find out?*

So, "No, Naomi, I'm pretty
damn sure I was spot on.
No one noticed me when
I was there. Why would they
miss me when I was gone?"

*The universe doesn't revolve
around you. Me, me, me.
Tiresome. I've talked to your parents,
and your sister. If you'd died,
they would've been devastated.*

*Did you know your mom spent
hours and hours e-mailing
your photo to law enforcement
agencies? That's how the police
knew who you were when they
found you, lying there frothing.
Had you been just another hooker,
who knows how hard they would
have tried to resuscitate you?*

Derailed

By dimpled blond Naomi.
So much for sympathy.
So much for trying to justify
the dumb moves I made.
I'll try to pacify her, paint
my face with contrition.

"You're right. I was totally
selfish, and I'm sorry I hurt
my family." As the words
fall from my mouth, I realize
they're maybe true. "I'm just
a stupid girl who fell in love
with the wrong man."

> *Tell me about him. What*
> *was so special about this*
> *guy that made every ounce*
> *of common sense desert you?*

"Br—Bryan is to die for.
Cute. Smart. Drives a cool
car. Mostly, he treated me
like I was the most amazing
girl he'd ever met. He swore
I was beautiful, and made me
believe it. No one else has
ever done that for me."

Okay, that sounds lame. Totally TV.

I Don't Out Bryn

To Naomi—I call him
Bryan. Bryn is a peculiar
name, one that stands out,
and even as hurt and pissed
as I am, getting him in trouble
(he could go to prison
for a very, very long time)
isn't on my "to do today" list.

Don't ask me why not.
Part of me would genuinely
enjoy seeing him locked up
in a cell with some beefy guy,
looking for a little action.
I'd probably pay to watch.

Despite that, the biggest
piece of schizo me remains
head-in-the-clouds in love
with the bastard. How is that
possible? I'll never forget
hours and hours, curled up
in a corner, stomach knotting,
body shaking beneath beads of salt

sweat, waiting for him to bring
powdered relief, cursing the day
I met him, weeping at my need
for him, screaming into the silence,
"Please come, Bryn. Please
come and make love to me!"

A Poem by Eden Streit

Screaming into the Silence

No one to hear
the brittle cries
but shadows thrown
against the walls and

I

burrow my face into
the quilts to shut out
the demon dance.
This nightmare I

can't

escape walks and breathes
beyond the confines
of sleep, and with it
a monster impossible to

forget,

grinning. Leering.
Whispering lust-infused
ballads through serrated
teeth. He carries in

his

hand a perfect strawberry,
offers it like treasure,
and when I bend to taste
it, he smashes it into my

face.

Eden
Walk Straight

Was a godsend to me, maybe
even literally. I'd been sleeping
on the streets, crashing behind
Dumpsters, offering myself up
to passersby for meager money,

barely enough to eat. I would
say "survive," but that requires
being alive, and I was one of
the walking dead when I threw
a plea skyward, "Please, God,

please, if it's your will, show
me the way out." It wasn't God
who actually answered, but
a priest in the Catholic church
I had sleepwalked into.

How can I help you? he asked,
trying not to look disgusted by
the odor clinging to the awful
Salvation Army clothes I wore.
I didn't know how he could help,

but once he had no doubt about
my circumstances, Father Gregory
knew exactly how. He sent me here
to Walk Straight, a rescue for teen
prostitutes intent on a better life.

Teen Prostitute

How can I ever reconcile that
title in front of my name? It's so
contrary to everything about me—
the straitlaced daughter
of an evangelical preacher and his strict,

overbearing wife. Mama. At least
she was until she sent me to hell on earth,
a reform school of sorts called
Tears of Zion, where they isolated me
in a tiny room, only a Bible for company.

Barely fed me. Rarely bathed me.
Forced me to meditate on my sins—
chief among them falling in love
with Andrew, the Catholic boy with
attitude and spiritualistic belief beyond

the ken of my hellfire and brimstone
parents. With love as my sin, it was
only proper that my redemption
would come at the hands of a devil,
my savior Jerome, a Tears of Zion

apostle with a sick appetite for sex
with young girls like me, who he wanted
to own. I did what he required in trade
for an escape route across the desert—
my path to prostitution when I fled from him.

I've Confessed None

Of that to the great people here
at Walk Straight, a place founded
by an ex-prostitute determined
to help reshape the tomorrows
of teens who want out of "the life."

My caseworker, Sarah (who still thinks
I'm "Ruthie") has been after me for
information. To live here, my legal
guardian has to sign off on it. I was
never arrested, so I'm not in the juvenile

justice system, therefore not a ward
of the state. When I first arrived
here, I told them my parents
were dead. That lie is catching up
to me. Walk Straight has been patient—

their goal is to take kids off the streets
and give them a safe place to live.
But there are legalities involved.
I'm scared to return to Boise and live
under my parents' rule again. I'm also

terrified of seeing Andrew, who I love
more than anything in this world,
because he'll want to know why—and
where—I vanished last spring.
I just don't know how to tell him.

I've Been Courage Building

For weeks, and today is the day
I'll give Sarah the information
she needs to ruin my life the rest
of the way. But it's the only real
roadway into the future. I truly wish

Andrew could be there, too, but
he deserves someone better than me.
Someone clean. Unbroken. Worthy
of a love so intense it will leave her
breathless. Suddenly, my eyes sting.

>   *You okay?* asks Shayleece, noting
>   the onslaught of tears. She's one
>   of thirty-two Walk Straight girls—
>   about my age, with dark-chocolate
>   skin and huge espresso eyes.

We haven't talked much, but then
neither of us is the talkative type.
"I'm all right. Just thinking
about someone back home."
We are at lunch, which today

is a delicious (not) tuna salad
sandwich. I never cared for tuna,
anyway, but in this setting, with
everyone eating it at the same
time, the fish smell is nauseating.

Shayleece doesn't seem to notice.
Someone special, huh? Bet it's a guy.
She waits for my nod before
continuing. *Like a real boyfriend?*
Ooh, girl! I want one of those someday.

Okay, maybe she *is* the talkative
type. I remain tight-lipped, except
to say, "He's the most amazing guy
in the world." If I think one more
time about him kissing me beneath

the broad Idaho sky, I'll go completely
crazy. It's the best memory I own,
but when it rises, smoke, I choke
on the knot that forms in my throat.
I'm suffocating at this moment.

I don't want to talk about Andrew,
so I refocus the conversation,
which I guess is what we're having
between bites of yucky tuna sandwich.
"You never had a boyfriend?"

> *Oh, hell no. My mom, she would*
> *have killed me. Sex for love, which*
> *means for free? Nah, she wouldn't*
> *have put up with that for one second,*
> *and Daddy would've killed the guy.*

Now That She's Opened Her Mouth

It's going to be hard to slam it
shut again. Because when I ask,
"You mean your mother knew
you were turning tricks?" she has
no compunction about sharing

> her entire life story with me. *Oh,*
> *yeah. My mom's the one who put*
> *me out on the track. Well, she did*
> *it for Daddy. See, she was one of*
> *his "wifeys," too. And know what?*

> *Daddy was maybe my real daddy,*
> *ain't that a hoot? Mom was fourteen*
> *when she started tricking, and he was*
> *her man, so she didn't use no protection*
> *with him. She was fifteen when she had me.*

"Wait. Your mom *wanted* you
to prostitute? How old were you?"
My own mother insisted I had to
get married before I even allowed
a boy to kiss me, let alone . . .

> *We needed the money for rent and*
> *stuff. I was thirteen, but no big deal.*
> *One of Daddy's friends broke me in*
> *when I was nine. As Daddy says,*
> *tight pussy costs a pretty penny.*

Unless You Can Coerce It

Crush what's left of a little girl's
childhood into dust. I know
it happens, but it's hard to picture,
and she doesn't even seem that upset
about it. How can that be possible?

> Shayleece finishes her sandwich,
> chases the last swallow with a big
> gulp of chocolate milk, starts on
> her giant oatmeal raisin cookie.
> *Who broke you in?* she asks bluntly.

"You mean who did I give
my virginity to?" I realize few
enough girls here actually gifted
it to someone. Maybe only me.
"My first time was with Andrew."

> *He your boyfriend?* Her voice
> drips incredulity, but when she
> assesses my body language and
> finds only truth reflected there,
> she asks, *So how you end up here?*

"Want my cookie?" I shuttle
my tray across the table so she can
enjoy the second dessert. "This will
probably sound stupid, but I think God
sent me here. See, this priest—"

No. I don't mean here at this table.
I mean in Vegas, in the life. I never
saw you out on the track. Daddy
woulda loved getting hold of you.
He's always scouting for white girls.

I don't really want to talk about
Tears of Zion with Shayleece,
so I tell her, "It's a long story. Let's
just say I had no choice but to run
away, and the trucker who picked

me up hitchhiking was headed
in this direction. I've got a question
for you, though. How did *you* wind
up at Walk Straight? Does your mom
know you're here?" I watch her stuff

the last bite of cookie into her mouth.
My mom's dead. A few crumbs fall
from her lips. *Daddy makes his girls give*
him five hundred every day. Mom was
short too many times. He got mad, beat

her down. I got home right as he put
the gun to her head. I ran 'cause Daddy
saw me, but didn't know where to go.
A girl out on the track told me 'bout this
place. She said they'd keep me safe.

The Sex Trade

Is a violent business. Pimps
competing. Pimps keeping their
girls in line. Big city, small town,
makes no difference. "Did the cops
ever find out who killed her?"

> *Oh, hell yeah. Word got around*
> *on the street, and you know, one*
> *person said something to someone,*
> *probably someone who runs other*
> *girls, and eventually it reached*

> *the police. Plenty of Daddy's DNA in*
> *that place. Then my counselor here*
> *made me fess up about my pimp, so*
> *now they've got him for murder and*
> *for trafficking children. I still qualify.*

That busts her up, and the way
she laughs, head thrown back
as she squeals and snorts, makes
me grin, despite the fact that it
isn't funny. Am I still a child?

> *Okay, well, it looks like lunch*
> *is over. Thanks for the cookie.*
> She pushes back from the table,
> stands. *If your boyfriend really*
> *loves you, he'll forgive you.*

On Weekdays

We're required to attend classes
both a.m. and p.m., the goal
being to earn our high school
equivalency certificates so we can
move on to productive jobs and

become solid members of society.
That's assuming we stay long
enough to make all that happen,
and I don't think I will once Sarah
contacts my parents. Then again,

I can't imagine returning to Boise
High, pretending to be an ordinary
junior, a little behind on credits
because . . . Exactly why? Beyond
school, what about church? Papa's

church, where he preaches everlasting
hellfire for infractions as insignificant
as divorce or using birth control. How
can I sit there and listen, all the while
remembering the things I've done?

How can I bask in the glory of God
when I've trolled the streets on Satan's
arm? Shayleece claims Andrew will
forgive me. But how can I forgive myself,
or expect the Lord to offer redemption?

These Thoughts

Intrude on my concentration
this afternoon. I'm happy when
I can leave US Government behind
in favor of library hour. I requested
computer time yesterday. I don't know

if they bother to monitor what
we view online. Probably. Doesn't
matter to me. My tastes are benign.
I check e-mail first, always hoping
for some little word from Andrew.

I'm not disappointed. *Hello, my heart,*
he writes. *Hope you are well and
that you're coming home soon. Wherever
you are is too far away. God, I miss
you. I dream about you every night.*

*Sometimes those are good dreams.
You and me, here on the ranch,
playing with Sheila (who's not
a puppy anymore . . . funny how
fast they grow into dogs!), or just*

*sitting on the porch, watching
the cottonwoods flicker in the breeze.
But then come the nightmares
where I see you in the distance, faint,
but no matter how hard I try or how*

fast I run, I can't catch up to you,
and when I reach the place where
you were standing, you're gone.
Vanished, just like you disappeared
from my life. Please come back to me,

or at least tell me where you are so
I can come find you. I promise, no
matter what has happened, we'll make
things right again. I don't care what
your parents think. All my love, Andrew.

Beautiful words. I want to believe
them, need to trust in him. But how?
The love we shared ran marrow deep,
but the Eden he knew died behind
the walls of Tears of Zion. "Ruthie"

is who I am here in Vegas. Walk
Straight needed to call me something,
so I offered my middle name, Ruth.
Sarah added the "ie" to make it feel
"friendlier." Less biblical, for sure.

But I don't want to be Ruthie
anymore. She represents a short
chapter of my life I'm determined
to edit out. And if I'm no longer Eden,
who'll I be if I return to Idaho?

Heart at War with Head

I think about how to respond.
At some point, I'll have to break
down and tell him the truth. Not
possible to construct a solid future
on a foundation of dishonesties.

Doing it this way would give him
time to consider the implications
and change his mind about wanting
me back in his life. He wouldn't
even have to write a reply to say

goodbye, he could simply excise
me from his life with his silence. Plus,
I don't have to look into his eyes,
absorb the hurt and anger that will
surface there if I admit the ugliness

face-to-face. I'm a coward. Too
cowardly, in fact, to come clean
right now. To keep moving forward,
I have to maintain at least a minimal
amount of hope that Andrew and I

can be together again. Still, I need
to give him something, so maybe
a bare-bones explanation of why
I simply evaporated one day.
The story begins with Mama.

Backward in Time

That's where I take him, not so
far back, not really though
it feels like years ago, and what
has transpired between then and
now has aged me more than months.

"Dearest Andrew. I am safe, for
now, in a shelter in Las Vegas.
I do hope to return to Boise, but
I'm not sure when, because I told
them my parents were dead,

something I plan to rectify today.
I won't tell you everything now,
but want to confide some of it.
Remember the last time I saw you?
My family was at church, at least

I thought so. But when I got home,
Mama was there, and I was sure
she'd beat me again. Instead she brought
me into the kitchen, made tea laced
with sleeping pills, and as I passed

out, she blamed Satan for me falling
in love with you. I woke up eleven
hours later, out in the middle of
the Nevada desert, at a rehab
center called Tears of Zion. . . ."

I Describe

My routine, the lack of sustenance
and human company. Underline
the hopelessness I felt when I learned
my time there had no set termination
point. Now comes the hard part,

but without it there's no explanation
for how I got here. "All I could think
about was finding a way to escape,
to get back to you. One of the orderlies
had a crush on me. God forgive me,

but I promised he could be my boyfriend
if he helped me get away." I won't give
Andrew the disgusting details; he can assume
them or not. "It worked. When we stopped
for gas, I hid from him. A nice rancher

gave me a ride and I wound up in Vegas.
I tried to call you, but your phone was
disconnected. I didn't know my parents
had you arrested until your mom told
me. I'm so sorry. For everything."

I spend a few minutes stressing over
how to sign off. "Love" isn't strong
enough, and he used the preface "All my."
I choose, "I'll never stop loving you,"
hit send before I change my mind.

A Poem by Cory Bennett

The Disgusting Details

Of life in hard-core juvenile
lockup don't really need
to be repeated. My brother
Cody would never let me
live it down. I won't argue
the system got it wrong, that

                                              I'm

not qualified to be here.
Break into a home,
then whup the owner's
ass until she's lying

                                              still

on the ground,
they'll put you away
if they catch you. Problem
is, there isn't

                                              a kid

in this place
who won't walk away
tougher, meaner, calloused,
no hint of child left

                                              inside.

Cody
Imprisoned

I thought a lot about being locked up
when they first sent my little brother
to jail. Not saying Cory didn't deserve

it, or that it didn't maybe save his life.
The path he was headed down
could have ended with him slamming

face-first into a brick wall. But it made
me a little crazy to consider the day-
to-day of containment in a little cement

room, only let out for meals, classroom
bullshit (like anyone there gives a fuck
about school), and an hour of exercise.

Yeah, that pretty much seemed like hell
to me. But, with luck and good behavior,
Cory will be released one day. He didn't

manage to kill the woman he knocked
senseless, and since she recovered, he'll only
be incarcerated until he turns eighteen.

The cost of my indiscretions, which
should've resulted in nothing but pleasure,
was life, in prison in a useless body.

One Day Blurs

Into the next, a huge brown smear
of hospital shit. There's nothing to do
but watch TV, hour upon tedious hour.

The food sucks, but even if it was gourmet
I'd avoid it because eating only means
someone's gloved finger massaging

my anus to make me take a dump. Not
that I can feel it, but knowing that's what's
going on is more than enough to drop

me into a cavern of depression, a place
I fall into regularly, with or without
a latex-sheathed pointer exploring my ass.

Mom brings me books, and the unread
pile continues to grow, along with a stack
of magazines. *Sports Illustrated. People.*

National Geographic. No *Hustler*, not that
it would do anything but remind me
what a worthless excuse for a man I've become.

No, my life will never be the same,
and worse, my future as a complete human
being was stolen by that low-life fucker, Chris.

Federico would tell me to shut the hell
up, cancel the pity party and get to work.
His idea of work? Learning to sit up.

Equilibrioception

That's another word for balance,
and apparently I've got a problem
with that. First of all, I've been lying

here for weeks, rolled side to side
from time to time so I don't get these
nasty things called pressure sores—

wounds caused by staying in one
position for so long your bones
poke through your hide. I've seen

pictures. Disgusting. The worst thing
is, since I can't feel the wear and tear,
they could get infected before I even

realize my skin is rotting away.
But there's more. To keep from falling
over, your eyes, ears, and proprioceptors

have to work together. Proprioceptors
are sensors that tell you where your limbs
are positioned in space. Like, your right

arm is over your head, or your left foot
is two inches off the ground. And since
my legs don't have a clue where they are,

things get a little tricky. Federico insists
it gets easier with practice. Too bad
sitting up isn't on my to-do list at all.

This Will Be the Day

That's what he said, and I do
believe he meant it. Best of luck
with that, old buddy. He's yanked

the sheets back, exposing most
of my uselessness, slack and pale
as the Cream of Wheat they tried

> to make me eat for breakfast.
> *Okay now. The process is fairly*
> *simple. Put your elbows flat*

> *on the bed beside you and push*
> *down, bending your head and*
> *shoulders forward.* He stands there,

waiting, but I don't bother to try
and move. What's the point?
"Don't feel like it. Maybe tomorrow."

> His expression is priceless.
> *Look, Cody. Time keeps ticking*
> *forward, and the rest of the world*

> *isn't on hold waiting for you to*
> *get on board. You're not going*
> *to die, and the quality of your future*

> *living is entirely up to you. I believe*
> *you want to get up on your feet*
> *again, and I also believe we can*

absolutely make that happen.
Scratch that. You *can make that*
happen. People with worse injuries

than yours have *made that happen.*
But it takes heart and courage.
Out of breath with the effort of not

convincing me to budge an inch,
he lingers there, hands on hips,
with such genuine bewilderment

on his face I almost feel sorry
for him. But not anywhere near
as sorry as I feel for myself.

"Look, dude. I'm lying here with
a tube hanging out of my dick, leaking
piss into a plastic bag. That dick,

by the way, is totally useless for
anything worth getting excited about.
Yeah, yeah, Dr. Harrison told me

ninety percent of men with incomplete
injuries, T12 and lower, get it up, and some
higher than that, too. But that's not the real

problem, is it? Not like I want to go
above and beyond, just to whack off.
How many girls go looking for cripples?"

Half-Sad

Half-annoyed, that's how
he looks now, like he needs
to dig for words of wisdom

> but the shovel needs sharpening.
> *It's "disabled," not "crippled," and
> so you know, there are millions*
>
> *of couples living with disability.
> Not only that, but there are plenty
> of perfectly healthy partners who*
>
> *don't have sex regularly.* He winks
> conspiratorially. *You could ask
> my wife, but she'd probably lie.*

That actually makes me smile,
and I almost consider rewarding
him with the behavior he's seeking.

> But then he has to go and ruin
> the moment. *So, do you have
> a girlfriend? Someone special?*

With a stunning burst of memory,
the face of an angel materializes
from the ether. "Not anymore."

> He's gone too far, and backpedals
> quickly. *You don't know that, do
> you? Have you talked to her?*

Are You Out of Your Mind?

That's what I want to ask him,
quite loudly, but yelling is too
much effort. "Not since before . . ."

> *Look, at the very least, let's work
> on mobility. You don't have to do
> anything but roll onto your side.*
>
> *I'll handle the heavy lifting, and
> while I do, why don't you tell me
> about your girl? What's her name?*

"Ronnie," I answer without
even thinking. "Well, Veronica,
but everyone calls her Ronnie."

Federico rolls me onto my left
side, begins manipulating my right
leg. This isn't new, but I sense more

> movement than before. *Ronnie.
> Is she pretty? Bet she is.* Bend.
> Lift. Backward. Forward. As

he continues the routine, I find
myself describing the girl who
still possesses my heart. "She's not

pretty. She's beautiful. Her hair
is the color of obsidian, and shiny
like it, too. And her body. Man,

it's amazing. You've never seen . . ."
I skid to a halt before I mention
her glorious tits. "But there's so

much more to her than that.
She's—was—my rock." My rock,
when my stepfather, Jack, got sick

and died. My rock when Cory melted
all the way down into a puddle
of booze-inspired anger. My rock.

And then I went and fucked it all
up with drugs and gambling and
financing those by offering myself

up for sale. Invincible, that's what
I believed I was. Untouchable.
Such conceit! And now, look at me.

Hard to maintain an air of vanity
while being posed like a nude mannequin—
bend, lift, backward, forward, flip,

and repeat. Federico finishes each
side by massaging my legs and feet,
all for the sake of circulation. Too bad

I can't feel it. Ronnie used to do that
for me, and boy, did I love . . .
Next thing I know, I'm sobbing.

Even Better

Suddenly, my right foot jerks. Ouch!
But, wait. Movement? "Hey, what
was that?" Does that mean more

   brain connection than we supposed?
   The action was involuntary. Federico,
   it seems, missed it. *What was what?*

"My foot just twitched. Hurt like
hell, too. That's a good sign, right?
Like, maybe you're all totally wrong

   and my spine just had to heal more?"
   But Federico shakes his head.
   That's called spasticity. We've been

   wondering if it would affect you.
   It usually doesn't first occur until
   several weeks post-injury. See,

   your muscles have memories, and
   even without an intact circuit board,
   they try to repeat learned behaviors.

   The bad news is, it can be painful,
   or at the very least, annoying.
   The good news is spasticity

   can actually be helpful with bowel
   and bladder behaviors, and many
   SCI patients utilize it to help them

stand and even walk. One day
at a time. If it becomes a real
problem, there are drug therapies,

so be sure and let a team member
know if the pain is too much.
Team member: one of the nurses,

doctors, physical therapists,
psychologists, and social workers
assigned to my case, just a number

among many on their busy lists.
Federico waits to see if I'll spasm
again, but when that doesn't happen

right away, he spreads the sheet
back up over me. "So, if spasticity
is nothing but my foot remembering

how it used to move, and I'm still
paralyzed, why could I feel it? And
how could it possibly be painful?"

He shrugs. *With incomplete*
injuries, it's always possible some
feeling will return. Besides,

the brain is an incredibly
complex machine. Sometimes
its will trumps common wisdom.

Go Right Ahead

Burst my fucking balloon.
The truth is a sharp pin,
and I tumble back down

to earth. "Hey. My brain
tells me I'm hurting. Can
you give me something

for that? You must've
worked me too hard. Or
maybe it's just spastic me."

> He looks unconvinced,
> but then he decides, *Tell*
> *you what, Cody. I'll send*
>
> *in a nurse, but only if you*
> *give me your word that*
> *tomorrow you'll cooperate*
>
> *and help me get you sitting*
> *up. We've got a long way to go,*
> *and it starts with you upright.*

I'd say anything for the key to
oblivion, and besides, as my Kansas
kin might say, my word ain't worth

a pile of manure, so it's a no-brainer.
"I solemnly swear if you eradicate
my pain I'll try to sit up tomorrow."

Nurse Carolyn

Who remains my favorite filly
in a stable of Thoroughbred
caregivers, tries to rip me off

at first, offering acetaminophen,
but I'm not going for that.
Federico isn't overseeing,

so I'll use my latest, greatest
excuse. "Please, Carolyn.
Did Federico tell you? Spasticity

has reared its nasty head, and
I'm in a lot of pain right now.
I need something stronger

than Tylenol!" I wait for her
stern face to soften, and it does
almost immediately. Score.

> *Oh, all right, as long as*
> *the on-duty physician concurs.*
> *I'll check and be right back.*

She isn't gone long, and
when she returns it's with
a healthy (or not) dose of codeine.

> *Dr. Cabral gave the okay*
> *this time around, but there are*
> *better pain management methods.*

I understand spasticity can
cause quite a bit of discomfort,
but so can opiate dependency.

As your rehab progresses,
I'm sure your doctor will
recommend alternatives.

Pill swallowed, agreement
is easy. "I understand. Thanks
for caring, Carolyn." I reward

her with my very best smile—
the one that swears all will be
well, though that, of course, is a lie.

Okay, then, I'd better get back
to work. You aren't the only
needy patient around here.

As she leaves, the codeine kicks
in and I find myself inexplicably
drawn to the pendulum of her narrow

hips, thoroughly disguised by baggy
powder-blue scrubs. "You're an idiot."
I scold myself for the transference,

which is also impotent transference.
Obviously, the will of my brain
is trumping its common sense.

Rocking

In the cradle of the poppy,
all the bad feelings slip away.
Why am I lying here again?

Where am I, anyway? White.
Everything's white, and quiet,
like a winter-quilted mountain

meadow, except it's warm. I like
it warm, and now I know this
can't be snow, because the air

doesn't sting my nose. Inhale.
No sting, but there is perfume.
Apples. That's it. Baked apples,

rich with cinnamon and brown
sugar, and I realize I'm dreaming.
Weird, when you're aware

you're not treading time in the real
world, but rather wandering
another dimension. A drift of apples

fills my nose, and a satin caress
(surely not Federico's!) slides
along the skin of my legs. Legs.

Why does that word bother me?
Not important. What is worthy
of my attention is the force field

rising up around me, a halo
of well-being that can only be love.
I search for the source. Nearby,

she must be nearby. My rock.
There, in the mist, a shadow,
approaching, and growing as

it nears, solidifying. "Ronnie?"
It's no more than a whisper, and
escaping the fog, comes an answer.

> *I'm here, Cody. I waited for you,*
> *but almost gave up hoping that*
> *you'd come back to me. Wake up.*

> Her voice is smooth and rich
> as frosting. But I still can't see her.
> Now she urges, *Open your eyes.*

I do and the dream dissolves.
Bedside, in the flesh, is, "Ronnie."
I start to throw back the sheet,

remember where I am, how I am,
who I've become. "Go away. I
don't want you to see me like this."

> *Too damn bad. I have no clue*
> *why you decided to throw "us" away,*
> *Cody, but I won't let it happen.*

A Poem by Alex Rialto
The Dream Dissolves

Every dream does,
but hope saturated this one,
and a tiny piece
of me tries very

hard to

believe my cards
have been re-dealt.
The thought of nurturing
an innocent soul makes love

rise

in me like nothing else
ever has before, not even
lying next to Ginger, wrapped
in the warmth of her sighs.
I am lifted high

above

the landscape of my life.
But now I fall again, desert
scrubbed of sustenance,
without the promise of
my baby, who chooses

surrender

in favor of time with me.

Ginger
Time Drags

Here at House of Hope,
where everything is regimented,
little variation to any given day.
They say that sameness

is necessary to meeting
expectations, that it's good training
for real-world situations like
keeping a job. Up at six thirty a.m.,

dress for the day, make our beds,
straighten up our rooms. Breakfast
at seven, finish by seven thirty.
Load the dishwasher, if it's your day.

If not, lucky you, fifteen minutes
to read or stare into space before
chapel, where you'll stare into
space even longer. House of Hope

is a Christian home, and morning
prayer meeting attendance is mandatory.
Saving souls. That's what they believe,
and hey, if it works that way, more

power to the Power. The concept
of God is foreign to me. Not even
Gram subscribes to the notion,
at least, she's never mentioned it

to me if she does. Personally,
I'm just happy House of Hope
has rescued my body from abuse.
If there's anything resembling a soul

residing inside me, it probably
does need a little assistance, but
I'm pretty sure listening to Pastor
Martin yak at us won't make

that happen. Doesn't matter.
It's easier than scrounging a living
taking my clothes off, and for the girls
who somehow still *do* believe,

his words seem to offer comfort,
don't ask me why. He sits on
a stool in front of the group, as if
standing would be too much effort.

> *The amazing thing about our Lord,*
> *Jesus Christ, is his bottomless*
> *supply of love, and all you have*
> *to do to receive it is ask.*

That doesn't sound so bad, but he
won't stop there. He never does.
Because, although he would argue
this, Pastor Martin's all about judgment.

And ... His Engine Fires

First, he straightens his back,
builds himself real tall, tilts
his chin toward his nose. Red
alert: serious stuff headed this way.

> *Now, you probably think*
> *you've experienced love,*
> *but unlike the men many*
> *of you have known, Jesus*
>
> *doesn't ask for favors in return,*
> *at least not that kind of favor.*
> *All he requires of you is to*
> *accept him into your heart,*
>
> *and to pray for forgiveness*
> *for your sins. You can do that,*
> *can't you? The robots group-nod.*
> *Then let us pray. Heavenly Father,*
>
> *please search our hearts, and*
> *find repentance there. We admit*
> *we have sinned. Forgive us and*
> *allow us to walk forward cleansed*
>
> *of our transgressions. Infuse us*
> *with your light. Fill us with your*
> *love. In Jesus's blessed name, amen.*
> We. Us. Our. All-inclusive.

Why Does Everyone Insist

On lumping us all together
under the "troubled youth"
label? I guess our stories
might sound similar,

but to us, they are unique
and personal, despite
the ugly things we have
in common. Most of our

childhoods were marred
by rape, often by older men.
But those might have been
a stepfather, grandfather,

older brother, neighbor,
teacher, priest, doctor,
foster parent, policeman,
or complete stranger.

Faces. Bodies. Odors.
Skin textures. Voices.
Mannerisms. Methods
of attack. All different,

and scratched into our
memories and, worse,
our psyches. We are who
we are because of them.

Post Prayer

We attend classes. I balked
at first, knowing I'd be leaving
House of Hope before I'd complete
a semester, but my counselor

did her job and convinced me
I shouldn't get any more behind
than I already am. She even got
hold of my high school in Barstow

and found a way for me to finish
up the classes I was most of the way
through when I ran away last spring.
I worked a little magic. That's how

she put it when she told me I could
complete geometry, world history,
and sophomore English and receive
credit for them. When I go home,

I'll take online classes, work at
my own pace and hopefully complete
my junior year pretty much on schedule,
or at least by the end of next summer.

I could then, if I wanted, go back
to high school for my senior year
and graduate like a regular kid.
But how do I pretend to be normal?

To Be Perfectly Honest

I've never exactly felt "normal,"
thanks to the circumstances
of my life. And, to be even more
honest, I actually feel more

normal now, knowing how many
other girls' lives don't fit the usual
definition of the word and yet
share so many strange facets.

There are more imperfect diamonds
than flawless stones. So, what
the hell? I'll give it a try, and do
my best to keep moving forward.

Hey, with luck, maybe Pastor
Martin's shtick will rub off and
I'll make the journey "cleansed
of my transgressions." Wouldn't

that be brilliant? Meanwhile,
I'm working diligently to finish
my assignments quickly and earn
decent grades. It's the first time

since I was a little kid that I've
felt compelled to excel at something,
and I'm discovering my mind
is every bit as important as my body.

My Love for Language

Has been rekindled. I first found
it back in Barstow, in Ms. Felton's
creative writing class. The one
where I met Alex—all spiky hair

and heavy eyeliner and I thought
she was amazing before we ever
hung out together. And maybe
I'll have to write that memory

> for Ms. Cox, who teaches English
> with a heavy lean toward creative
> writing. *Every one of you has stories*
> *to share with the world,* she says,

> *and you must tell them the way only*
> *you can. If I asked you all to write*
> *the same story, still it would be*
> *different from one another's because*

> *each of you will tell it in your own way,*
> *choosing specific words and syntax.*
> *That is your voice, and it's as unique*
> *to you as the voice you speak with.*

In reply, most of the girls groan,
but they claim to hate writing,
anyway. A few of us take up
the challenge, and I embrace it.

We Write

Happy memories. I struggle
to come up with one of those,
and find it buried beneath
a deep pile of resentments.

It was the first Christmas
we spent with Gram, and there
was a tree—a real tree, our first!—
with ornaments we made ourselves.

Not beautiful by any means,
but spending that time as a family,
stringing popcorn and cranberries
and making paper chains, was new.

We also write sadness,
and I don't have to look too hard
to pull a short chapter from
my personal history. I only had

to go back a few weeks ago,
to the day Alex and I parted
ways. Although, as I admit
in my paper, she and I had truly

split quite a while before our
formal goodbye, and that's where
I found the true wellspring
of my sorrow. Faded love.

This Morning

Ms. Cox has a new assignment.
Today let's write about fear.
First, an exercise. I want you to
concentrate on sensory details.

So take out a piece of paper
and tell me how fear smells.
How it tastes. How it sounds.
How it looks. Feels. One or two

sentences for each sense, and
be creative. You are artists,
painting pictures with words.
Fear isn't pastel. Be bold. Brave.

This should be easy. For all
the sadness I've experienced,
fear is a more present companion.
I have to take a couple of deep

breaths to breast stroke through
the recollections. Now I pick up
my pencil and write. Fear smells
like nicotine-tainted fingers, playing

with an unwashed pecker poking
from piss-damp boxers. Bold?
I think so. I continue. Fear tastes
like the whiskey-soaked lips of your love,

whispering a long goodbye.
That one is fresh, and personal.
Fear is the sound of fingernails,
scratching linoleum, seeking escape

from the monster clawing behind.
Nothing brave about that,
but it's something I know well.
Fear looks like a crow, circling closer

and closer until its black pearl eyes
come even with your own. Heavy
with symbolism, but also drawn
from experience. Fear feels like

waiting for the phone to ring,
certain the caller will inform you
that your little brother is dead.
Definitely not pastel. That memory

is bloodred, and though I try
really hard not to let it surface,
sometimes it does—a sharp photo
of Sandy lying in the street after

being hit by a motorcycle.
I should have been there, watching
him instead of hanging out downtown.
Thank God he survived, and healed.

We Go Around the Room

Sharing what we've written.
Some girls clearly didn't get
it, and their papers are mostly
blank. Others scribbled madly.

From Lena: *Fear is the sound
of my father's belt, unbuckling.*
Plenty to think about there.
Sometimes I'm glad my father

didn't stick around long enough
for me to get to know him well.
If he was married to Iris, he must
be the world's biggest loser.

From Brielle: *Fear tastes like
the oily, smoky barrel of a gun.*
Another bold picture for you,
Ms. Cox. Is that what you expected?

And from my roomie, Miranda:
*Fear feels like a snake, wrapping
around and around your throat
and squeezing tighter and tighter*

*until the light goes all the way
out.* And after that comes a gang
rape. Wonder if Ms. Cox might
prefer something more in sepia.

If So

She doesn't mention it, or
even look surprised at the things
she's heard, including what
I wrote. The other girls aren't

shocked, either, although
my "fear smells like" sentence
does elicit a fair amount of laughter,
mostly because the majority

of girls here have been in that
exact situation. Which makes me
wonder about Ms. Cox and her
relative lack of reaction. Was she

ever in the life? Thinking about
it, I'm guessing no, or she probably
would have changed her last name.
That makes me giggle, so I'm glad

> the other girls are still laughing
> about unwashed pecker and piss-damp
> boxers. But now, Ms. Cox reins us in.
> *Okay, since you've got solid*
>
> *sensory details to bring this story*
> *to life, I want you to write about*
> *a time when you were frightened.*
> *Make your readers feel your fear.*

Won't That Depend

On who my readers are?
I mean, if I wrote about
my "breaking in" by one
of my mother's men,

the story wouldn't bother
these girls, though it might
scare the hell out of some
innocent virgin somewhere.

Oh, well. Ms. Cox never
mentioned audience, so I'll go
with whatever first comes
to mind. I have to think for

a few minutes. Fear. I close
my eyes, fall backward in time.
Way, way back into childhood.
I was a kid once, wasn't I?

And there was a time long
before moving in with Gram
when Iris was still "Mommy."
We moved around, spent lots

of time on military bases,
living with a lineup of men,
and I find myself on a lopsided
sofa, watching cartoons.

I Start My Story There

Mommy says I'm a big girl, so I'm in
charge while she's gone. Mary Ann's
asleep in her dirty old crib. Her diaper
smells like poo, but it's dark outside,

and the light is burned out so I can
only see by the TV. Scritch-scratch.
What's moving across the floor? Ew!
Giant brown bugs, two of them, with

clicking shells and antennas that twitch
sideways. I pull my feet up onto the couch,
which smells like cigarettes and beer
and something I don't have a name for,

but it stains the cushions crusty white.
Suddenly, there's banging on the door.
Iris! Let me in! It's Wes. Where's his key?
I start to get up, but with a loud crash,

the door flies open. Where the fuck is Iris?
That makes Mary Ann wake up, crying.
Wes stomps closer, eyes wide and weird,
reflecting the TV's glow. His mouth leaks

booze-stinking spit and he screams, I said,
where's your fucking mother? I draw back
against the arm of the sofa, try to crawl
into the crack there, but Mary Ann's wailing

makes Wes mad. <u>Shut up!</u> he yells, shaking
the rail, which only makes her cry harder.
He reaches into the crib, but I know he'll hurt
her. "No! Stop. I'll take care of her. Mommy's

next door at Steve's." Ken spins, and I think
he'll leave us alone, but he grabs hold
of me, tucks me under one arm, and now
I smell onion sweat. I'm facedown, watching

the ground move below, dizzying. Tread
the steps, across the dead grass, toward
the neighbor's, Wes's anger beating palpably.
<u>Hey, Iris! I've got your little girl!</u> Bam!

He kicks in the door, and there's Mommy,
and now I notice the knife in his hand.
<u>You been screwing around, whore?</u> He puts me
down, but doesn't let go. Instead, he holds

the blade to my throat. <u>Come here, Iris. It's you
or her.</u> I see Mommy smile. Feel a sharp sting.
Look down as red dollops fall onto my shirt . . .
The story ends with shirtless Steve, who

went out the bedroom window, around
the house, and sneaked in from behind,
resting his pistol against Wes's temple.
Iris laughed and laughed and laughed.

A Poem by Bud Parnell
My Story Nears Its Conclusion

Not quite two years
since my sweetheart let go
of her pain, emptied
these rooms of love, and

I

still hear her whispers
fall soft against my pillow
in the deep indigo sea
of night. How do I ignore the

hunger

to hold her again, spend
just one more hour together?
And my son, my Seth.
If I could change a thing
it would be the need for you

to leave

the path to damnation
you chose. I sit, drowning
sorrow in a bottle, look out
over the fields, harvested
and soon fallow, consider
the coming freeze and

this

I wonder: is the blossoming
pain in my chest more than
just a broken heart? I pull
a weary breath, knowing
my time is short in this

world.

Seth
Choreographing a New Show

Is apparently time-consuming.
David has been working overtime,

which bothers me not at all. I enjoy
his company, but I'm not lonely

without it, and when he comes home,
despite the long hours he puts in,

he seems energized. Maybe it's just
passion for creation, or maybe it's got

everything to do with white lines
snorted in dressing rooms. Probably both.

I'm glad he refuses to maintain a stash
here, or I might be tempted to indulge

far more often than I do. I like the cool,
numbing escape; love the delicious rush

of goose bumps and shivers. But not
enough to lose the "me" I've worked hard

to find and encourage in a more positive
direction. Coke is more addictive than

alcohol, and that's saying a lot. I'm trying
desperately to keep a handle on both.

At First

I thought the reason David won't keep
drugs in this place was because he worried

about getting ripped off by his staff
or me. Turns out, he's just paranoid

about losing the house in a raid. But,
if he were to think about it logically,

law enforcement must have some idea
about what goes on here at the parties.

Seems like all the city's movers and
shakers attend them, and that probably

includes a politician or ten, and maybe
even a keeper-of-the-peace or two.

Even without actually witnessing
him use, it's not much of a stretch

to conclude famed choreographer
David Burroughs has a tidy drug habit

himself. Ah, show business, especially
Sin City show biz! Sexy girls. Sexy boys.

And enough stimulation to keep both
going all hours of the day and night.

To Keep

From falling into the same trap,
I have to stay busy, and not just with

Have Ur Cake entertainment. I need
something wholesome in my life, so

I'm volunteering at a center serving
LGBTQ youth. At eighteen, I'm old

enough to work here, but young enough
so queer teens will feel comfortable

hanging out with me. I can't officially
counsel them, but I can share my own

experiences and try to help them become
more at ease about living in their unique

gay skins. For kids sleeping on the street,
there are showers and food, as well as

an Internet café and ways to have
fun, including movies and games.

Not all YouCenter clients are homeless.
Many have parents, the majority of whom

have no clue how to talk to their kids
about what it means to be gay.

Some of our teens haven't yet confessed
their sexuality to anyone beyond

these walls. They come, looking for
answers, but more often, they come

in search of communion with people
like themselves. People like me, and

most of the staff. The great thing for
me is, I'm actually building friendships

with gay people who aren't bartering
their bodies to survive. I almost feel . . .

Dare I think it, let alone say it out loud?
It's only when I'm here, not at David's,

not while sitting in a bar, waiting for
a "date." Only here. Normal. There.

Thought it out loud. The last time I felt
anything close to this was so long ago

I didn't know enough to consider myself
different. Once I did, however, it became

pretty much all I could think about.
I'm different. I'm weird. I'm damned.

One Excellent Thing

About volunteering at the YouCenter
is it doesn't bother David at all, so not

only can I come here at will, I can also
use it as an excuse when Lydia calls.

Today, however, I'm really at the center,
and currently playing a game of pool

with Charlie, aka Charlene, who is not
only one pretty cute lesbian, she's also

kicking my butt. "Hey, man. Who taught
you to shoot pool? I think I need a lesson."

> Bam! She sinks another one. *My dad.*
> *Back when we still used to talk.* And . . .

> Ka-blam! In goes the eight ball. Game
> over. She looks up, smiling. *Had enough?*

"Hell, no. Rack 'em up, woman.
But I get to go first this time."

> *Sure. Like it will do any good.* She dances
> around the table, collecting balls from

the pockets. "I don't talk to my dad, either,"
I tell her, drawing a bead on my break.

*You don't talk to him, or he won't talk
to you?* She watches me spectacularly

miss the shot. *Don't choke up on the cue
so much. You shoot like a girl, by the way.*

That makes me laugh. "I want to shoot
just like you do, and you're a girl."

*Some people would argue with that
observation. And don't change the subject.*

"Fine. My dad kicked me out last year,
two months before I graduated, in fact.

So instead of finishing high school,
I ran off to Las Vegas with my partner

at the time. . . ." No need to confess
the lurid particulars. "Now, Dad refuses

to talk to me. I've tried calling several
times. He asks if I've decided I'm straight,

and when I can't tell him yes, he suggests
a heart-to-heart with God, and hangs up."

*I'm sorry. My parents, at least, will let
me stay until graduation. We don't converse*

*much, but we quit talking before I came
out. You're not from Vegas, then?*

I shake my head. "Indiana born and
raised right there on the farm . . ."

The last word lifts a cloud of nostalgia.
Were the crops good this year? I tilled

the fields right before I left. Did Dad
get the harvest in by himself okay?

I have to stop thinking about home.
"But is *anyone* actually *from* Vegas?"

Charlie raises her hand. *Yup. Believe
it or not, one or two of us came into this*

*world right here in Sin City. It's funny,
because everyone assumes anyone living*

*here must be liberal and morally bankrupt.
Well, they haven't met my dad, who's about*

*the most conservative asshole who ever
lived. Not one hundred percent sure*

*about his morals, but I think he's got
at least a few left intact. How about you?*

What Is She Asking?

"How about me, what?
Do you mean, am I liberal?

Or morally bankrupt?"
Her answer is a massive shrug.

Okay, then. I have to think
about how to respond. Let's see.

Gay? Makes me a liberal,
at least in Indiana, where

leaning left is not exactly
celebrated. Gun rights? Used to

go hunting with my dad, and
target shooting with a black

powder rifle kind of turns me
on. Probably conservative.

Enjoys a good buzz?
Could go either way.

"Politically, I suppose I'm
a white line kind of guy. . . ."

Oops. Freudian slip. "Uh,
meaning middle of the road.

Call me an Independent, I guess,
not that I'm registered to vote."

> She bristles. *You* are *eighteen,
> yes? Because, left, right or*

> *"middle of the road," you have
> a voice, and damn it, we need*

> *more queer voices shouting
> that we won't be ignored, and while*

> *we might be underrepresented,
> we're no less consequential*

> *than all those straight, white
> evangelical voters who somehow*

> *believe they matter more than
> anyone who doesn't look or think*

> *or dissect biblical scriptures
> exactly the way they do. Get it?*

"Jeez, Charlie, catch your breath
before you turn blue. I know

you're right. I just haven't gotten
around to it, but I promise I will."

Passionate

That word describes Charlene
Tate, and it's only one reason

I like her so much. Maybe
the biggest one is because

she likes me, and has zero
ulterior motive for palling

around with me. It's been a long
time since I've had a friend, and

now I second-guess myself. "Hey,
Charlie. We're friends, aren't we?"

> She glances up from the table,
> confused. *Well, sure. Why?*

> *You're not going to ask if you
> can borrow money, are you?*

"Do you have any?" God,
she's funny. "Just kidding.

No, I was just thinking how
nice it is to make a new friend.

Then it struck me that you
might not feel the same way."

Especially Not

If she actually knew everything
about me. Which brings us back

to moral bankruptcy. Who am I
really? Indiana Seth, or the Seth

I've forced myself to become?
I realize suddenly that Charlie

is standing there, waiting, hands
on her hips, as if I missed something

important. "I'm sorry. Lost in
my thoughts. What did you say?"

> *I said friends are hard to come by,*
> *so I'm happy we met, as long as you*

> *realize I'm pretty much always broke.*
> *So . . . what were you thinking about?*

I retreat again into half-truths.
"Unlikely friendships. Chance

meetings. Getting my butt whupped
at pool by a girl. And home." That

is the complete truth, and I know
I've got to try harder to reach Dad.

Unlike Charlie

My wallet is comfortably fat,
so I invite her to get a bite with

me, which turns out to be a good
thing because by the time I get home

the Friday night festivities have already
kicked into gear. This time, the party

is relatively small—mostly the cast
of David's new show, I'm guessing,

plus significant others and hangers-on.
Immediately, I climb out of my "regular

gay kid" disguise, move into the role
of party boy. As usual, David holds court

poolside. I grab a drink from the bar,
head over to say hello, working hard

to look like I absolutely belong here
after questioning that idea for the past

several hours. David's entourage
consists of dancers—men and women,

and all stunning. Handpicked as much
for beauty as for the talent they must

possess to have made it this far
in such a cutthroat market.

The show's producer is also here,
so David is distracted, entertaining

his moneyman, and that's all good
by me. I let him know I'm home,

withdraw to a quiet Adirondack chair,
away from the revelry, where I can

better meditate with my bourbon.
I'm looking up at the auburn night

sky, wondering where the hell the stars
are hiding, when a husky voice behind

> me inquires, *Want some company,*
> *or would you rather be alone?*

He materializes from the shadows,
and I think he must be a Greek god,

with copper skin and topaz eyes
and soft waves of burnt-sienna hair.

"Please." I gesture toward the adjacent
chair. "Make yourself comfortable.

I'm Seth." I offer my hand, and
when he accepts it, we both smile

> at the exchange of energy. *Great
> to meet you, Seth. I'm Micah. You*

> *sure I'm not interrupting communion
> with the universe or something?*

"Nothing as lofty as that, and I'm
happy to have someone to talk to

besides God, who I'm pretty sure
disowned me a while ago, anyway."

> *Oh, I doubt that. God tends to favor
> the most beautiful of his creations.*

I've never before experienced
instant mutual attraction, but I'm

pretty sure that's what this is, unless . . .
I don't want to sound paranoid.

How do I ask? "So, how do you
know David? Are you in his show?"

> *I am. I'm a principal.* There's pride
> in his voice. *What about you?*

We Talk

Until the party breaks up—hours.
Micah's twenty, and from California,

where it's mostly okay to be gay.
He's confident. Strong. Straight-up

gorgeous, and for whatever reason,
he's impressed by me, despite

> the fact I have no real direction.
> *You're only eighteen. You don't have*

> *to know where you're headed yet.*
> *Maybe I can help you find your passion.*

Little doubt about that, at least
if we get the chance, and I'm certain

we will. The chemistry between us
is palpable. I'll have to be careful

that it escapes David's notice. I wait
for him to go inside before inviting

Micah back into the shadows.
I haven't kissed a boy, lips on lips,

since Loren. But I'm kissing one
now, and it's soaked with promise.

A Poem by Kyra Lang

Into the Shadows

That's where Whitney
needs to fade,
like the vampire she is.
People might think
it cruel that I can find

no

sympathy for the sister
who was once my playmate,
if never quite my friend.
But, while I do

hope

she can claw her way
out of the pit she jumped
into, eyes wide open,
I see little need

for

offering my hand,
only to have it bitten
again and again and again.

Whitney's

a hungry bloodsucker,
willing to drain this family
dry in her misdirected search
for love, and any expectation of

redemption

dissolves like a rainbow
in burgeoning sun
when I look into her eyes.

Whitney
One Thing About Rehab

You're pretty much guaranteed
to meet new dope connections,
in case that happens to interest
you, considering why you're here.
The funny thing is, if you want
illicit substances, you don't have
to go very far. They're on-site.

Rumor has it they come in with
one or two members of the staff,
but more often on our weekly
Sunday visiting day. And when
they arrive that way, they might
be hidden in flower wrappers
or the hem of someone's skirt.
Mostly they're pills, but I hear
every now and again the Lady
will make an appearance. I can
leave the pills alone, but I'm afraid
if I see heroin I'll give in to temptation.

Of course, I'd need money, at least
after the first time, and I have no
available cash. So maybe I'll be
okay. I really don't want to take
that ride again, but I'm not the strongest
person in the world, and just thinking
about dropping down the shaft
into purgatory makes my mouth water.

I've Tried

Talking to Naomi about it,
in fact asked for a meeting
today to discuss it specifically,
but she can't bring herself to
agree that there could reasonably
be a problem. Her response:

> *Have you actually seen drugs
> in this facility? No? Then I suggest
> you keep quiet about that possibility
> until you do. We work extremely
> hard to maintain a drug-free
> program, and even a hint of
> impropriety could make our job
> a lot more difficult. Understand?*

"Sure." I say it, knowing that's
what she wants to hear. But when
her expression turns smug, I change
my mind. "It's just, I'm worried
if someone offers me powdered
goods, I won't be able to say no."

> *That's why you're here—to learn
> how to say no. What happens
> when you leave? Do you think
> all drugs will magically disappear?
> You have to want to stay clean,
> and you have to reach deep down
> inside to find strength of character.
> Let's give you some tools to do that.*

A Half Hour Later

I've got "tools in my recovery
toolbox," as Naomi put it.
They sound pretty basic to me,
and I'm relatively sure I could
have written this list on my own:

One: Find a trusted acquaintance
I can confide in, especially
when I feel like backsliding.
Programs like Alcoholics or
Narcotics Anonymous would call
this person my "sponsor."

Two: Join one or both said programs.

Three: Avoid old friends who might
tempt me down the rabbit hole.

Four: Make new, wholesome friends,
who'd never, ever use and abuse.

Five: Work very hard on rebuilding
relationships with my family.

Six: Keep in mind the times I'll
be more likely to succumb—when
I'm tired, lonely, hungry, or angry.

Seven: Find fun in simple things.
Dancing. Biking. Swinging.
Singing. Long walks on the beach.

There Are Problems

With all seven tools.

One: Who the hell might
that be? I don't trust one single
soul on this pathetic planet.

Two: Sit around confessing
my history and feelings to strangers,
most of whom are just as messed
up as I am? Not going to happen.

Three: If I do that, I won't have
any friends at all. Everyone
I'm comfortable around hangs
out through the looking glass.

Four: See three.

Five: Rebuilding relationships
is a two-way street. Only Mom
seems interested in reconstruction.

Six: Even if I force myself to
eat three massive meals every
day and get the requisite eight
hours of sleep, I'm almost always
lonely, and regularly pissed off.

Seven: Long walks on the beach
will forevermore remind me
of how very much I miss Bryn.

Not Sure

How it's possible
to miss the person
who brought me down
in such a profound way.

He lied to me, and not
only that, but he lied
about loving me, and
that is unforgiveable.

He used me, almost
all the way up. Pimped
me out for his own
selfish purposes. Hurt
me by allowing me to
be abused by a long
parade of johns.

He hooked me on
the vicious Lady, to
keep me at his mercy
completely, and within
that addiction, he made
me suffer. He swore
I was beautiful, and
then he made me ugly.

I won't forgive him.
But how do I forget
him when I can't fall
out of love with him?

I Don't Mention That

To Naomi, who's heard it
before, and won't accept
my emotional attachment
to a man she views as evil.
She isn't totally wrong.

Neither do I argue tools and
toolboxes with her.
She's only doing her job,
and it doesn't include
convincing me, just repeating
the stuff she tells everyone.
Before I can leave, however,
she tosses a wrench at me.

> *One last thing that might*
> *help your recovery, especially*
> *in the early stages, when*
> *things are likely to be most*
> *difficult. Find a purpose, and*
> *I don't mean just returning*
> *to school and getting decent*
> *grades. Try volunteering*
> *somewhere—at an animal*
> *shelter, or maybe mentoring*
> *a child who needs help learning*
> *to read. Retrain your focus*
> *away from yourself, toward*
> *others. Happiness requires*
> *cultivation. I'm here to show*
> *you how to plant seeds of change.*

Planting Seeds of Change

Sounds good, and that's what
I tell her, right before I go.
But the truth is, I'm scared
of change. Every time I try
it, something goes wrong.

Still, I'll be out of this place
in a few days. I've only been
here three months, and I'm not
sure I'm ready to go, but there
it is. Rehab costs a ton, and while
Mom would probably like to see
me stay longer, Dad's paying
the bill, and I don't think
he believes seeds of change
have actually been planted.

Maybe he's right, because
the idea of going home scares
the crap out of me. What if I
go ahead and relapse right here
instead? Would he have to let
me stay then? Wow. I might
have found the solution.

There's still the problem with
having no cash. What could I
barter? The answer comes rushing
at me, slams against my gut.
Duh. My body is a commodity.
I just have to find the right dealer.

Now That a Different Seed

Has burrowed into my brain,
it sprouts and grows quickly.
I've overheard this girl, Dana,
talking about disguising
her highs. I seek her out, hoping
Naomi et al. will be happy
I'm making a new friend.

I find her, just finishing breakfast,
plop down across the table.
"Hey. Delicious cardboard
pancakes, yeah?" She looks up
from her plate, offers a smile.

> *Frisbees, you mean?* Dana
> swallows what's left of hers
> anyway, then asks, *Did you
> need something from me?*

"I was wondering if you might
happen to know where I could
score something to help me sleep.
Every time I actually doze off,
these goddamn nightmares wake
me back up. I'd give just about
anything to stay out an entire night."

> She looks me right in the eye,
> trying to figure out where I'm
> coming from. Whatever she sees
> seems to satisfy her. *I might.*

But that's all she says, so I go
ahead and add, "The only problem
is I don't have any money, so I'd
have to work out a trade."

She studies me harder. *What
do you want, and what can
you give in exchange for it?*

I shrug. "Powder or pills,
doesn't really matter. What
I've got is a talent for great
sex." Still, she makes me wait.

*How old are you, anyway?
And are you really sure you
want to fuck up your rehab?*

"I'm sixteen. Age of consent
in California, so whoever is safe
that way. And yes, I'm sure, or
I wouldn't be asking. Will you
help me, or point me to someone
else who will? I'll be generous."

*My delivery arrives on Sunday.
She reaches her hand across
under the table, rests it on my knee.
So have you ever been with a girl?*

The Unexpected Question

Gives me pause.
I figured she'd hook me
up with a male staff
member who'd cut loose
with a finder's fee.

The truth is, though
I've been with more
men than I want to
consider, I haven't ever
had sex with a girl.
But how hard could
it be? "Of course."
The lie slips past
my lips like custard.

> *You're pretty. I can*
> *spare a couple of pills.*
> *No powder. Too risky.*
> *Sunday night, my room,*
> *after lights-out. I promise*
> *you'll sleep like a baby,*
> *no dreams, good or bad.*
> *Until then . . .* She flicks
> her tongue, serpentlike.
> *You can dream about me.*

Now That I've Determined

A course of action,
I can hardly wait to put
the car into gear, even if
it might mean motoring
over a very steep cliff.

I've chosen a dangerous
route, and yet I feel safer
than I did an hour ago.
Not like my morals
are going to take a hit.
Guys. Girls. What can
it possibly matter?

I suppose I might have
believed I could put
Las Vegas all the way
behind me. But something
like that tails a person,
teeth bared for the bite,
doesn't it? Guess I'll have
to develop a tough butt.

God knows the rest of me
is tougher. I think back
to Lucas, how devastated
I was learning he never
cared about me at all.
I was just a little girl
seven months ago.
What am I now?

I Don't Feel Guilty

Until Sunday, when I, too,
have a visitor—my mom,
who arrives all excited about
the prospect of my coming
home at the end of the week.
We sit out on the patio,
bundled against the chill.
The sun does its best, but
it's no match for the sharp
November breeze.

> Mom doesn't seem to notice.
> *So, I've talked to your school,*
> *and it's no problem for you to*
> *start midterm. They'll bring*
> *you in for an assessment next*
> *month to see how far you've*
> *managed to catch up, okay?*

I nod, robotlike, knowing
it doesn't matter at all what
they've got planned. Safe.

> *You won't believe this, but*
> *I'm actually going to attempt*
> *to cook Thanksgiving dinner.*
> *I've been taking some culinary*
> *classes, and I think I can manage*
> *it, with your and Kyra's help.*
> *She's flying home for the weekend.*
> *I want us to feel like a family.*

Yeah, well, good luck with that.
I half listen to her talk about
everything she's got planned for me,
though she frames it with the word
"us." Through the window, I see
Dana talking with her visitor,
who might be her sister. They
look alike. All I can think about
now is what's coming later,
and anticipation creeps along
my spine, manifesting itself
in a huge crop of goose bumps.

> Mom notices me shiver. *Cold?*
> *Let's go inside. I should probably*
> *think about leaving anyway.*
> *Whitney? I want you to know*
> *how proud I am of you for*
> *hanging tough in the program*
> *and digging yourself out.*
> *I was so scared for you. And me.*
> *I know I haven't told you enough,*
> *but I love you very much, and*
> *I promise to do better as a mother.*

She gets to her feet and I join
her for the short walk to
the front door, noticing
Dana's wink as we pass.
Despite guilt, game on.

Fortuitously

Dana's room is only three doors
away from mine. I wait almost
an hour after lights-out before
venturing down the hall and
slipping inside. She waits for me
in bed, two little tablets in hand.
"What are they?" I ask, hoping

> for the exact answer she gives.
> *Oxycodone. You into opiates?*

Oh, darling, if you only knew.
"I'll try anything once." I pop
one, put the other into my pocket
to save for right before our next
drug test. Tonight I'm going to
sink down, down, down. It's a slow,
lovely drop, and oh, how I've longed
for this feeling! Denial is pointless.

> *Okay, baby. Payment required.*
> *Take off your clothes. Sex is better*
> *naked.* She watches me strip, pulls
> back her covers, and I shimmy in
> beside her already nude body.
> *There's a pretty girl. Kiss me.*

The one thing I never did with
a john was kiss them, or let them
kiss me. But, even as a form of payment,
kissing Dana isn't so bad. In fact, it's nice.

Maybe it's the oxy, or maybe it's
because she's a girl, not in spite
of that fact, or maybe it's just because
I've missed being intimate with anyone,
but the heat of her skin, which is satin
soft, and the rich perfume of her
femaleness turns me on completely.

No, I've never been with a woman
before, but everything feels familiar,
from the curves of her heavy breasts
to the invitation between her slim thighs,
and my mouth and tongue and fingers
know exactly what to do to pay my debt
in full. She signals the end with a shudder

> and quiet moan, then draws me
> into her arms, laying my head
> against her chest, where I can hear
> the stutter of her heart. *That was
> outstanding. I'll expect you back
> tomorrow night.* When I start to
> question her, she shushes me.
> *Those are eighty-milligram oxys,
> and go for thirty a pop. How
> much do you think you're worth?*

Good question.

A Poem by Andrew McCarran
How Much Is It Worth

To discover the girl
who infuses every day
with light, even when
she's not here—it's enough
to know she's woven into your

life,

a luminous ribbon.
A promise of happiness.
How much can be forgiven,
when the excuse

is

existence, no other way
to reach tomorrow?
Morality becomes

meaningless

when you're wandering
the streets, the way home
lost to you. Forbidden.
What is the future

without

hope for a rainbow
on the far side of the storm,
no hint of sunshine
to shimmer through the gray
in a world emptied of

Eden.

Eden
Last Week

I chickened out. I swore to
myself I'd tell Sarah everything
she wanted to know about
my background: Boise; Pastor
Streit, Assembly of God minister,

not to mention my father; evil, in
Mama disguise; my younger sister,
Eve. I hope she's okay. She always
was smarter about dealing
with our parents than I. She'll be

a freshman this year, at least
if she pretends to do exactly
what Mama tells her, and
wouldn't our mother be surprised
to know that my little sister

is every bit as rebellious as I am?
Was. The rebellion has kind of
been shaken out of me. Damn.
That thought makes me sad,
because it means Mama won.

So yeah, I took the coward's way
out. Kept my mouth shut, and
now I regret it, mostly because
I just got another e-mail from Andrew.
He's the only person in the whole

world who can help me rebuild
my confidence, which makes
perfect sense, since he was the one
who built it for me in the first place.
Knowing he thought me worthy

of his love was all I ever needed.
And now, he cyber promises
he'll love me, no matter what.
*My beautiful Eden. Desperation
drives people to places they'd never*

*ever go otherwise. Whatever
horrors you suffered in the desert,
whatever lengths you decided
were necessary to remove yourself
from that place, I stand firmly*

*in your corner. You don't need
forgiveness. The person I must
learn to forgive is myself. I could
see trouble brewing, and I chose
to love you selfishly. I won't make*

*that mistake in the future. I promise.
I'd give everything I own to hold
you again. Tell me how to find you.
Tell me what I have to do to get
you back in my life. Your Andrew.*

My Andrew

Straightforward, like Andrew
himself. I wish I could believe
it can be as easy as telling him
where to find me. Come to Vegas.
I'll meet you just off the strip,

where I once gave a tooth-impaired
guy a BJ for twenty dollars.
Of course, if *you* want oral sex, no
charge other than your continued
misplaced faith in me. In us.

I need to be pragmatic. Believing
in miracles is what led me here
to start with. "Hey, Almighty, giving
source of love, please bless the unlikely
love I've found with Andrew.

Remember how I asked you that,
not even a year ago? Remember the faith
I invested in you, despite the example
my father, 'your representative on
earth,' demonstrated on a daily basis?"

Am I actually talking to God, and
not only that, but talking out loud?
Glad there's no one close by to hear me.
Pretty sure everyone at Walk Straight
has given up any notion of him, if they

had one to begin with. Little
evidence of God in the backseat
of a john's car, or some seedy
motel room, and even less in
the eyes of your pimp when he's

beating you while ranting about
your failures as a good little
prostitute. Almost every girl here
tells a similar story of being scooped
up by some predatory man when

it was obvious they had nowhere
else to go. Runaways, most of them.
I suppose if I'd been on the street
for very much longer, some smooth-
talking guy would have latched

onto me, convinced me I'd be safer
in his care than on my own. A few
more days, struggling to eat and
clean the ugliness from my body,
I probably would have been grateful

for the intervention. Instead, I found
a helpful priest. So maybe God was
watching out for me after all. I whisper,
"Father, forgive me. And if it's your
will, please bless Andrew and me."

My Counseling Session

Is after lunch, which I can't eat
because of the nerves tap dancing
in my stomach. I practically crawl
to Sarah's office, coaxing myself
the whole way to go ahead and tell

my entire tale of woe. I knock on
the door, hoping something has called
her away, but no such luck. Instead,
she invites me in with that chirpy
voice, and I have no choice but to

      comply. A whooshing fills my ears
      as I sit across the desk from Sarah.
      She takes one look at the way I'm
      shaking and gushes, *What's wrong,*
      Ruthie? Did you see a vampire?

That makes me giggle. "A vampire?
Don't you mean a ghost?" I must look
as pallid-faced as I feel. "Anyway, no.
I didn't see either. It's just . . ." Go on.
Reach deep for the courage you need.

"I think it's time for me to tell you
some stuff. First of all, my name
isn't Ruthie. It's Eden. Eden Ruth Streit,
and my parents aren't dead (at least,
I don't think so), and I'm from Boise. . . ."

Ice Broken

It all comes gushing out,
as if a dam breaks inside
me. I rush the telling,
sure if I slow down I'll grind
to a complete halt. I notice

Sarah nodding, but she stays
silent, like she intuits my fear
of stopping before the climax.
I know this can't surprise her,
that she's heard plenty of awful

things before, but when I get
to the part about Tears of Zion
and Jerome, her eyes grow
wider and wider, and when
she finally gets the chance to

> speak, she says, *I've just been*
> *reading up on teen boot camp*
> *horror stories. Your Tears of Zion*
> *wasn't mentioned, but there are*
> *several similar places that*
>
> *invoke conservative religious*
> *values to abuse their clients.*
> *Most parents, however, don't have*
> *any idea about their practices,*
> *which include isolation, denial*

of food, water, and the ability
to use the bathroom. Sometimes
they get shut down, but usually
they just move and set up shop
somewhere else. It's very hard

to regulate them because often
they operate as "private schools,"
which have a whole different
regulatory process than, say,
rehab facilities or public entities.

Thank you, God! She believes
me! A huge knot of tension
tumbles from my shoulders,
and a warm wave of relief
washes over me. Still, tears

spill onto my cheeks. "I thought
everyone would think I was
lying. The only thing is, Mama
knew what was going on, and
she left me there anyway."

Are you sure, Ru—I mean, Eden?
From everything I read, parents
rarely have a clue about what
goes on in these places. Why
would your mother leave you if . . .

She Trails Off

Noticing the way my face
turns to marble. "I guess
you'll have to ask her that.
I assume you'll need to be
in touch with them. But

do you really have to?
I'm so scared that if you
send me back to Boise,
they'll make me return
to Tears of Zion. Mama

says I'm possessed, claimed
by Satan, and she really,
truly believes that. Please,
please, find a way to keep
me at Walk Straight. I'll do

anything—work here for free,
or go to work somewhere else
and pay you to let me stay.
Whatever it takes. I can't go
home!" But now, she's shaking

> her head, no. *I wish I could
> tell you okay, Eden, but the law
> is very clear that I must report
> your whereabouts to your legal
> guardians, who happen to be*

your parents in this case.
They have a right to know
you're alive and safe. Besides,
what about your young man?
She's completely missed the point.

Still, I knew this was not
only possible, but probable.
I'll find a way to make it work.
And she's right about Andrew,
if nothing else. "I understand.

Do whatever you have to do.
But is there a way for me to
maybe talk to a judge about
emancipation?" The word swims
out of my subconscious.

That is a possibility. As long as
you're at least sixteen, as per
Nevada law, you can petition
the court. You're seventeen, yes?
And when will you be eighteen?

"I just turned seventeen
last month. Right before I
came here, in fact." A birthday
to remember, alone on the street,
sleeping behind a Dumpster.

I Learn

The requirements
of emancipation,
which are pretty
much the same in
Idaho as in Nevada:

Must be at least sixteen.
Check.
Must be living away
from your parents.
Check.

Must have the financial
security to be independent.
Almost check.
Walk Straight can
help me find a job.

Must stay in school
until you're eighteen.
Check.
And this is where
things get tricky.

Both mother and father
must agree to let the child
emancipate.
Guess there's only one
way to find out.

I Also Learn

The pros and cons
of emancipation.
Pro: You can enter
into contracts without
a parent's signature.

Con: You can be sued
if you violate said contracts.
Pro: You can also sue
someone, if that's a priority.
Yeah, me? Sue who?

Con: Cannot drop out
of school without written
permission from
the school board. No problem.
I want to be educated.

Pro: Can go to the doctor
of your choice and parent
doesn't have to okay
treatment. Wonder if that
includes mental health.

And just FYI: Still can't vote
until age of majority; can't drink
till twenty-one. And worst
of all, can't marry without
parental consent until eighteen.

Which Brings Me Back

To Andrew. Everything seems
to. Six months ago, I believed
we would marry as soon as I
turned eighteen. Yes, I knew
that was young to make such

a momentous decision, but
the overwhelming love we felt
for each other trumped common
sense. Now, I don't know if
even the deepest affection

can overcome the reality
of who I am, what I've become.
This isn't a romance novel,
not that I've ever read one.
Mama would have gone off

the deep end had she ever
found me in possession
of a steamy confessional.
Wonder what she'll say when
she finds out what's become of me.

If she suspected Satan's handiwork
in my relationship with Andrew,
she'll have no doubt at all that
he's holding court inside me
once she's privy to why I'm here.

I Look at Sarah

Who stares back at me, and I see
something in her eyes. Something
dark. Hidden. Something like
a secret. Suddenly I know. "You
were in the life once, weren't you?"

> No hesitation. *Yes, Eden, I was,*
> *although the circumstances were*
> *somewhat different from those*
> *of most of the girls here. Once*
> *upon a time, I was a world-class*
>
> *gymnast, used to having all eyes*
> *on me. After a horrible fall,*
> *I could no longer compete or*
> *perform, but I still had a great body,*
> *and I was only nineteen. I did get*
>
> *a few TV commercials and stuff,*
> *but not enough to cover the drug*
> *dependency I'd developed after*
> *the injury and beyond. Someone*
> *suggested escorting with a high-*
>
> *priced service. Believe it or not,*
> *many failed athletes end up there,*
> *and celebrity has its advantages,*
> *including the level of clients who*
> *are willing to pay top dollar for it.*

She's so open about it, it's scary.
Why didn't I suspect it before?
"How long did you do it? And
what got you out? And why are
you here?" So many questions!

Sarah takes a deep breath.
I escorted for a little over three
years. I can't say it was an awful
experience because, like I said,
the men who pay upwards of

a thousand dollars an hour for
your company tend to be looking
for exactly that, with fringe benefits,
of course. For the most part, they're
respectful, even kind, if a little kinky.

What got me out was two things.
The first was my boyfriend, who
found out what I was doing and
issued an ultimatum: Stay where
I was, or stay with him and he

would support me through rehab.
The second was watching younger
and younger girls being moved into
the business, and really coming to
understand just what was at stake.

Which doesn't exactly explain
how she ended up here. "But why
did you get involved with Walk
Straight? You were already an
adult when you started escorting."

> *Yes, and there was some rather*
> *ugly lobbying being done by adult*
> *sex workers who don't like the term*
> *"sexual exploitation" because they*
> *say there's no coercion involved.*

> *But I saw teens who were promised*
> *the world and forced out on the streets.*
> *Maybe not where I was, but nearby.*
> *I decided to get my degree in social*
> *work and lobby on the other side.*

I glanced at her left hand, find
no telltale ring, ask the question,
though I'm afraid of her answer.
"So, what happened with your
boyfriend? Are you still together?"

> *No. But I'm with someone different*
> *now. He fell in love with me despite*
> *knowing about my past. It's all about*
> *the man. But trust me, you can't hide*
> *from the truth. It's persistent.*

A Poem by Veronica Carino
The Truth Is Persistent

Once, I believed it possible
to hide lies behind a wall
of plausibility, but the facade
always crumbles. The only way to

                                    help

rebuild any semblance
of trust's to come clean and
plunge into apology, hoping
you don't drown. I've always
managed to float, but that's

                                    me

and the depth of Cody's
deception is hard to reconcile.
When the details first became clear,
I thought it would be impossible to

                                    find

the compassion to go on
caring. But when I saw him
leaning into the opened arms
of death, a fierce sort of

                                    forgiveness

surfaced, transcending anger
and resentment, buoyed
by the tenacity
of my indestructible love

                                    for him.

Cody
How Do I Believe

Love is still possible
for a creature like me?
It's not just the half-man

that I've become who's
undeserving of the devotion
of someone like Ronnie,

or anyone at all. It's the person
I already was—the one
responsible for the rest—

whose right to even exist
I question. He's a liar.
Cheat. Hopeless addict.

Always seeking the easy
way out, and unable to admit
the horrible mistakes he was

making, despite the evidence
mounding right under his nose
and stinking like dog shit.

And now. Now there's no way
to turn back the clock and
choose another path, let alone

fix what he's done to his family,
his beautiful girl, his so-called
friends. Himself. All ruined.

Busting My Pity Bubble

Mom walks through the door, and
for once, all smiles. In fact, she's
humming. "What's up with you?"

> She comes over, kisses my forehead.
> *Your social worker has accomplished*
> *some magic. Apparently, Jack's*
>
> *medical insurance is still in force for*
> *you and me, and with Nevada expanding*
> *Medicaid under the Affordable Care Act,*
>
> *your bills here are pretty much covered.*
> *Plus, she found a rehab hospital*
> *with some charitable giving "angels"*
>
> *willing to take care of whatever costs*
> *insurance won't cover. You can move*
> *there and start your rehab as soon as*
>
> *your doctors say you're ready. It's*
> *supposed to be an amazing place, and*
> *I hear the food is a lot better, too.*

She laughs as if that's the funniest
thing ever. Hate to burst her own
bubble, but, "What if I don't want rehab?"

Her mouth snaps shut, and suddenly
she looks about seventy years old. "Can't
you just put me in a home or something?"

Yes, she can. Your own *home, but not*
till after your inpatient rehab. After
that, there will be more rehab, so shut

your mouth and for God's sake, quit
feeling sorry for yourself. Ronnie stomps
into the room and across the floor,

looking every bit the part of a pissed
little girl. Man, she is something.
Why did she have to come into my life

just as it was ending? She reaches the bed,
nods once at Mom, and plops her cute
little behind right down on the mattress.

It strikes me that she and my mother
have never met, except for in passing
at Jack's funeral. "Mom, this is—"

Your mom and I have met, interrupts
Ronnie. *In fact, together we have*
formed the Cody Bennett Fan Club

and Two Woman Cheer Squad.
Our mission is to get your ass out
of that bed and on your feet again.

Mom's Expression

Changes to smug.
I really don't get it.
I will never stand on

my feet again. My
head begins to twist
side to side. "Not

going to happen and
you know it. Why
don't you just leave

me alone? Go find a real
man. Someone who'll
love you the way you

deserve to be loved.
Seriously, Ronnie. I'm
a sinking ship. Don't

go down with me when
the lifeboat is empty
and waiting for you."

> Ronnie turns to face
> me straight on. *Last
> time I looked, assault*
>
> *was a crime punishable
> by jail time. Consider
> yourself lucky I'd rather*

not experience lockup,
or I just might slap you.
Instead, I'll do this. . . .

With zero regard for
my mom's presence,
Ronnie leans into me,

covers my mouth with
hers. Her lips are sticky
with cherry-flavored gloss.

The kiss is a slow ride
to heaven, and transports
me back to the post-funeral

afternoon we spent in bed,
sponging comfort from
the heat of our intertwined

bodies. If Mom wasn't
watching, I'd try to assess
the boner I must be wearing.

Muscles have memories,
right? Hey. What happens to
a catheter when your dick

gets hard? The sudden
thought makes me pull away.
Still, I say, "Thank you."

Hurt Surfaces

In her eyes, and her face grows
taut in response. *Thank you?*
That's the best you can do, Cody?

I know exactly what she wants
to hear, but if I say it, if I make
it real, I'll just open us both up

to disappointment. Mom looks
almost as eager as Ronnie for me
to admit it, and that makes it harder

yet. "Mom, could you please give
us a few minutes alone?" Her nod
is reluctant, but she leaves the room.

Once she's retreated, I hold out
my hands and Ronnie takes them
into her own. "Veronica Carino,

you are the most amazing girl
in the entire universe. And the fact
is, I fucking love you more than life

itself, which is why I want you to
find the person you deserve, and
that is so not me. . . ." She tries

to interrupt me again, but I shake
my head vehemently. "Listen to me!
It's not just because of my legs."

I pause to gather the courage
to continue the sordid confession,
and Ronnie actually sits there

patiently, not saying a word,
eyes glistening. "Please don't cry,
or I'll never be able to do this.

Look, it isn't just my 'condition.'
it's the stuff I was doing that
resulted in my being here. I told

you things that weren't true, and
didn't tell you things that were true,
and all I did for months was lie to you.

I didn't mean for any of it to happen,
but I was gambling, and couldn't stop,
and when I tried to dig myself out,

the only way I could come up with
was . . ." Goddamn it, how can I tell
her this? Fuck it. Just go for it. Push

her totally away. "The only way I could
come up with was working for an escort
service. That's what I was doing when . . ."

> I let my voice trail off, certain I've said
> more than enough to make her run.
> Instead, she looks me in the eye. *I know.*

Okay, I Did Not Expect That

Her acknowledgment is a complete
surprise, as is her calm acceptance.
"How?" Does Mom know, too?

> *From Vince. He told me everything,*
> *at least everything he knew, and*
> *the police, too. That guy, Chris,*
>
> *was at the poker game, remember?*
> *He followed you to that hotel room.*
> *Killed his girlfriend, and the other*
>
> *man. They said you were lucky*
> *you didn't die, too. He definitely meant*
> *to kill you. Oh. I'm not sure you know,*
>
> *but the other guys at the game were*
> *all called in as witnesses. It wasn't hard*
> *to track Chris down. When the cops*
>
> *knocked on his door, he went out*
> *a window. There was a high speed*
> *chase out into the desert near Red Rock.*
>
> *Finally the dude ended up stuck*
> *in the sand. He jumped out of his car,*
> *shooting. The cops took him down.*

"He's dead?" Her nod brings
relief, and also elicits a small sense
of satisfaction. Extremely small.

He Got What He Deserved

But you couldn't exactly call it
an eye for an eye. It was a two-
for-one deal, and that doesn't touch

what he did to me.
I hope it hurt.
I hope he screamed.

Most of all,
I hope he didn't die
quickly. I close my eyes,

picture him lying
on a bed of hot sand,
bleeding out slowly,

listening to the cops
discuss the relative merits
of glazed versus jelly

doughnuts while a dozen
buzzards circle above him,
edging lower and lower as the cops

move into the shade to wait
for the coroner, who's sitting
in an air-conditioned office—

Earth to Cody

Ronnie's gentle urging elevates
me out of my trance. "Oh. Sorry.
I was just thinking about . . . him."

> Let's talk about you and me instead.
> I'll admit I had a pretty tough time
> when I found out about the stuff
>
> you were doing. But then I started
> thinking about me, and where I was
> then—getting high, cutting school,
>
> hanging out on the strip with my
> friends, and fighting with my parents
> when they called me on it. Who knows
>
> how far I might have gone if I'd kept
> down the same path? Not to say
> I'm perfect now, but it was a wake-up
>
> call, and one I seriously needed.
> I love you, Cody. I should've seen
> you were in trouble. Should've asked.
>
> You probably wouldn't have admitted
> it. Forthrightness (that's a word, yeah?)
> isn't your best thing. That has to change.

I'm Speechless

Is she really going to stay with me,
despite my treachery, not to mention
my disability? "Does this mean you'll

give me another chance? That you
forgive me?" I can't believe she'll jump
right in and agree, and she doesn't.

> In fact, she sits for way too long,
> silently studying my face. Finally,
> she says, *I'm not sure forgiveness*
>
> *is possible, Cody. Trust is the core*
> *of commitment, and my faith in you*
> *has been shattered. Whether or not*
>
> *it's repairable will take time for me*
> *to decide. But if I walk away now,*
> *I'll never know for sure, will I?*

She, at least, could walk away.
Which kind of brings me back to,
"What are you, some kind of saint?"

> Ronnie spits laughter. *You know*
> *me better than that.* Now she turns
> serious. *What I am is in love with you.*
>
> *What I've learned is just how resilient*
> *love can be. You can beat it, pound it*
> *into pulp, but killing it is hard to do.*

Little flickers of hope sizzle
like sparklers inside me. Can it really
be possible to move forward from here,

finish school, build a career, with
a girl as perfect as Ronnie by my side?
Can love even survive, let alone thrive,

immersed in the dreary details
of living with someone like me?
"But what about . . . about . . . ?"

> *I don't know, Cody. I've never*
> *considered myself especially strong,*
> *and I'll have to be, won't I? This*
>
> *isn't just a storm. It's a freaking*
> *tornado, and it's doing its best*
> *to blow our world apart. I guess*
>
> *the question is, do we kneel down*
> *and let it wipe us out, or hang on*
> *tight and work our asses off to rebuild*
>
> *what we can and start again?* She stops
> to draw breath, and I'm struck by
> the way the curves of her breasts expand

and contract, expand and contract.
Hey. What are you staring at? Good
to know your eyes work okay, I guess.

Yeah, My Eyes Work Fine

But other things don't work at all,
and the truth is, sex with Ronnie
was an important part of who "we" were.

"I so want to believe it's possible
to have some kind of future with you.
But you have to understand that

my legs aren't the only things
that might be lost to me. I mean . . ."
I take a couple of deep breaths.

"My favorite memories are lying
in bed with you, holding you close,
touching you, and you teasing me,

making me hard, but making me wait
so it would last a very long time.
And then, being inside you, God!

You are just so incredible, all I want
is to make you feel half as good as
I feel, remembering. What if I can't?"

> She has listened patiently, those
> pretty eyes never veering away
> from mine. Now she says, *I liked*
>
> *that, too. But it isn't what made me*
> *love you. Besides . . .* She grins.
> *Abstinence makes the heart grow fonder.*

We Laugh Together

Warm. Soothing. Remembered.
And that invites another kiss.
Honeyed. Luscious. Reinvented.

> She puts on the brakes too soon. *Better*
> *stop before someone takes a picture.*
> *Besides, we've got work to do.*

Déjà vu. "Uh-oh. I don't think
I like the sound of that. That's what
Federico says every time I see him."

> *I know. And he swears you refuse*
> *to cooperate. Just to be clear, with*
> *me you have no choice, and from*
>
> *what I hear the PTs at the rehab*
> *hospital don't take crap from patients,*
> *so you'd better be prepared to give*
>
> *it your all. I've been doing some*
> *research, and I want to share a few*
> *videos with you.* She reaches into
>
> her backpack, extracts a tablet, and
> turns it on. *First, there's a website*
> *you should check out. It's got a ton*
>
> *of interviews with people with spinal*
> *cord injuries, both paraplegia and*
> *tetraplegia—that's the new word for*

quadriplegia, did you know that?
Apparently she thinks I haven't heard
anything these people keep telling me.

Mom hustles back into the room
just as Ronnie starts touring the site.
She pauses to show us several short clips

of SCI patients, doctors and therapists.
Visiting hours officially end during
the marathon, but apparently my team

thinks this is more important than
rules. Maybe they're right. My biggest
takeaway from the session is knowing

I'm not alone with either my injury
or my reaction to it. It's normal
to feel like a freak when that is, in

fact, what you've become. Still,
every single one of them insists
it's possible to move on and create

a fulfilling future. It's a regular
SCI house party. Wonder how much
is bullshit. Hey. Wait. What if

they're all ringers, not paralyzed
at all, just paid to say they are, and
no worries because hey, it gets better?

Go Ahead, Label Me Cynical

Okay, considering that website
is an SCI resource clearinghouse,
they're probably mostly legit.

> *I've bookmarked that site for you,*
> *but now I want you to watch this*
> *video. It's by this amazing woman. . . .*

It's a long glimpse into the rebound
of a lady who broke her neck in a car
crash. They told her she'd never so

much as move her fingers again,
but by sheer strength of will, and
forcing herself to tap into her muscle

memory, she managed not only that,
but using swim therapy, taught herself
to walk unassisted in water, where gravity

can't interfere. Ronnie holds my hand
until it's over. "That's incredible.
Only problem is, I'm not that strong."

> *Don't say that. You are, and I'll be*
> *here to help you.* She places the tablet
> on the table next to the bed, stands

> and pulls back the sheet, not even
> wincing at the too-obvious tube. *First*
> *things first. It's time for you to sit up.*

A Poem by Iris Belcher

Sitting Up

Who'd have thought this
simple thing would become
an impossible chore?

I'm

very sure I managed it
while in my crib,
when my bones were still
pliable, my muscles soft.
Yet here I am today,

not

able to prop myself upright
for more than an hour at
a time. I'm only thirty-four
and being tugged toward
a distant doorway I'm not

ready

to enter. My mother
won't say it to my face, but
I notice the blame in her eyes,
know when Ginger comes
home I'll see it in her, too, only
magnified, and I will carry that

to

the cold sandy pit
they'll lower me into
without forgiveness when I

die.

Ginger
I Keep Thinking

About Iris dying, withering
into the dried-up flower she's always
aspired to be. I keep thinking
I need to manufacture the tiniest

spoonful of sympathy—elixir
for me. No amount of medicine
can help her now, and I don't feel
the slightest bit bad about that.

Instead, I keep wishing she'd go
ahead and take that long, scary walk
before Gram can manage to pick
me up. Gram tells me it's a matter

of days now, that the final paperwork
giving my grandmother custody
of all of Iris's children will arrive
any time. Does our mother have any

regrets, other than doing the guy
who infected her, obviously without
protection? Considering the state
of her deterioration, that had to have

happened seven or eight years ago,
probably soon after Porter was born.
Baby Sandy was carried in her HIV-
infected womb. Luckily, the stats

were in his favor, at least that's what
Gram told me when I asked why
he wasn't born positive. *Only one
in four babies will pick up the virus*

in utero if the mother goes untreated,
Gram said. Iris didn't even suspect it.
Ob-gyns don't test for HIV as standard
procedure, but even if they did,

Iris wouldn't have known because
she never was one for prenatal care.
I remember her whining when she
was twin-carrying Honey and Pepper:

> *All those tedious office visits,*
> *and the outcome will always be*
> *the same. It's just a way to take*
> *money from people who don't have*
>
> *enough to start with. You're healthy,*
> *right?* Somehow, all six of us
> mostly were, despite the fact that
> Iris smoked at least a pack a day.

Well, healthy except for Mary Ann's
asthma and Porter's heart murmur
and my ridiculous attraction to the very
substances I hated to smell on Iris.

Iris Has No Regrets There

I'm sure. She loved smoking.
Needed to drink. But what
about any of the rest? Does
she realize Sandy might have

come into this world cursed
with a shortened life span?
Does it bother her at all?
What about leaving her kids

behind when she heads on
down to the brimstone-heated
whorehouse? Oh, and how
does she feel about putting me

up for sale? Does she carry
even the smallest thimbleful
of remorse for that at all?
My guess is the only thing

she's sorry about is having
cut her life in half. I suppose
it's a little sad that she'll die
before her thirty-fifth birthday.

Wonder if the kids even know
she's dying. Wonder if they'll miss
the mother who's been nothing
but a negative presence in their lives.

I Only Hope

She never auctioned off my sisters.
Mary Ann would tell me if it happened
to her, not that I can do one damn
thing to change it. And now a big

old knife of guilt rips through me.
Running away accomplished zilch,
especially considering where Alex
and I ended up. It was totally selfish,

and what if it only opened the door
to one of the kids being traded
for cigarette money? I could probably
forgive the fact that Iris was a sex

worker, but making one out of me,
and profiting from the rapes
that ground my childhood into
oblivion? What do I say when

I see her? "Hey, Iris, I'm home.
I'd like to tell you I'm sorry
you're dying, but that would be
a lie. Could you hurry the process,

please?" And how much do I confess
to Gram? I haven't said a word to her
about why I ran off. Do I want her
to hate her daughter as much as I do?

Play It by Ear

That's what I'll do, like every
girl here, pretty much. One day
feeds the next, and the routine
grows exponentially more boring.

I never really learned how to deal
with routine. We've always moved
around a lot, never put down roots
in a town or school, Iris chasing

dreams with penises, one after
another. You can't keep friends
like that, which is why I'm so close
with my sisters and brothers.

Alex was the first outside person
I'd ever truly connected with. God,
I miss her. But I guess she's moved
on with her life, totally independent

of me. For all the texts I've sent her,
she's only bothered to answer a few.
I try one more time now. HEY GIRL.
STILL PUKING IN THE MORNING?

BEEN THINKING ABOUT U AND
HOW WE MET. DID I EVER TELL
U I NEVER HAD A REAL FRIEND
BEFORE U? MISS TALKING TO U.

NOT THE SAME SWAPPING
STORIES WITH STRANGERS.
HEARD SOME GOOD ONES
THO. WELL, SO BAD THEY'RE

GOOD. ALWAYS THOUGHT
I WAS STREETWISE, BUT I
NEVER REALIZED JUST HOW
DIRTY THOSE SIDEWALKS

CAN BE, SPECIALLY FOR KIDS
EVEN YOUNGER THAN U AND
ME. PEOPLE WANT TO CLOSE
THEIR EYES TO WHAT'S GOING

ON JUST OUTSIDE THEIR DOORS
OR ONE BLOCK OVER. HEH. NOT
LIKE I'M TELLING U SOMETHING
U DON'T ALREADY KNOW.

DO ME A FAVOR? TELL ME
SOMETHING I DON'T KNOW.
LOVE YOU. TALK TO ME!
I leave it there, with the less-

than-subtle plea to stay connected,
if only virtually. Despite it all,
how can she toss "us" away so
easily? Did she totally forget me?

I guess this is the downside
to loving someone. When they cut
you loose, pretend like you don't
even exist, how do you say goodbye?

I Tuck My Cell

Into my pocket, go on inside.
It's Saturday—no homework, so
most of the girls are busy doing
crafts, which House of Hope

sells online to help finance
their programs. Next Thursday
is Thanksgiving. The cornucopias,
scarecrow wall hangings, and pumpkin

and turkey candles were finished
in September. We've been working
on Christmas decorations since
I've been here. I'm not really

the crafty type, but pasting sequins
on glass ornaments is easy enough,
and it's better than hanging out
in my room. I slip into a chair

next to Brielle, one of the few girls
I've bothered to get to know. I'm leaving
soon, so have done my best to avoid
making friends. But there's something

special about her, and you can't
always silence attraction. "You've
got glue stuck to your head." It clings
to the burnished copper waves

like ice. Brielle tosses her hair
back over her shoulders, looks
at me with striking gray-blue eyes.
Good thing it's Elmer's, huh?

*But remind me to wash it before
I try and brush it. Hard enough
to keep my ends from splitting.*
Her ends are perfect. Her hair

is definitely a vanity, but that's
not a bad thing. Every girl here
struggles with self-confidence,
which is how pimps and other

masters of violation maintain
control—by beating it out of us,
verbally and/or physically.
"Are you kidding? I'd kill for hair

like yours. If I try to grow mine
out, I kind of resemble one of those
dogs with fur like a mop, which
is why I keep it cut short."

She laughs, and I love the way
it sounds. Gentle. Sweet. Pure.
*I think those dogs are cute, but
I happen to like your hair short.*

The Chime

Of her laughter touches a place
inside me. Half of me wants to
hug her. The other half tells me
to run before I get hurt again.

But I'm just so, so lonely. I need
to feel like somebody cares,
and not because they're related
to me, which, with the obvious

exception of my mother, means
they pretty much have to care.
Of course, I'm probably totally
wrong to think Brielle might be

interested in hooking up with me.
I've caught her staring a few times,
and when I smile at her, she always
smiles back. Is that meaningful?

We both turn our attention to glue
and sequins and ribbon and beads,
but as we work, I slide my leg
over so it's barely touching hers.

Nonchalantly, of course. Game
on. Her move. It comes swiftly.
She tucks her shin behind my calf,
shimmies it softly up and down.

Exquisite little shivers trill
through my body. Man, it's been
a while since I've experienced
anything even close to this.

When I first got together with Alex,
I questioned whether it was sexual
identity or just the need to be held
tenderly by someone. I think I just

found the answer, cleared up
any sense of confusion. I still can't
be sure it doesn't have a lot to do
with the way I've been mistreated

by men, and maybe one day I'll change
my mind, so for now I'll just consider
myself bi, leaning toward women.
Right now I find myself leaning

toward the girl on my right. "Want
to take a walk later?" I ask, sure
despite our tangled legs that she'll
say no. "It's gorgeous outside."

> *No.* The word deflates my happy
> bubble. But then she qualifies,
> *Not later. Let's go right now.*
> *I'm feeling claustrophobic anyway.*

We Put Away

Our craft supplies, clean the table.
There aren't a whole lot of rules
here at House of Hope, but respect
for others is required, and this qualifies.

We can take off if we want; the doors
are unlocked during the day and
only bolted at night against danger
outside them. Brielle and I sign out,

so the staff understands we're gone.
Should we not return, the proper
authority will be informed,
but very few girls who leave

don't come back. For most, there's
nowhere better to go. Right now,
a test-the-waters stroll is in order.
"See? Isn't it great today? I think

November must be the best month
in Vegas. Still warm, but not melt-
your-makeup hot." We start along
the sidewalk, and before very long

> Brielle reaches for my hand.
> Our fingers link, and we don't care
> who sees. *Do you wear makeup?*
> *I've never noticed it before.*

"I used to wear it all the time, but
there's no reason to here, you know?
Besides, it reminds me of a place
in my life I'd rather not revisit."

We are beyond sight of the House
of Hope windows. Brielle stops,
turns so we're facing each other.
I understand. I've got one of those

*places, too. But I think it's good
to talk about it. My grandpa always
used to say that keeping secrets
chews you up from the inside out.*

*I'll tell you about my place if you
tell me about yours. But first . . .*
Her kiss, like her gentle demeanor,
is so different from Alex's—soft,

sweet. Tempting. It doesn't last long—
not close to long enough—but we are
very aware of traffic, some of it
slowing to gawk. One guy even beeps

and yells encouragement. Brielle
pulls away, face slightly red. *Sorry.
Hope that was okay. I just wanted
you to know how I feel. Was it okay?*

I Love That She's Worried

I love that she cares enough to ask
permission rather than expecting
me to respond the way my body
most definitely has. "It was more

than okay. It's been a long time
since I've kissed anyone. The last
person I was with quit kissing me
before she tore us apart. Thank you."

She shakes her head, and her eyes
insist she does not understand.
"Thank you for showing me
there is still beauty in the world.

All I've seen for most of my life
is ugliness. So, okay. Let's walk
and I'll share my story with you."
We tour the neighborhood, finally

come to a park with shade trees
and a playground that seem out
of place in Las Vegas. By the time
we settle at a picnic table, sitting

very close, and comfortable that way,
Brielle knows the circumstances
of my arrival at House of Hope. When
I finish, she boosts herself up on

the table, facing me and putting
my eyes level with the full curves
of her breasts. She leans forward
until her eyes are even with mine.

>   *God, that so sucks. I can't believe*
>   *your mom is that evil. And I'm*
>   *sorry your girlfriend left you like*
>   *that.* She kisses me again, and this

time there's no one watching,
no reason not to escalate into
the red zone, all the way to
breathless. "Holy crap. You're hot."

>   She smiles. *Ditto. So, fine. Guess*
>   *it's my turn for confession. I didn't*
>   *know my dad, either. But my mom,*
>   *she was pretty cool. She worked hard*
>
>   *to take care of me, but then she got*
>   *sick. I was fifteen when she died,*
>   *and they sent me to foster. The first house*
>   *was okay, pretty nice, really, but they*
>
>   *decided they didn't want to take care*
>   *of teens so I got moved. I don't know*
>   *how people like Rick and Claudia*
>   *manage to pass background checks.*

The Rest of Her Story

Is about what I expected. Seems
Rick had quite a thing for teenage
girls. When he got too friendly,
Brielle told him she was a lesbian.

One night he decided to "fix her
little problem," and to help convince
her he brought a gun into her room,
forced it into her mouth and gave

her the choice. Suck the thirty-eight,
or suck him. Then he proceeded
to do his best to "turn her." Acutely
aware that the pistol was nearby,

Brielle didn't fight, but she ran
away later that night and was on
the street for a couple of days
when a proactive cop picked her

up before one of Vegas's numerous
pimps could. Her caseworker
believed her tale, and she ended up
at House of Hope, better off than

many girls in similar situations.
Unlike me, she'll be here at least
a year, until she turns eighteen.
Which complicates things.

A Poem by Micah Lerner
Complications

Rarely have I allowed
myself to tumble
for someone, but it
appears I've taken a

                                    hard

stumble, and finding my feet
again is proving difficult.
It's not that I don't want
the experience, but

                                    time

is a luxury I have no way
to indulge, and why
did it have to be this guy
I was destined

                                    to fall

for? I mean, Seth's kept
by the very man who gave
me a chance to jump-start
my career, here

                                    in

a place where dreams too
often die, sucked dry
of hope by a city that
celebrates sin in favor of

                                    love.

Seth
I Didn't Expect

To fall in love again, and definitely
not here in Vegas, here in David's care,

here where I must be careful not to
expose that fact to anyone. Not even

Micah. Not yet. I mean, he has to suspect,
and if I dared trust my feelings, I'd swear

he's in love with me, too. When we're
together, the outside world melts away,

and it's just the two of us there. Despite
our different backgrounds, we have so

much in common, from our taste in movies
and books, to our favorite cuisines.

And where our opinions differ, we're willing
to compromise. For instance, I'll put up

with Broadway music and he'll take a listen
to country. Not sure we've totally swayed

each other, but we do agree broadening
horizons isn't a bad thing. He makes me

feel—dare I say it out loud?—hopeful.
Like there's a real future available to me.

Of Course, As Soon as I Think

That way, the reality of my situation
slaps me upside the head. To have

a real future with Micah would mean
deserting David, which could very

well lead to problems for Micah, unless
David was willing to let me go, and who

knows when he might get sick of me?
But then I'd need a place to live, which

would require an income. And if I were
to commit to Micah, I'd have to leave

escorting behind. What else can I do?
I didn't even graduate high school.

I suppose a minimum wage something
would be possible, but I'm used to living

well. I'm sure I could get my GED, but
then what? College? Paid for how, and

to study what? I'm just a gay hick farm
boy loser. So who am I fooling? There's

no hope of escape for me. For now,
I'll just pretend to believe in possibilities.

It's Thanksgiving

And I'm helping out at YouCenter,
which is hosting a big turkey dinner

this afternoon for kids with nowhere
else to go. David doesn't especially

care about the holiday, other than
the fact that most people spend it

with their families, rather than in
casino showrooms. Hell, even Have

Ur Cake expects a slow evening.
Guess L-tryptophan and pumpkin pie

bloat aren't especially conducive to
the desire for paid sex. Tomorrow,

Black Friday, johns will probably be
looking for deals. Meanwhile, kitchen

work is mostly keeping my mind off
my future. I've always enjoyed cooking,

though I've never attempted anything like
an entire Thanksgiving dinner. Good

thing Charlie's here to help. "This stuffing
smells incredible," I tell her. "My mom

makes plain old cornbread with onions.
I bet the sausage really spices it up."

Sausage. The word entices a memory—
Dad and me joking about venison

sausage and haute cuisine. Wonder
who's sharing Dad's table tonight.

Wonder if I should try calling him
one more time. Charlie stops humming.

> *Sausage, my dear, makes the stuffing.*
> *That, and fresh rosemary. Of course,*
>
> *I prefer it cooked inside the bird,*
> *but I would have had to be here by*
>
> *six a.m. to make that happen. Baked*
> *in a casserole will just have to do.*

"Is your mom a great cook? Where
did you learn your way around a kitchen?"

> She snorts. *My mom is the frozen*
> *food queen. No, my grandpa taught*
>
> *me. But I love it. In fact, I've been*
> *thinking about a culinary arts degree.*

"You mean like go to school to learn
to cook? But you already know how."

> *I don't know everything. Besides,
> you can also take restaurant*

> *management, which basically
> gives you a business degree.*

> *With the right credentials, you can
> make bank, especially if you get hired*

> *by a big casino or something. I'm
> not going to be a doctor or a lawyer.*

> *But that doesn't mean I don't want
> to earn a good income. Why not*

> *make it doing something I love to
> do anyway?* She slides the big pan

of stuffing into the oven, closes
the door with a satisfied smile.

Huh. I like to cook. "Is a culinary
arts degree, like, major expensive?"

> *Depends. Le Cordon Bleu is pricey.
> But College of Southern Nevada isn't.*

Think Outside the Box

Mom used to tell me that. Still,
she probably would've laughed

at the notion that a person might
be able to make a decent career

out of cooking, and Dad would
have chuckled right along with her.

I'm sure a short-order cook's paycheck
couldn't approach what I make on

a single night escorting. But what
about overseeing a five-star kitchen?

Definitely something to think about,
especially if things get serious between

Micah and me. And if not that, at least
I'm thinking outside the box, rather

than flinging myself into a big pond
of pity. Funny how when I think about

home any culture I managed to absorb
from Carl and David dissolves and rural

Indiana takes over. Home. Back home.
Home sweet home. No place like home.

Around Two P.M.

People start trickling in, knowing
dinner is supposed to be served at three.

I'm familiar with many of the faces,
but some are new to me, and some

interest me for whatever reasons.
There's a butch girl who can't be

more than twelve. Surely she's not
homeless, right? Surely she has family

somewhere who cares? I asterisk
a mental note to ask Charlie about her.

Ditto the girl, maybe a year younger
than me, coming through the door now.

She's pretty enough to model, except
she looks so scared. Not sure there's

a market for that. Oh, but wait. What is it
about her? She's lanky, and wearing heels

that make her even taller. Is that why her gait
is awkward? I nudge Charlie. "Who's that?"

> *Pippa. Born Philip. You should talk*
> *to her. She could use a friend like you.*

Born Philip

That explains a lot. But transitioning,
or just cross-dressing? Only one way

to find out, at least if she feels like
sharing the information with me.

Once dinner is on the table, I make
sure to take the seat next to Pippa.

It isn't hard. No one else has chosen
it. "Hi. I'm Seth. Mind if I sit?"

She looks at me nervously, with dark
eyes enhanced with expert makeup.

> *Uh . . . No. I mean, I guess so. If you
> want to.* Her gentle voice is more

male than female, but it belongs
to a boy, not a man. "I'd like to . . . ?"

> She understands the implied question.
> *Philippa, but you can call me Pippa.*

> She passes a big bowl of cranberry
> sauce, skips it herself. *You work here?*

"Volunteer," I correct. "I haven't seen
you here before. Are you new to Vegas?"

Not really, but kind of new to YouCenter.
I ran into Charlie downtown. She told me

about it. It's nice to be around people
who don't think you're a freak, you know?

"I do know. So, where you from?
I mean, if you want to tell me. Oh,

and please pass the gravy." I notice
she skips it. "What? Don't like gravy?"

Love it. But I'm watching my weight.
I'm from Provo, which explains why

I'm in Vegas. Other than Salt Lake City,
which is more open-minded than most

people realize, Utah isn't exactly trans-
friendly. Las Vegas was a cheap ticket.

We take a few minutes to stuff food
into our mouths. "Man, Charlie, you can

cook for me anytime!" Everyone nods
and murmurs agreement, and Charlie

beams. *You ain't seen nothing yet,*
she replies. *Wait till you taste the pie.*

Pippa Skips the Pie, Too

But seems content enough watching
me devour pumpkin cheesecake.

Afterward, everyone helps clear
the tables, and a few step forward to

wash the dishes. Pippa and I grab cups
of coffee and wander outside to sit

on a bench haloed by the duskish light.
"The days are short. Almost December."

> *I hear they've already had snow*
> *in Utah. It definitely fell early.*

"I used to like the snow, but we only got
four or five inches a year in Perry County.

Sure did get cold, though. Not like here,
where they think fifty degrees is cool.

So, anyone missing you in Provo? Do
your parents know where you are?"

> *Incredulity spikes her laugh. They*
> *couldn't give two fucks about where*
>
> *I am. They stopped worrying about*
> *me years ago, when I wouldn't quit*

insisting God put me in the wrong
body. My mother says God doesn't make

mistakes, but I identified at three. All
I wanted was to play with my sister's

Barbies. All my father wanted was to
beat the girl out of me. Couldn't do it.

Different fathers. Different states. Different
religions, I'm guessing. Similar attitudes.

"My dad didn't beat me when I came
out, but he completely disowned me.

I can't imagine what he might have
done if I'd told him I was a girl in

a boy's body. Gender dysphoria is not
in his vocabulary. Are you transitioning?"

Pippa nods. Started hormones, and
I've done a few rounds of electrolysis,

but that's so expensive. I want to go
all the way at some point, though.

A girl doesn't need a penis. In fact,
it's counterintuitive to who I'm becoming.

"Do you have a safe place to live?
How are you supporting yourself?"

Let alone affording estrogen
supplements and facial hair removal.

> *I have a little studio, yes. Not much,*
> *but it's cozy and clean enough. As for*
>
> *how I pay my bills, you can probably*
> *guess. No back alley blowjobs, not*
>
> *anymore. I'm not proud of it, but I've*
> *no other way to make that kind of money,*
>
> *and I'm saving up for procedures.*
> *Besides . . .* She smiles. *What better*
>
> *excuse to shop for pretty clothes?*
> *I'll quit someday, once I've become*
>
> *the woman I was meant to be. In*
> *the meantime, I'm surviving. But mark*
>
> *my words. Philippa Young will make*
> *something special of herself one day.*

"I believe you. Until then, never
apologize for doing what you have to."

I Don't Mention

My personal connection to "doing
what you have to do," but I do offer

Pippa my friendship. "Anytime you
need to talk, you can call me, okay?

Be really careful out there. This city
is crawling with creeps, and some

of them are dangerous." I take time
to study her face really closely.

"You're lucky. You have amazing
bone structure. You won't need

surgery there. In fact, you could
model. Have you considered it?"

> What girl hasn't? Actually, I'd love to
> find work dancing. The one real gift
>
> my parents gave me was dance classes,
> and my teachers told me I have talent.

"Believe it or not, I might have an in
for you. And not pole dancing, either."

> She smiles. I'd do that, too, except . . .
> Yet another reason I don't want a dick.
>
> But I'd give my left nut for a chance
> to dance. Nah. I'd give both of them.

Which cracks me up. "I can't promise
anything, of course. But I do know

some people." I don't mention names,
nor my living arrangement. "I should

go. You've got my number." I head
on inside to say goodbye to everyone,

then call for David's driver to pick
me up around the corner. No one here

knows where I live, or with whom.
Once we're on our way home—scratch

that, back to David's house—I call
Micah, careful not to say too much

within earshot of Percy. "Hey. Hope
you've had a great Thanksgiving.

Would love to hear from you. Please
call me later." Way to be ambiguous

when what I really want to be is in
his face, followed by him in mine.

And what I wish is I was on my way
back to a home Micah and I share.

Home

I check the time. Six p.m. here in the Pacific
zone, two hours later in Indiana. Dad will

probably still be awake. Hands shaking,
I dial the number I committed to memory

years ago. One ring. Two. Three. On four,
a machine answers. *Can't answer the phone*

right now. Please leave a message. Dad's
voice. Strong. Clear. Loved. Now, the beep.

"Hi, Dad. Happy Thanksgiving. Hope you
spent it with Aunt Kate or someone. Sure

do miss you. How did the harvest go?
So you know, I'm thinking about going

back to school. Maybe getting a degree
in culinary arts. Las Vegas is in dire need

of decent venison sausage. Love you." Huh.
Aunt Kate. Dad's sister. Haven't thought

about her in a while, but she always was
decent. Kind. Wonder if she'd talk to me.

As we pull into the driveway, I make a
note to track down a way to reconnect.

A Poem by Renée Lang
Reconnection

How do you glue
back together
a relationship torn into
scraps like paper?
Where do you find

trust

buried in a stinking heap
of epic past failure?
Losing a child
to illness or accident

is

a bitter tonic to swallow,
but losing one
to personal indifference
would be too

hard

to reconcile, and I've come
much too close—
within the width
of an eyelash—

to

doing exactly that.
I've been given a second
chance with my Whitney.
But how do I

rebuild

her faith in me?
How do I prove my love?

Whitney
Free

From the confines of rehab, and
scared through and through
to be without overseers, unless
you count my family. Yeah,
and how did that work out
last time? Okay, they're doing
a good job of pretending
to care about how I'm feeling.
Well, Mom and Dad are, anyway.

Kyra acts like I'm a dark cloud—
something to draw the blinds
against. She's probably said
two dozen words to me over
the past two days, and those

she barked. *Don't talk
with your mouth full.
Get out of the bathroom.
Put some decent clothes on.
God, look at your arms.
How could you?*

Except for that, nothing.
I'm glad she's flying back
to Vassar on Sunday.
Long-distance silence
is preferable to
the in-your-face kind.

My Arms Are Tattooed

With long silver scars—damage
from shooting up over and over
in the same general location, once
I forgot to care about hiding it.
What did I know? Not like drug
programs teach you how *not* to inject,
when they're warning you about
using at all. Not like I thought
I'd ignore that advice and go walking
with the Lady. She calls to me,
and I'm terrified. I'm weak.

I didn't take that second oxy
back in rehab, not because I
tried to be strong, but because
I lost it somewhere, and figured
that must have been a sign.
It made me take a long look
at myself, and I hated the view.
Once a junkie, always a junkie,
that's what I keep hearing.
But the dope doesn't have to win.

And I can reclaim my body,
abused and broken as it might
be, I can take ownership of it.
Dana thought it was hers for
the price of two pills—pharms
that would slide me back into
the arms of the Lady. Instead,
I pulled away. That time.

It's Weird

Being back in my room.
My room, but not like I left
it. Apparently, Mom thought
I needed a fresh start, so she had
it painted a pale lilac with purple-
and-crimson paisley borders.

It's pretty enough, but not
something I'd choose. Given
free rein, I'd likely pick black,
to match my mood. It's hard
to come home, be confronted
with rules, most of them meant
to keep me from making the same
mistakes that almost killed me.

I understand the need for them,
but they're suffocating me, and
I've only been here a few days.

Yesterday was Thanksgiving.
Talk about strange.
Mom did do the cooking,
and did ask for help from
my sister and me. Way back
when I was just a little kid
we worked in the kitchen together.
But it's been years, and since
then holiday meals have either
been prepared by hired help
or, more often, eaten out.

So, the Turkey Was Dry

The dressing was bland.
And the rolls were underdone.
The best thing was the pies,
apple and pumpkin,
and they came in a box from
our favorite bakery—
Dad's contribution.

Hey, at least he was here,
not hiding out in San Francisco,
his Turkey Day habit
for the past couple of years.
He was even nice at dinner,
and managed the entire meal
with only two glasses of wine.
Mom needed three, but
stayed pleasant enough.

It's like my parents decided
the only way to save me
was to save themselves.
Not that I'm at all sure
it's possible for their marriage
to be resurrected. It was dead
and buried before I left.

Sobering thought.
Maybe that's how
they should've left
it. If it all nose-dives
again, will that be on me?

Today Is Black Friday

A day when any sane person
stays holed up at home, or goes
to the gym to work off a few
calories. But not the Lang clan!
We're going to the mall, and
calling it an adventure.

At least, that's what Mom's
calling it. Dad, who's driving,

> says, *You realize this is insanity?*
> *Look at this parking lot. How*
> *far are you ladies willing to walk?*

Kyra (speaking to the family
in general, not to me specifically)

> claims, *This is a total nightmare.*
> *I bet Coach is already sold out.*

Me? I'm just going along
for the ride, and because
they're scared to leave me
alone in the house, not
that I blame them.

The stores opened early,
but none of us is the type
to rise before dawn so we
can stand in mega-lines,
just to fight the inevitable
crowd, which might actually
thin out later in the day.

We did skip breakfast
instead of working out
to make up for calories
consumed yesterday. Fueled
only by coffee, we hit the mall
a little after ten, including
a six-minute walk in from
the far edge of the parking lot.

Dad was right. This is insane.
The sheer number of people,
all in one place, threatens
to overwhelm me. It's like Vegas
on steroids, only for all its nasty
underbelly, Sin City's facade
is beautiful. Nothing particularly
attractive about Capitola Mall
even without all the jostling.

A guy walking by turns to stare
with eyes that don't quite track
and suddenly I'm carried back
to another day here. I came with
Paige, and we went on a weirdo
watch—that's what we called it—
and ran into one hot creeper
loitering outside the Gap, looking
for stupid girls like me to recruit
into his stable. Wonder how many
pimps are hanging out here today.

I Spot a Possible Few

As we push and shove
our way into the throng,
a determined Kyra carving
a path to Coach, I'm pulling
in air as if through a pillow.
"Mom," I try, but it's a weak
attempt, and she can't hear it
above the clamor. "Mom!"

It's Dad who falls back,
takes a long look at me.
What's the matter? Now
he grabs my hand, and his

skin is hot and I can't stand
the touch of a man—any man,
really, but especially not this Vegas
wolf, who rushes me and I feel his grasp
at my throat, and he's telling
me that he doesn't pay for sex
and now he's cursing,

Fight, you goddamn whore!
Fight or I'll kill you.

"Leave me alone!" I scream,
and even above the din,
people hear. People stare.
People think Dad is hurting
me. Dad. The realization
of what just occurred punches
me and I fall to my knees.

"I'm sorry. I'm sorry. I'm so
sorry." It's a chant. "I didn't
mean it. I'm sorry. I'm sorry."
Finally, I chance looking up.
People are still staring, but
they've pushed away,
forming a wide circle, giving
me space. And now I see

> Dad encouraging the crowd
> to *please move back. Can't
> you see she needs air?* His
> mask is calm, assertive, but
> his voice trembles, denying
> the disguise. *Are you okay?*
> he asks, and I know he wants

to help, but he's definitely scared
to touch me again, so I stretch
my hand toward his. "Please?"
Still, I have to reach deep inside
for the courage not to recoil
when his fingers close around
my wrist and gently pry me
up from the dirty tile floor.

> Once I'm on my feet, he lets
> go of me immediately. *What
> just happened, Whitney? Do
> you want to talk about it?*

Before I Can Answer

A security guard wades in
between us. *Is this man
bothering you, young lady?*

"No, sir. This is my father.
I just had a bit of a panic
attack, that's all. Sorry for
causing a scene." The guy
looks unconvinced, but nods
and returns to patrolling for
shoplifters, dine-and-dashers,
and maybe the odd flasher.

Now that I'm so obviously
safe, the crowd goes back to
scouring stores for bargains,
despite the fact that most of
the good ones are long gone.
Which reminds me, "Kyra
must have found something
good at Coach after all. She
and Mom have been gone
a while." Thank God Kyra
didn't witness my little scene.

Don't change the subject, says
Dad. *Was that a panic attack?
Have you had them before?
You about gave me a heart
attack, Whitney. Are you okay?*

How Many Times

Is he going to ask me that?
Maybe until I answer?
"Yeah, Dad, I'm okay."
Sure I am. For the moment.

"It's just when you grabbed
my hand, it reminded me of
something that happened in
Vegas." I've been mostly silent
about the stuff that went on
while I was working for Bryn.

The focus has been the H, and
fighting addiction. My parents
know I'd been lured into the life
by a panderer—Vegas Vice was
clear about that. But no one's
asked for the details, and I sure
haven't volunteered them.

"I think it was a panic attack.
First, I couldn't breathe. It was
all the people, all the noise.
And then . . . I don't know.
No, I haven't had one before.
I think maybe I just need fresh
air. Is it okay if I go outside?"

> *I'll go with you if you want.*
> *And anytime you need to talk,*
> *please know you've got my ear.*

I Haven't Talked to Dad

In a very long time.
I wouldn't have any idea
what to say to him now.
Would he want to know
that I met Bryn, the phony
"fashion photographer"
who convinced me to run
away so he could pimp me out,
right here in this very mall?

No, probably not. I attempt
a joke to lighten things
up. "I don't have your ear,
Dad. I can see both of them,
one on either side of your
head, and they look firmly
attached." I smile, signaling
humor, but he doesn't get it.

>   *All right then. Let's go*
>   *outside for a while.*

"You don't have to come
with me. I'm fine on my own.
I'll just go find a place to sit
in the sun and watch people
behave badly for a while.
Catch up to Mom and Kyra,
and text me when you're ready
for lunch. I'm getting hungry."

He's Reluctant

To leave me on my own, but
I convince him a few minutes
solo are just the medicine
I need. Awkward thought:
What I wouldn't give for that
oxy right now, or better yet,
a ticket to the Land of Nod.

Stop it, Whitney. Guess I'd
better consider finding a sponsor
after all. Weak moments like this
are exactly why they invented
them. I step out into the cool
coastal morning, where the sun
hints at its presence behind
a gray mist. There's really
no place to sit, except on
the sidewalk—too dangerous
today. So I lean back against
the side of the building, take
deep breaths of sea-flavored air.

Suddenly, a familiar laugh
comes floating toward me from
the parking lot. The annoying
nasal giggle belongs to Paige,
my onetime best friend. I squint
to find her. Yes, there she is,
and she's with . . . Skylar?

Okay, I Get

That it's been almost eight months
since Paige and I went to the party
that basically ruined my life—
the one I left, destroyed by finding
Lucas cemented to Skylar. The one
Paige was too busy making out
with some random guy to take me
home from, so I called Bryn, who
was all too happy to use the excuse
to worm his way into my pathetic life.

But Paige and Skylar are as different
as blue and red. Or at least they were.
Can people change so much so quickly?

Backpedal.
Of course they can.
I pretty much define the concept.
I've been to hell and back.

As they near, it's easy to see who
did the changing. Paige, who always
carried a spare few pounds, is thin
enough to wear those skinny jeans
well. Her hair's styled into short
spikes, and her makeup is plastered
on. Head to toe, she's Skylar's
twin, except if anything, despite
the weight loss, her boobs are even
bigger. Skylar, it pleases me to witness,
has yet to grow an observable pair.

I Hold On to the Thought

As they hit the sidewalk
together, almost straight
in front of me, yet somehow
don't seem to notice I'm here.
Better fix that. "Hey, Paige.
Long time no see, huh?"

> Her jaw totally drops.
> *Whitney? Oh my God,*
> *girl, where have you been?*

> Skylar can't help herself. *Yeah.*
> *And what happened to you?*
> *You look so . . . so rough.*

Rough? My hair has grown
out. My skin's mostly clear.
And I'm wearing a cute long-
sleeved sweater, which covers
the tracks. I ignore the bitch.
"Most recently, I've been in rehab.
Before that, I was in Las Vegas.
With Bryn. Remember him?"

> Paige wrinkles her forehead.
> *You mean the photographer*
> *guy? The one who was stalking*
> *you here last year? What were*
> *you doing with him all that time?*

I have to be careful. Whatever
I say *will* get around. "Modeling,
of course. He had a lot of contacts
in Vegas. But you know it's a dirty
business. Lots of drugs and stuff.
I kind of got in over my head,
so I ended up in rehab. Old story."

> *Wow. Sounds exciting. I want*
> *to hear more. Are you coming*
> *back to school?* asks Paige.

"That's the plan." I wince at
the hard nudge Skylar gives her.
Before they escape, I have to dig,
"How's Lucas? You two still together?"
Not like I don't know the answer.

> Skylar shakes her head. *Nah.*
> *I decided he's not my type.*
> *We have to go. See you around.*

> *Call me,* says Paige, turning
> her back. As they walk away,
> I hear her say, *Wonder what*
> *kind of drugs she got into.*

> *Wonder what kind of modeling*
> *she was doing,* responds Skylar.

Wouldn't she like to know?

A Poem by Eve Streit
Not My Type

That's what I told him.
Did he believe it was a lie,
or could he look through
the windows of my tears,
see beyond the words to

        the truth

behind them? I wanted
to know what it was like
to fall in love, conveniently
forgetting the facts

        of my

sister's disappearance.
Incorrigible. That's what
my parents called Eden when
they tossed her to the jackals,
where her limited

        experience

did not equip her for what
followed. I know because
they've done the same to me—
forced me into isolation
at Tears of Zion, where Father

        is

the heavy hand of God,
or so he claims. All I did
was give my heart away.
Punishment like this is

        incomprehensible.

Eden
Thanksgiving Is Weird

On a personal level, it is the first
I've ever spent away from home,
where the pattern never deviated.
Papa hates turkey, so Mama
put a huge ham in the oven

at ten a.m. exactly. Then the Streit
family went visiting faithful church
members to remind them that thanks
is better shared. We prayed together,
Papa collected a Thanksgiving

offering, and often we left with
food, too, most generally homemade
rolls or pie or maybe even a sweet
potato casserole. By the time we'd get
home, the ham was ready and Mama's

cooking was finished. It was brilliant,
really, and, of course, the whole
plan was Mama's idea. Cooking,
especially baking, isn't her favorite
pastime. And after all that earlier

praying and talking and collecting,
we'd sit at our own dinner table
in silence, which is how most meals
at our house are experienced.
Quietly communing with ourselves.

But Here at Walk Straight

Noise fills the dining room—
girls talking and laughing and
sharing stories of Thanksgivings
past. The majority of those aren't
beautiful, yet they are comforting

because of experiences they have
in common. For many, the best
thing about the day is their pimps
understand that men usually spend
it with their families, rather than

trolling for sex. Fewer customers,
less money, not the girls' fault,
they get a pass. By the time we
get to dessert, everyone's guard
is down, and Rhonda, who's

> usually standoffish, offers
> a memory. *My mama, she all into*
> *skag and she spend a lot of time*
> *in jail, so I had to take care of*
> *my little brother. That's why I'm*
>
> *on the track. I don't know nothing*
> *else. Quit school in sixth grade.*
> *Had to, you know? Never had no*
> *pimp, only me. Mama, when she not*
> *locked up, she work the streets,*

and she told me what to do, and
where to find johns, and how much
to make 'em pay. It's not so hard,
not usually, but you know sometimes
a guy go a little crazy or whatever.

So one time, one Thanksgiving,
Mama was gone and Oscar was
hungry, no food but stale cereal
in the cupboard. I tell him to watch
TV, I'll be back soon. I go out,

and yeah, it was real slow but after
a while along come a black-and-white,
and this old cop stop to see what's what.
"What you doing out here?" he ask.
"Don't you know what day it is?"

I tell him, yeah, but I gotta feed my kid
brother, hoping maybe he let me go,
maybe for a blowjob or whatever.
He say, "Get in," and that made me
scared, but you know what he did?

He drove to Denny's, bought four
turkey dinners, two pieces of pie,
gave it all to me, and a twenty, too.
Didn't ask for nothing. "Feed your
brother," he say. "Happy Thanksgiving."

After That

A lot of cop stories are passed
around, few enough as feel-good
as Rhonda's, though there are some:
Cops who looked the other way.
Cops who offered numbers to

services and rescues like Walk
Straight. One cop who played
protector when he saw a john
on a rampage. But mostly, we hear
about cops who were quick to haul

the girls in. Cops who let them off
in trade for squad-car sex. Two girls
told of cops who chose the role of
pimp, both eventually busted and
made to leave the force. Across

the board, what the girls learned
was not to trust men who wore
badges. Back home in Boise, most
cops I met were fresh-faced hometown
boys, and friendly enough, at least

on the surface. Wonder how many
were hiding dark secrets. I go back
to my room, plop into bed, thinking
about the lies people carry, and
what's to gain by shedding them.

Such Thoughts

Lead to a night of underwater
dreams—struggling to swim up
from the deep without drowning,
finally sputtering to the surface
just about daybreak. On the far

side of the room, my new roommate,
Hana, snuffles softly. Tia, my last
roomie, snored like a bulldozer.
She's been gone two weeks now—
decided the straight and narrow

wasn't for her, and went back to her
pimp, despite the fact that she wore
the scars of his cigarette burns and
his tattoo on the back of her neck,
signifying his ownership. We weren't

close, but I hope she'll be okay, or at
least as okay as you can get, renting
out various parts of your body.
Hana is a soft-spoken Korean American.
She's been here four days now and

I still don't know her whole story.
We're just getting used to seeing each
other in the mirror, and to the unique
sounds of our voices and breathing
patterns. The rest will come with time.

Except, I'm Not Sure

How much time I have left
here. Just got unhappy news
from my counselor, who finally
heard from Mama. Apparently,
she's decided to arrange a reunion.

> *She'll arrive tomorrow.*
> Sarah's eyes hold sympathy.
> *I tried to ask about emancipation.*
> *She told me her relationship*
> *with you is none of my business.*

"Of course she'd say that."
Dread drops into my stomach.
"I'm not ready to go, Sarah. Oh
God, I'm so afraid. Will I have
to leave with her if she insists?"

> *Unfortunately, you would.*
> *Walk Straight can't keep you*
> *if either of your parents wants*
> *you with them instead. Not unless*
> *we can prove extenuating*

> *circumstances like sexual abuse*
> *or neglect. But from what you've*
> *told me, there was neither in*
> *your home. As for Tears of Zion,*
> *that's a different can of worms.*

If my parents couldn't send me
back there, could I deal with living
at home for a year? If I had to,
yes. "What about Tears of Zion?
What if I brought charges?"

> *After we last talked, I did*
> *a little research. Tears of Zion*
> *calls itself a religious retreat*
> *center, not a boot camp or*
> *rehabilitation facility, which*

> *complicates things. The easiest*
> *way to shine a spotlight on*
> *the place would be to allege*
> *that one or more staff members*
> *were responsible for abuse.*

> *The problem with that is, unless*
> *the director—what's his name . . . ?*
> She opens a file to check her notes.
> *Oh yes, Samuel Ruenhaven. Unless*
> *he was personally involved, he could*

> *simply fire whoever was accused,*
> *and it would probably be business*
> *as usual. That said, there were prior*
> *allegations of neglect against him,*
> *though in Idaho, not Nevada.*

Hope Surges

First, because she believes
me enough to dig deeper.
Second, because maybe there
is a solid answer. "Really?
Against Father? What happened?"

> I rethink the question before
> she can answer it. Nothing
> happened. *He settled out of*
> *court, then dismantled his*
> *Idaho operation and moved*
>
> *to Nevada, where his name*
> *hadn't been blasted all over*
> *the media. This was years ago,*
> *of course, before the Internet*
> *made finding information so easy.*

Hope abates. "So no one
will take me seriously
if I come forward?" Beyond
my personal fate, Father and
his disciples need to be stopped.

> *I wouldn't say that, Eden.*
> *For all we know, someone*
> *else might find the courage*
> *if you go first. Or maybe*
> *someone else already has.*

Just cueing in law enforcement
would be a good thing, and
if the media gets hold of it,
at the very least there will be
public scrutiny, something

I'm sure Mr. Ruenhaven would
not appreciate. But he'll have
to change the way he conducts
his business. The question is,
do you want a spotlight on you?

Okay, I hadn't considered
that. I won't be publicly outed,
will I? I'd have to give
details about Jerome, and
the things I accepted, even

encouraged, to escape Tears
of Zion. And I'm sure, should
I accuse my mother of spiking
my tea, she'd be more than happy
to tell the world about her daughter,

who is not only incorrigible,
but also a harlot, in every sense
of the word. I don't know
if that's necessary yet. "I'll think
about it." And decide tomorrow.

Sarah's Phone Rings

I start to leave, but she gestures
for me to stay. *Are you sure?*
Urgency shades her voice. *When
was she supposed to be there?
I see. Okay, I'll ask around.*

She replaces the handset. *Have
you seen Shayleece? She had
a dentist appointment, but never
showed.* Worry creases her face.
Do you remember if she was at lunch?

"Actually, I haven't seen her
since yesterday. But she planned
to go to the dentist. She was excited
about getting that hole in her front
tooth filled. She hated it."

*That's what I thought. Maybe
the bus broke down? But then
she would have called, right?
Will you help me poll the others?
Maybe someone saw her go.*

A half hour later, all we know
is the last person who talked to
her was her roommate, Rhonda.
*That was last night. She was
going outside to have a smoke.*

Rhonda Was Asleep

Before Shayleece came back
in. *If* Shayleece came back in.
No one has seen her since.
Sarah goes to call the police
and report her missing.

A few of us volunteer to canvass
the neighborhood. We go in two-
person teams, in four directions.
I partner with Hana. We head east.
It's afternoon, post-school, and

we pass parents walking with
their children. A few older people
are walking their dogs, and there
are bunches of kids sitting
on car hoods or stoops, smoking

or making out. We ask every
person we come across if they've
seen our friend, with little luck.
It's starting to get frustrating.
It's starting to get worrisome.

> One elderly woman asks for a
> description, nodding her head.
> *I think I might have seen her
> just a few minutes ago. She got
> in a car with some other youngsters.*

Hana and I look at each other.
A few minutes ago? Couldn't
have been her. Still, I ask, "Do
you remember what kind of
car, or what color it was?"

The lady scratches her thin hair.
*I was all the way over on the far
side of my grass, and I don't see
so good anymore. But it was a big
car, and I'm sure it was gray. Or blue.*

We thank the woman and, as soon
as we're down the block, bust up
laughing. *Probably didn't need
to worry,* hiccups Hana. *Bet her
hearing isn't so good, either.*

But now the heavy gravity of
the situation sinks back in.
"Shayleece wouldn't run off.
Where would she go? Besides,
she likes it at Walk Straight."

We keep going until the light
begins to pale, then circle back,
the chances of finding out anything
useful fading with the sun. Dinner
this evening is unusually quiet.

Sleep Is Evasive Tonight

Playing tag with worry
about what the morning
will bring. Usually, I fall
straight into dreams but
an odd slant of moonlight

through the blinds disturbs
the darkness, and the silence
is punctuated by Hana's gentle
snoring. I haven't noticed it
before. Now I can't not hear

it, even with a pillow over
my ears. It reminds me
of my sister. I've thought
about Eve a lot lately, and
now, with Mama coming

tomorrow, a collection of
images mash together in
my head: Eve and me giggling
together in church; Papa
halting his sermon to chastise

us; Mama glaring, Mama
accusing, Mama handing
me a cup of tea; Mama's
face smearing, blurring;
the face of Father Samuel

Ruenhaven swimming
into view; Father staring,
Father chastising, Father
forcing me to pray; Jerome
leering; Jerome coaxing;

the luscious taste of ripe
strawberries; calloused
greedy hands touching
places meant for no one
but the boy whose face

I cannot find. I sit up,
lean back against the wall.
Something's wrong.
Really wrong. Every
nerve in my body tingles,

on full alert. I don't know
what this means, except
there'll be no sleep at all
tonight. Quietly, I slip out
of bed, search for clothes

in the dark, take them down
the hall to the bathroom,
and get dressed. The entire
building is asleep, so I tiptoe
to the rec room, wait for morning.

By First Light

My intuition is shouting a warning,
but can't give me details. I skip
breakfast. Can't possibly eat. When
Mama finally shows her face,
I look every bit as ragged as I feel,

> and the door to Sarah's office barely
> closes behind us before she attacks.
> *Look at you. Hmph. Ended up exactly*
> *as I predicted. You were determined*
> *to prove me right, weren't you?*

The old Eden would find an excuse,
even knowing she wouldn't be believed.
The new Eden has nothing to lose.
"*You* are responsible for my being here.
I didn't deserve what you did to me."

> *Of course you'd try to blame me.*
> *God will punish you for that, too.*
> *I had to see for myself just how far*
> *you fell. One thing's for certain, you*
> *can't come crawling back home. Stay*
>
> *among the filth, where you belong.*
> *It will probably please you to know*
> *you infected your sister with your*
> *disease, but Samuel will reform her,*
> *and she won't escape the way you did.*

A Poem by Vince Carino

Blame

Is a bullshit game,
and I'm a world-class
expert at gaming.

        Some

are easy, some not so much,
but you need rules to play
competently, and one of the

        things

you learn very quickly
about the blame game
is there

        are

no guidelines, no
predetermined directions
to an exit strategy. What's

        worse

is when the guilt
that evolves continues
to grow longer and deeper

        than

the original stab
of remorse. Had I been
responsible for Cody's

        death

I'd probably be over it
by now. But this will haunt
me until I go to my own grave.

Cody
You'd Think

Sitting up is something easily done,
and for most people, from the time
they're six or seven months old, it is.

Learning the skill is baby's play.
Relearning it has been one of the hardest
things I've ever attempted, not only

because I'm mostly numb from the waist
down, but also because my muscles
are seriously considering atrophy.

The most I've accomplished in some
twelve weeks is pushing the buttons
that call for the nurse or raise the bed,

and lifting silverware to my mouth,
when I feel like eating, which isn't all
that often. Federico's manipulations

keep me limber, but nothing close to
toned, let alone strong. We've mostly
managed to avoid bedsores, a plus.

But when Ronnie tried to help me
sit the first time, I couldn't. She enlisted
Federico, who showed me the ropes.

After several days of practice,
I can bring myself upright, unaided,
and move myself to the edge of the bed,

use my hands to swing my legs over
the side and stay there, mostly balanced,
for several minutes. I can't believe

such a little thing can give me such
a huge sense of accomplishment.
The determination to succeed doesn't

spark inside of me, however. Without,
as Ronnie calls them, my personal
cheerleading squad, I'd still be prone.

But between her, my mom, Federico,
and Nurse Carolyn, my free will has
been compromised, and truthfully,

sans Veronica Carino, the team would
not have near the influence as they do
with her spearheading my therapy.

She is a force to be reckoned with.
I just wish I knew why she's still by
my side after everything I've done.

A Stark Reminder

Of everything I've done walks
in the door this morning,
in the hulking form of Vince Carino.

Not sure why, considering his sister
is here practically every day, but
I never thought I'd see him again.

His approach is tentative, almost wary,
and so is my reaction to it—up come
my hackles. I feel like a caged coyote,

though the reason is watery. Vince never
did anything bad to me, except get
the best of me in poker on a regular basis,

and use me for my dope connections.
But I did exactly the same thing to him.
"Uh . . . Hey, Vince. What's up?"

He glances at the wheelchair parked
beside the bed. It obviously makes him
uncomfortable. Same for me, dude.

> I thought I should drop by and have
> a conversation that's overdue.
> First, I'm sorry about what happened.
>
> Not that it's my fault or anything.
> Assholes like Chris are a dime a dozen,
> and he got no more than what he had coming.

"Hey, you know, I don't blame you.
In the end, I'm the only responsible
person, not that I felt that way at first.

At first, I blamed everyone—Misty,
Lydia, my mom, my dead stepdad, and
even you, I guess. But when you wake

up to your life, changed forever in this
way, blame is easy. Figuring out what
to do next is the hard fucking thing."

> He nods as if he can relate, which is,
> of course, impossible. *Ronnie tells us
> she wants to help you, that she's willing*
>
> *to forget all the shitty stuff you did
> to her, and in spite of her being a very
> special girl. I want you to know that,*
>
> *two-legged, one-legged or legless, if
> you hurt my sister again, I will be
> happy to kill you the rest of the way.*

One thing about Vince, he's blunt. Cool.
I'll return the favor. "Even in the midst
of all the bullshit, I never stopped loving

Ronnie. Truthfully, one of the *only* things
I feel guilty about is letting her down.
I won't hurt her again. Not if I can help it."

He Studies Me Closely

Looking for hints of dishonesty,
ready to call my bluff. But this is
a solid bet. I mean every word.

> *Well, that's good, then. Because if*
> *I think for one moment you're playing*
> *her, just so she'll hang around until*
>
> *you get whatever support you can*
> *wring out of her, then decide to dump*
> *her . . . I told you what would happen.*

"Look, Vince. I never asked for her
help. In fact, I gave her every reason
to make a graceful exit from my life,

including coming totally clean
about the sewer I'd been swimming
in. I don't want her here because

she thinks it's the right thing to do.
I don't want her pity. I want her love,
something I don't deserve. But if

she's willing to give it, wants to invest
time and effort into what's left of me, I will
love her back, with all my heart. I can't

say what that means as far as the future.
I have to take it one day at a time, but every
day is a million times better with Ronnie in it."

His Grin

Is lopsided. Is it the first time
I've seen him smile, other than
his big-ass leer when he claims

a giant pot at the poker table?
*That's good to hear because
it means I can offer my help, too.*

*One, I have a friend who customizes
autos, and he's willing to look at
your car and see what he can do*

*to make it work for you. I know
buying another one is probably
out of the question financially.*

*Leon is talented. He'll get you on
the road. Two, I don't know what
your house is like, but I'm sure it'll*

*need some alterations for accessibility.
One of our cousins is a damn good
handyman, and he'll work for cheap.*

*I hear you're moving to a rehab
hospital soon. How long will you be
there? Do you know? Maybe he can*

*have everything finished before
you go home. And three, anytime
you need to talk, man, call me.*

What the Hell

Just happened? We went
from murderous threats
to offers of help in less

than five minutes. "Jesus,
Vince. I have no idea what
to say, or how to thank you."

> *Keep your mouth shut and*
> *stay good to my sister, we can*
> *be friends. I treat my friends right.*

My eyes sting suddenly.
Can't cry in front of Vince,
or he'll change his mind.

No one needs a friend who
spontaneously bursts into
tears. But that's exactly

what I do, and he looks
petrified. "S-sorry. It's just,
no one except maybe Jack,

my stepdad, has ever been
so kind to me. Not even Mom,
and that's supposed to be her job."

> *Yeah, well, don't let it get*
> *around. I've got a reputation*
> *to uphold, and "kind" isn't it.*

Okay, then. One question,
though. "This isn't because
you feel sorry for me, is it?

'Cause I don't want pity
from you, either. I'd be happy
to accept your respect, though,

and I'm more than willing to
earn that, whatever it takes."
He's quiet, thinking it over.

Finally, he says, *Since we're friends
now, here's a story I don't tell
many people. My high school*

*sweetheart was this amazing
girl. Smart. Gorgeous. Going
places. A week after graduation,*

*a semi hit her car. She survived,
but lost a leg, and her face wasn't
ever going to be as beautiful*

*again. I did everything I could
to persuade her life was still
worth living, but she killed herself*

*that summer. You want respect?
Get your ass up out of that bed
and onto your feet again. You can.*

Add Vince

To my cheer squad. Weird.
So goddamn weird. "Sucks
about your girlfriend, dude."

> *It was a tragedy. What about you?*
> *You've thought about suicide,*
> *yeah?* He looks at me intently.

"Strangely, no. I mean, I did
ask the Great Squash to please
haul my ass home to the pumpkin

patch in the sky, but he ignored
me, and I'm way too much
of a coward to do the deed myself."

> He laughs, but then grows
> serious. *But . . . All right, I know*
> *this is really personal, but any*
>
> *chance you can have children?*
> *Not that you need a dozen*
> *next month or anything, but*
>
> *historically the Carinos are big*
> *on offspring—you know, like*
> *populating the planet with Italians.*

"I don't need a dozen, ever,
and I'm not sure I'll even want
one or two. But I felt that way

before this, and if I change
my mind, apparently the semen
factory is still functioning. It's

the delivery method that's in
doubt. Anyway, you're not saying
you want me to knock Ronnie up?"

> His amusement grows. *You do,
> and I'll kick your ass. Unless
> that's what she wants one day.*

"Just so you know, my ass can't
feel a thing, so kicking it would be
irrelevant." Am I really joking

about this? "As for the rest,
I guess it's one step at a time
(figuratively, of course) for now.

Tomorrow is a long way away.
The challenge is figuring out
how to get through today."

> *Fair enough. Listen. I'm happy
> to get hold of your mom about
> your car and the house renovation.*
>
> *But would you please let her know
> I'm going to call, so she doesn't think
> I'm out to scam her or something?*

I Agree

And Vince says goodbye, and as
I watch his retreat an odd sensation
settles over me: contentment.

Not at my condition, or the things
that led me here, but at the vague
possibility of a meaningful future.

The first step is acceptance, that's what
they keep telling me, and I understand
that my only real choices are to accept

or take the quick way out, like Vince's
girlfriend. My seventeenth birthday
is still a month away, three days after

the current year melts into the next.
I should be thinking about football.
Junior prom. Geometry, chemistry,

and American history. Psychology.
I should be worrying about Christmas
and what to buy for Mom and Ronnie.

Those things are lost to me, but what
remains is more important, and vital
to my struggle to, as Vince said,

get my ass up out of bed and onto
my feet again. I've got love. Support.
And at least a couple of friends.

Funny, but I never really thought
about my friends—or lack of them.
I had lots back in Kansas, and I

probably would have qualified
some of the people I knew from
school here in Vegas as buddies,

but no, not really. And of the girls
I went out with, only Ronnie
qualified. As for Vince, I saw him

as a means to an end. I had it all
bass-ackwards, and in hindsight
I see everything I did, every damn

goal I set, revolved totally around
me. Why did it take something like
this to clear my vision, shine

a spotlight on what's truly important—
not money or dope or winning a bet,
but treasuring the people who love

you? Figuring that out is the upside.
The downside is I didn't get it while
Jack was still around, or before I could

step in and stop Cory's downslide.
But any chance of that has evaporated.
Ditto the happiness I felt moments ago.

A Sudden Jolt

Zaps my spine, electric pain
just south of my disconnection.
"Jesus!" I fling the word toward

the wall, and it bounces back, too
loud in the hospital silence.
The effort sends another bolt

down, where I have no feeling
to speak of. How is it possible?
My finger starts working the call

button again and again. Overkill,
and I know it, but I want relief now!
Footsteps come pounding and Nurse

Carolyn hustles in. *What's wrong?*
She hurries to the side of the bed.
Pain? What kind, and where?

I'm familiar enough with the vocab
to tell her, "Lumbar region, neuropathic."
The kind initiated by my short-circuited

nerves, rather than musculoskeletal,
which is muscle or joint discomfort,
caused by overloading them. This is not

overwork. "It's bad. Real bad. Please,
can you give me something?" She nods
and goes to get permission while I sit

here wondering if the source of this
searing static isn't my stressed-out
brain informing my body that I

deserve to hurt. Maybe I should
keep my appointment with the shrink—
the one I've been avoiding, as if I

don't need a psyche adjustment.
Carolyn returns with both meds
and my mom in tow. Mom watches

> me swallow a dose of relief, and
> waits for the nurse to go. *I need
> to talk to you about the house—*

"Hey. Ronnie's brother, Vince,
stopped by. He says he has a cousin
who can help with the alterations. . . ."

Another sharp stab in my lower
back makes me wince, and Mom's face
creases with concern. "Don't worry.

I'll be okay as soon as this pill
kicks in. Anyway, Vince says maybe
he could have it done by . . . what?"

> She pulls a chair over close to me.
> Takes my hand. *I didn't want to worry
> you about anything outside of here, but . . .*

But There's a Lot

To worry about, starting with Mom
hasn't been able to put in very many
hours at her already low-paying job.

She's behind on bills, chief among
them the mortgage. Jack's life
insurance kept her head above water

for several months, but she can't see
a way to satisfy the bank. She's thinking
about letting the house go to a short sale,

> which means we'll have to live
> somewhere else. *Uncle Vern will
> let us move in for a while. There isn't*
>
> *a rehab hospital close by, but there's
> a gym not far away. Hopefully we can
> find a decent physical therapist.*

"Go back to Kansas? No fucking way!
What will I do there? I can't farm. I can't
fix tractors. Hey, I know. Maybe I can

find work as a scarecrow." Anger carves
into me, a white-hot blade. "No, Mom.
I won't leave Ronnie or give up on my rehab.

I'll figure something out." Where can I
find a big wad of cash? Is there a market
for sex with a guy in a wheelchair?

A Poem by Brielle Scott

Scarecrow

That lovely name
is what I was called
in elementary school.
All it took was one

vile

boy informing everyone
on the playground
that my clothes were Goodwill,
and my face was

ugly

enough to scare
crows dead off a high
wire, and the other kids'

laughter

inspired a whole line
of barnyard jokes. It took
years to understand how that

defined

the way I looked at myself
and perhaps explained
why I changed myself so
drastically. I became one of

the painted

women I saw on TV,
and that inspired
all the wrong people to steal
piece after piece of

me.

And then Ginger came along.

Ginger
Stealing Time

To spend with Brielle has totally
been a challenge. You're not
supposed to hook up with other
residents here, and since we're all

girls, that isn't a problem for most.
At first, it wasn't an issue for us, either.
But kissing led to touching led to
the overwhelming need to explore

each other in the most personal ways.
And that means sneaking around,
something I hate. I'm an in-your-face,
this-is-me-take-it-or-leave-it kind

of person. I'd rather just let everyone
know that Brielle and I have connected
because this feels like we're living
a lie, and dishonesty sucks most of all.

Still, after dinner, rather than follow
the group down the hall to watch TV,
I go to my room, wait a few minutes
for the others to settle in, then I slink

the opposite direction, to Brielle.
She's waiting for me on her bed in
a fuzzy blue robe. She opens it, and
there is nothing underneath but

toasted-oat skin stretched over soft
flesh. She is all curves, a complete
contrast to Alex's taut, straight lines.
Turn off the light, Brielle whispers.

Darkness shades the room, but
not completely. The moon is bright
through the window, offering just
enough illumination so we can see

each other's silhouettes. Brielle
coaxes me closer. I'm nervous,
but more about someone finding
out than about what we want to make

happen. I approach slowly, peeling
back my blouse and dropping
my skirt to the floor. "What about
your roommate? Should we worry?"

> *No need to rush,* she purrs. *Sonya*
> *is cool, and I asked her to please*
> *give me an hour alone in exchange*
> *for some help with her algebra.*

"Good. I do appreciate a smart
woman, not to mention excellent
planning. But I've got something
more exciting than algebra in mind."

I Climb into Bed

Beside her, open my arms, and
she settles into them like a warm
mist. Her lips seek mine, and our kiss
is sweet and gentle at first, but quickly

blossoms into passion. Brielle rolls
onto her back, urges me on top
of her, and the skin-to-skin contact
lifts the rich scent of cocoa butter.

"Mmm. You smell like chocolate.
Hot chocolate." We giggle softly,
like little girls, though the response
of our bodies is all woman. With Alex,

I was never in control, something
that always bothered me. I take charge
now, and it's a feeling like no other
to give pleasure before asking for it

in kind. Emotion wells up, seeking
release along with the rise and fall
of her breasts. I don't dare admit
to having fallen in love, though,

not to her or to myself, so I find
other words, hope they convey
how very much I care: "You are
beautiful, do you know that?"

Unreasonably, her muscles contract
and grow tight. *Don't say that.
Don't lie to me. I'm ugly enough
to scare crows dead off a high wire.*

My initial reaction is to laugh,
but I stifle it, knowing she means
what she said. "When was the last
time you looked in a mirror?"

She sighs. *Every time I look in
a mirror I see that girl—the one
my classmates made fun of. I can't
find anyone else there. Just her.*

"That is so wrong. Whoever told
you that you were ugly was obviously
blind. I wish he—or she—could see
you now. You are amazing."

I kiss her to prove it, and she relaxes
again. "That's better," I soothe, then
spend thirty minutes convincing
her how wrong that person was.

I Only Think About Alex

Four or five times.
I try to keep my mind
solidly here with Brielle,
but comparisons seem

to be inevitable. Alex
made me take, take, take.
Brielle opens herself to
my giving. Truthfully,

I have always been on
the receiving end, whether
by invitation or because
I had no choice. This is so

new I might have no idea
how to enjoy it, except it's
instinctive. My own joy
comes from making Brielle

sigh with pleasure, and at
last cry out that yes, this
is right, and yes she feels
beautiful. And I love

that I can do that for her
when I couldn't manage it
for Alex. I am turned on,
alive, because I am powerful.

Post-Pleasure

No time to revel in afterglow,
we slip back into our clothes
before Sonya can return to claim
her bed. "I wish we could sleep

together." Thinking about it,
I've rarely slept alone. Before
I left Gram's, there was always
at least one sister tucked in beside

me. And then there was Alex,
who I loved to snuggle up against,
though as time went on, she pulled
away from me more and more.

> *That would be nice,* says Brielle.
> *But that will probably never
> happen, and it makes me sad.
> Why did we have to connect now?*

"The natural cussedness of things,
that's what my gram used to say.
It's like the good stuff always hits
at the exact wrong time. Sucks."

> She comes over, slides her arms
> around my neck, kisses me sweetly.
> *Are you really leaving day after
> tomorrow? Why do you have to go?*

I push her gently away, look
down toward the floor so I can't
see the sadness in her eyes. "Gram
needs me. And I have to figure

out who I am. I don't know who
that is, or who I want to become.
I only know who I was, and this place
is a constant reminder of yesterday's

Ginger, the one I have to leave
behind. I just wish I didn't have
to leave you, too. I never expected
to care about someone again."

Brielle pushes closer, lifts a hand,
and her fingertips flutter against
my cheek. *I'll go you one better.*
I never expected to care for anyone,

period. I've worked very hard to
avoid it, in fact, which is why
everyone thinks I'm cold. Maybe
I am, but it's because I'm afraid

of getting hurt. Love wasn't meant
for people like you and me. You
have to be strong and brave to fall
in love. And maybe a little stupid.

Before I Can Figure Out

How to reply, we hear footsteps
outside the door. Brielle pops up
onto her bed and I hustle over
to the cracked vinyl chair near

the window, making sure my
clothing is straight and buttoned.
My butt is barely planted when
Sonya comes in, humming

> a Maroon 5 song I recognize
> from back when I still listened to
> music. She stops when she sees me.
> Considers. Smiles. *Oh. Hey, Ginger.*

I don't really care if she suspects,
so I meet her expression head-on.
"Hi, Sonya. Thanks for giving us
a little space. We were just talking

about how you have to be brave
to fall in love, or maybe stupid.
What do you think?" I address
Sonya, but give Brielle a wink.

> Sonya laughs. *I think you have*
> *to be stupid to hook up in a place*
> *like this. And if that leads to love,*
> *well, you get what you deserve.*

That Makes Me Laugh

Because I'm not sure if she's being
serious or totally sarcastic or even
if she means it in a bad way or good.
However she spun it, it's accurate.

"Know what? You're right. Okay,
I'll let you two tackle that algebra.
I've got some reading to do." I stand,
then turn to Brielle. "Gram says love

lives inside every one of us. We just
have to accept that it's there. Don't
believe it wasn't meant for you and
me. We deserve it more than most."

Deserving and accepting are two
vastly different things, of course.
I go back to my room, digesting
the past hour. There was making

love, yes, and it was new and
satisfying, in a whole different
way. Surprising. Something
I want to experience again.

But I think there was a fair
amount of love, the emotion, too.
I wish I was better acquainted with
it. How do I know if I'm right?

How Does Anyone Know

If they're right about love?
Pretty sure there's no way
around trial and error, and
hopefully learning from

your mistakes when it comes
to things like listening to
the arguments of your heart.
Argh! I'm so totally absorbed

in thinking about what just
happened with Brielle that it takes
several minutes for the scene
in my own room to solidify.

When I go inside, I notice
Miranda's presence. See,
from the corner of my eye,
that she's sitting on her bed.

But it isn't until I turn to look at
her that it becomes apparent
she's in shock, her Latina face
the color of oatmeal. "What is it?"

She doesn't say anything, but
offers whatever she holds in her
hand. It turns out to be a printed
page, ripped from the local newspaper.

MISSING TEEN'S BODY FOUND

That's what the headline screams.
I skim the story, which shares
the grisly details in lurid
tabloid fashion:

Shayleece Reynolds just turned seventeen.
She should have been struggling with chemistry
and reading Jane Austen novels. Instead,
the former child prostitute was found beaten,
raped, and left to die in a remote stretch of desert
north of Las Vegas. In a highly publicized trial
last week, Ms. Reynolds testified against

Lawrence Reynolds, her pimp and alleged
biological father (court-ordered DNA testing
has yet to return results) for murdering her mother,
another prostitute. Ms. Reynolds disappeared
on her way to a dental appointment and was
reported missing by staff at Walk Straight,
a child prostitute rescue group home.

It is believed her death was retaliation for
her testimony, which resulted in Lawrence
Reynolds's conviction for first-degree murder
and pandering a child under the age of fourteen,
which in itself carries a life sentence in the state
of Nevada. This case highlights the growing problem
of trafficking children for sex in Las Vegas and
across the US. Just last year, an FBI task force . . .

I Stop There

"Where did you get this?"
I've never seen any of the girls
look at a paper. Few enough of them
keep up with anything newsy.

> *From Belinda. I was outside*
> *reading when she drives up, stops,*
> *and opens her window. She doesn't*
> *say anything. Just throws the envelope*

> *with this inside. I don't know how*
> *she knows where I am, Ginger.*
> *How did she find me?* The message
> is clear: Keep your mouth shut.

Miranda is supposed to testify
against Papacito in a few weeks.
They've been building a case against
him and want to go to court before

the end of the year. "Did you tell
anyone?" She answers with a shake
of her head. "Why not? You have to!
They should take you somewhere safe."

> *Where? If Papacito can find me*
> *here, he can find me anywhere.*
> *He'll kill me, just like that other*
> *girl. I have to leave. I need to hide.*

"No, Miranda. Where can you hide?
You can't go home. Papacito knows
Ricardo, and your family would be
in danger. You don't have anywhere

else to go, do you? Better to let
your caseworker know, so . . ."
Her head swivels side to side.
"Listen. If you don't tell, don't

follow through and testify, Papacito
will get out of jail and go right back
to working those girls. You don't
want that to happen, do you?"

> She thinks it over, but not very
> long. *Doesn't matter who goes
> to jail, someone will make the girls
> work. Today, Belinda, tomorrow . . . ?*

Her eyes shimmer with frightened
tears. "Listen, I know you're scared.
I'd be scared too. But someone
has to make them stop—"

> *Not me! Why me? I'm just a kid.
> I can't change it. I can't change
> anything.* Rather than dissolve
> as expected, she goes totally blank.

It's After Hours

Only a single staff person here.
It's Bethany tonight. I'm afraid
to go looking for her and leave
Miranda alone, so I open the door,

call down the hall toward a couple
of girls headed toward the rec
room. "Hello? Can someone
please find Bethany right away?"

One of them waves assent,
and I turn back to check on
Miranda, who definitely looks
all "kid" right now. It's striking,

really. I mean, we just threw
her a fourteenth birthday
party, complete with balloons
and cupcakes. But turning

tricks makes you ancient
inside. I think it ages your soul.
If there's such a thing as
reincarnation, Miranda will

come back as a thousand-
year-old newborn, and in this
life she's already an elderly
woman wrapped up in a child's skin.

At the Sound

Of footsteps approaching, I step
out into the hall to intercept
Bethany and give her a heads-up.
I offer the basic info, then add,

"She's thinking about running.
You have to call her caseworker
or she'll be gone by morning."
And probably disappear forever.

> *I'll see if I can get hold of her,*
> agrees Bethany. *Meanwhile, keep*
> *an eye on Miranda. I'll be right*
> *back.* She scurries away and I

return to my room as requested.
Miranda looks catatonic, but at
least she's staying put. I decide
to check my messages, not sure

why, and I'm surprised to find
one from Alex. My heart stutters
happily. At least, until I read it.
MY MORNING SICKNESS IS OVER.

THE BABY DECIDED HELL WAS BETTER
THAN LIVING WITH ME. I MISCARRIED.
AND I DECIDED LIFE ON THE STREET
IS WHAT I DESERVE. DON'T TEXT ME AGAIN.

A Poem by David Burroughs

Living with Me

Is a privilege, one I reserve
for boys with exceptional
talents. It is well within

                            my

power to make or break
not only careers, but also
the very lives of young

                            men

and women, here in a city
spun on a web of connections.
The partners I choose

                            represent

my taste, and I handpick
them carefully.
Intellect is high on

                            the

list of requirements,
though I don't want them
better educated than me, and a

                            beautiful

body like Seth's trumps worldly
experience. In fact, I prefer
schooling them. Some

                            people

might disagree,
but breaking in a novice
definitely pleasures me.

Seth
Winter Approaches

Back home, it arrives, jacketed in ice.
Here, the only change of seasons

is sizzling to lukewarm and back again.
People tell me Las Vegas is no stranger

to snow, which makes me laugh. A few
flurries blowing down into the valley

from the surrounding mountains does
not a blizzard make. Still, even a pitiful

few snowflakes might shake me out
of this mood. I know it has everything

to do with Christmas coming. I've
never spent one away from the farm,

and nostalgia is suffocating me.
Familiar carols play in endless loops

in every store I happen into. It's almost
enough to keep me sequestered at David's.

But I'm even more uncomfortable there.
The parties have grown old. It takes

ever larger quantities of drugs to get
high. Ditto alcohol to dull the buzz.

Sex with David has become worse
than routine. It's how I imagine it must

be for couples together for decades—
a series of excuses followed by a single

let's-just-get-this-over-with encounter,
repeat the cycle. Even David must be

totally bored by the process. It feels
like things here are coming to an end.

But I don't dare make the first move
to disintegrate our relationship until

I've sorted out the far side. My bank
account is healthy, but won't last long

if I have to invest in a place to live
in Vegas, where a decent apartment

will set me back a minimum grand per
month, and I'd really prefer something

better than decent. I guess I've become
spoiled by living comfortably. Scratch

that. By living extremely well. How do
I give that up? Do I even dare try?

The Main Thing

That makes me want to try is Micah.
Our relationship has grown beyond

infatuation all the way to serious love,
and it's killing me because I just want

to be with him. If his show was dark
tonight and circumstances were different—

yeah, right—I could spend the entire evening
with him. Nice dinner. Take in a movie.

Go home and straight to bed, where sex
would be anything but boring. Fall asleep

in each other's arms. But he's dancing
and David's entertaining, and as for me,

the sex I'll have, but not enjoy, will be paid
for by Peter from Kansas or Oklahoma

or New Mexico, who's here for a roll
on the wild side. We're connecting at

Liaison, a relatively mainstream gay
nightclub housed inside a major casino

right on the strip. One thing I've learned
is to meet these guys somewhere very

public first, to gauge demeanor
and hopefully avoid problems once

we go upstairs or next door or down
the street to wherever they're staying.

A couple of times I hooked up with creeps
who wanted rough play and figured

since they were paying premium rates
I'd be happy to accommodate. I will,

to a point. But I do have limits, and stuff
like fisting or asphyxiation are high on

my no-can-do list. It's another good
reason to maintain a certain level of

muscle mass. I may be gay, but I can
fight my way out of a bad situation

if need be. Luckily those two men
weren't interested in getting *that* rough.

We compromised instead. And while
I didn't get the hefty tip they promised,

I still got paid for my time. There's
a learning curve to the escorting business.

Intuition

Becomes your best friend, and mine
tells me Peter from Wherever is safe

enough. The slender fortyish man is sitting
at a table for two, looking a bit unnerved

by the hunky guys dancing onstage.
I know it's him by the Stetson he wears—

our prearranged sign—and greet him
confidently. "Hello, Peter. I'm Seth."

> His eyes swing my direction and assess
> me curiously. *Oh. Yes. Hello. Um . . .*

> He stands and offers a weak handshake.
> *Please. Sit down. Drink?* At my request

for bourbon, he goes to the bar, returns
with two whiskey sours. It's well liquor,

which suggests that the bundle he'll drop
to spend time with me is beyond his budget.

Or maybe he's already dropped a wad
investing in slot-machine play. Either

way, I'll request payment up front.
I sip my drink and he gulps his, gaining

confidence and growing bolder.
You're different than I expected.

"Really? You're not disappointed,
are you?" He drains his glass to ice

before he answers. *Oh, no. Not
disappointed. In fact, I'm pleased.*

*I kind of thought you might be more . . .
effeminate, I guess. I mean, I did*

request a . . . He lowers his voice.
A top. But you're exactly right.

Okay, a little strange. There's some
kind of story here. Another drink,

and he tells it, slurring slightly.
See, when I was a kid, there was this

*guy who lived around the corner.
He looked a lot like you, except older.*

*I used to ride my bike by his house
and one day I got a flat out in front.*

*He was working in his yard and
offered to fix it. I followed him around*

back to his shed. There were lots
of pictures on the wall—not naked

ladies, like most men have, but guys
in the buff, doing unmentionable things.

While he fixed my tire, I kept staring
at them. I didn't even know penises

were meant to do anything but pee.
Finally, he says, "You know, it feels

really good to have someone touch
your wiener. I'll show you if you want."

He showed me, and it did feel really
good. I kind of knew it was wrong,

but that made it even better. I went
back a few times. At first it was just

hand jobs. Then he taught me oral.
One day, he wanted to demonstrate

"the very best way." I was only ten,
and penetration hurt like hell. Plus,

it made me bleed. My mother noticed
my underwear, and that was that.

What Peter Wants

Is for me to play dirty old neighbor.
Hey, it's his cash, and I do ask for it

up front before we head to his room,
which happens to be at the Mandarin

Oriental, a short walk from the club.
We go up to the twelfth floor, to superb

accommodations. Apparently Peter
is flush after all. Maybe he just likes

cheap booze. He pours two deep
glasses of Jack Daniel's before going

to the bathroom to get ready. I return
most of mine to the bottle, turn on

the TV and find a country music
channel. I'm betting Peter is a country

kind of guy. If not, I am, and I get
to be in charge. I take off my shirt,

leave the jeans on so I can order him
to unzip them. I also take a quick whiff

of powdered encouragement from
a little bottle hidden in my sock.

By the time he wobbles back,
I'm ready to go. Ready to play dirty

neighbor who has gay porn hanging
on the walls of his shed. "Come here,

kid. Get down on your knees." And,
we're off, Toby Keith warbling in

the background. Peter has come prepared
with a number of toys, including his favorite

vibrator. If I wasn't buzzed and expecting
a very good tip, I'd have a hard time

stomaching the coming play. Instead, I
jump into the game and an hour passes

before I know it. Little boy Peter finishes,
completely satisfied. "If it's okay, I'd like

to clean up before I go." He nods mutely,
and doesn't even put on his underwear

again before shuffling over to say hi to Jack
Daniel's again. I take a quick shower,

       and as I'm leaving, Peter says,
       I'm not even gay, just so you know.

Could Have Fooled Me

Then again, who knows? I've read
that a lot of men who don't identify

as queer enjoy a good male-to-male
romp once in a while. Apparently,

some of them don't believe it's cheating
on their partners if they have sex with

a man instead of another woman.
I guess you can justify anything, as

long as you have psychological
parameters firmly in place. Whatever.

As far as I'm concerned, cheating
is cheating. And suddenly, I'm struck

by a fierce attack of guilt, despite
the eleven hundred dollars in my pocket.

No way can I go home to Micah
after performing the way I just did

with someone else. I've got to get out
of this business before I lose any more

of Seth. Wonder if I can regain what
I've lost of him already if I do quit.

In Need of Fresh Air

And time to eliminate Peter from
my mind, I wander down to the far

end of the strip, then cut down a side
street to the monorail station, where

I'm sure I can catch a cab. I'm almost
there when I hear a couple of male

voices yelling and, just underneath
them, soft pleading. Shit. Last thing

I need is to get involved in a row,
but someone is getting pummeled.

I move closer, and sure enough, back
up against a building, a female form

is on the sidewalk with two large men
standing over her, and I can see her arms

        raised to try and protect her face.
        Fucking fag! screams one of the dudes.

        I don't let no queer touch my dick.
        I'm gonna kill you, fucking whore.

Ah, shit. Now I have to do something,
don't I? First thing is pull out my phone

and dial 911 to report an assault
in progress. Now I hear the victim

> wheezing. *Please. I'm sorry. Take*
> *my money. Please. Leave me . . .*

Oh, man. I recognize her voice.
"Pippa!" I yell. "Is that you?"

> *H-help me.* Now she falls silent
> and her body slumps, motionless.

Still the men beat her. Kick her. Stomp
on her. Goddamn it! "Hey, assholes!

You like beating up girls?" They
straighten, turn toward me.

> *This ain't no girl, dickwad,* says one.
> *Besides, what business is it of yours?*

"She happens to be my friend.
But even if she wasn't, I'd have

to kick your ass." Two against one.
Bad odds. But I have no choice,

so I wade in, hoping they don't rob
me when they're finished wasting me.

Adrenaline Pumping

I hold my own for a while, and
barely feel the blows that connect.

Luck is with me in a couple of ways.
One, neither man seems to have

a weapon. And two, by the time
I'm actually losing the battle, a siren

is closing in. A huge set of knuckles
opens my forehead just above my left

eyebrow. The dudes take off running
as I drop to my knees, blood dripping.

I crawl over to Pippa, pull her skirt
down over her exposed crotch

before the cop can see it. She's
unconscious, breathing shallowly,

and bleeding a lot worse than I am.
I'm glad she can't see her face.

Son of a bitch! The cruiser pulls up
parallel to the sidewalk, and an officer

gets out, strolls over to take a peek.
You call this in? What happened?

"Can you, like, possibly arrange
for an ambulance or something?

In case you haven't noticed, they
messed her up pretty good."

He actually bends over to check her pulse
and see if she's breathing. *I probably*

should. You stay right here. I'll need
you to give me a statement, okay?

He saunters—yeah, that's the word—
back to his car. I sit, pull Pippa's face

off the sidewalk and into my lap,
try to stroke her hair smooth. I know

she'd be mortified for anyone to see
her like this. "It's okay, lady," I soothe.

"You're safe now." She moans softly,
so maybe she hears me. Suddenly,

I remember the bottle in my sock.
The cop is busy reaching for something

so I take the opportunity to remove it
and roll it off to one side. Just in case.

That Proves

To be a wise move. When the EMTs
arrive, one of them takes a look at

my face and decides I should go in
for stitches, which means I get to ride

with Pippa in the ambulance. They haul
her into the emergency room immediately.

I, on the other hand, get to wait for a while,
filling out paperwork, both for the hospital

and for the cop who impatiently followed
to bug me for that statement. Pretty

sure he thinks I was more involved with
the incident than happening onto it

by accident, but tough. What I write
is a truthful account of the facts as I know

them. By the time I finally arrive home,
forehead sewn back together and bandaged,

it's almost three in the morning. I expected
David to be worried. But he's fast asleep.

I, on the other hand, won't sleep tonight.
I go outside, call Micah, disturb his dreams.

A Poem by Bryn Dawson

Disturbed

That's what everyone
called me when I was a kid,
and truth is, they were

                                        right

though they didn't know
just how screwed up I was.
I believe the correct word
is sociopath. I was born in the

                                        wrong

century. Ancient Rome
would've been perfect for me,
as long as my circumstances
were royal. I mean,

                                        who

wouldn't celebrate having sex
with any number of slaves,
then trading them in
for newer models as soon
as boredom sets in? I

                                        really

wish I'd been born into
money, instead of having
to create an income stream.
Think of the opportunities, no

                                        cares

in the world except having
an exceptional time just being
alive and getting laid by pretty
young girls like Whitney.

Whitney
Despite It Being Saturday

I'm plugged into my computer,
where online learning is boring
me to tears. Yes, I've got lots of
catching up to do, if I'm to start
school again after the winter break
and reintegrate with my classmates,
now halfway through their junior year.

But even if I log in hours upon
hours, read every entry, learn
every math trick, pass every test,
how do I manage going back there?
What's the point? To pretend
I'm a regular kid again?

Even trying to reconnect
with Paige has been strange.
Yes, because she's friends
with Skylar, and that bitch
hasn't changed one little bit.
But it's more than that. For
as much as Paige has altered
her appearance, dropping
poundage and tinting her spiky
hair pink, once you get past
the Skylar-inspired conceit,
she's still the same inside as
before I left. Goofy. Girly.
She likes shopping. Texting.
Dreaming about the perfect guy.

But me? Oh, I'm different.
Once you've immersed yourself
in ugliness, wallowed in it,
sponged it up and internalized
it, you can't cough it back up
and spit it out. It becomes hard
to find beauty in anything.
No matter where I look, I find
evil lurking. A monster sleeps
inside every man. Cop. Mechanic.
Minister. It doesn't matter. I can
see the beast he hides. I won't let
one of them sneak up on me again.

How am I supposed to sit in
a classroom, hurry through
the hallways, change for PE?
How am I supposed to have
fun goofing around with friends
who have no concept of reality?
How am I supposed to stay clean
when the truth of what I've done
closes in around me, squeezing
hideous memories from the deep
recesses of my brain, and what
I really want is the kind of sleep
only the Lady can provide?

How am I supposed to trust
enough to fall in love, knowing
every guy is defective?

I Keep My K12 Program Open

(Still logging those online learning
hours!) while surfing the Web for
more exciting discoveries
than what chemistry can offer.

My news feed is full of them,
and the first story that catches
my eye is about a teen prostitute
whose body turned up rotting
north of Las Vegas. You know,
that could have been me, except
Bryn wasn't exactly the murder-
his-girls type. He was more
the help-them-OD type. Guess
I got lucky. The word makes
me snort. Yeah. Lucky. That's me.

Wonder how many girls just
disappear, sucked into the life
one way or another, only to die
at the hands of a pimp or a john,
no one to mourn them, or if there
is, those people have no idea
that their loved one met death
in such a brutal way. Is anyone
mourning Shayleece Reynolds?
Did anyone mourn her mother?

If I would've died there on that
stinking carpet, wonder how long
my family would have mourned me.

I Invest Four Hours

In schoolwork. Blow through
English and American history,
which aren't as boring as chem.
Dad says homeschooling isn't
a good path to college, but I
can't think past today, let alone
start plotting my future.

Mom pops her head in once
in a while to make sure I'm
performing, and when I finish
she has a surprise for me.

> *You've been working so hard.*
> *I thought you might like to go*
> *to the boardwalk. The rides*
> *are closed this time of year,*
> *of course, but there's Neptune's*
> *Kingdom and the big arcade*
> *and tonight is the holiday lights*
> *train. What do you think?*

She's letting me escape
the house? Surely not without
supervision. "You mean, go
alone or with you or what?"

> *No fun to do it alone. Why*
> *don't you call Paige and see*
> *if she wants to go along?*
> *I'm happy to spring for it.*

The Santa Cruz Boardwalk

Is right on the beach. In summer,
it's really fun, but during the winter
months the rides close down and
you're left with indoor amusements.
Still, there's music and food and
arcade games, which I used to love.
At this point they seem pretty silly.

So, of course, Paige wants to play
them. When I invite her to come,
I think for sure she'll turn me
down. Skylar, apparently, is tied
up elsewhere, however, because
Paige is quick to say okay.

Mom drops us off a little after
three. We watch her drive away.
"Before we go inside, can we take
a walk on the beach? My feet
haven't touched sand in months."

> *Las Vegas has sand,* she whines,
> but then agrees to a short stroll.

It's a crackling cool, clear blue
day, and the sound of waves in
the distance lifts a mist of nostalgia.
The last time I was near the surf
was the day Bryn took pictures
of me. How can I possibly miss him?

Paige must be psychic because
she chooses this moment to say,
*So tell me about modeling. Did
you make bank, or what?*

I'm good at off-the-cuff lying.
"Not really. I was still building
my portfolio by doing local shoots.
I was also partying a lot. It goes
with the territory." That part, at
least, is accurate enough.

*Skylar says you were probably
doing porn. You weren't, were you?*

"Skylar's a jealous whore. Tell
her I said doing porn would be
preferable to listening to her rude,
nasty comments. You can also
tell her she couldn't qualify to do
porn. She couldn't pass an audition."

*I can't believe your mom would
let you go to Vegas with that guy.*

"Mom's more open-minded
than you'd think. Okay, my feet
have touched the sand enough.
The train's at five. Let's get tickets."
I'm finished talking about Vegas.

We Could Skip the Train

Except Mom was really clear
that it should be part of the evening.
I think it's her own nostalgia.
We used to ride it every year
when Kyra and I were little.
Dad used to come along, too.

"You don't mind riding the train,
do you? Pretty sure Mom would
be disappointed if we didn't."

> *Are you kidding? Santa Claus*
> *and candy canes are two of*
> *my favorite things.* See?
> That's the old Paige right there.

We have to wait almost an hour
to board. As daylight fails and
the lights glitter on, I start to feel
pretty good. Like maybe I don't
really need a romp with the Lady
after all. But soon enough, we run
into a few people I used to know
at school. They all ask where I've
been and I feed them the same
tired story I shared with Paige.

After a while I kind of want to tell
them I was doing porn, if only
to see the shock in their eyes and
determine the velocity of rumors.

My Mood Improves Again

Once the locomotive gets
rolling through town. It chugs
through neighborhoods
where many people have
decorated their homes to
the max for the enjoyment
of the entire city, including
us holiday train passengers.

It's fun to watch the children,
especially the young ones,
whose eyes grow wider and
wider as they wait for Santa
to vacate the caboose and make
an appearance in the cars. Funny,
but I've never even thought
about having kids of my own.
I'd probably be a crap mother,
but, hey, you never know.

Was that just me, thinking
I might be able to have
something approaching
a normal life, after only
a few hours ago being very
sure that wasn't possible,
because of a train ride?

Maybe my mom knows
a thing or two after all.

The Arcade

Is crowded with families
enjoying everything from
pool to bowling to pinball,
plus a huge variety of electronic
games. Christmas carols loop
in the background, and the whole
place is done up with ornaments
and tinsel. It's fake, fake, fake.
But still, it's very pretty. I think
I'm starting to define "bipolar."

Before long, one thing starts to
stand out. I noticed it on the train,
too, where several women ignored
their excited children while vying
for the title, Crap Mother. "Why is
everyone so in love with their phones?"

> Paige quickly stashes hers. *What
> do you mean? Oh, look. There's
> a MyBoardwalk kiosk. Let's get
> some cards. They use those instead
> of tokens here now, so you know.*

I hand her some of the cash
Mom gave me, thinking about
people and their cell phones.
I guess maybe I used to text
a lot. But in Vegas I only used
my phone for business, and after

a while I hated when it rang.
Sometimes when it blares now,
it plops me right back in that
shit-hole apartment with Bryn.

We spend a couple of hours
on games. Bowl. Shoot pool.
I'm miserable at all of them,
but have fun, anyway. "Hey,
are you hungry? I'm starving."

> Get something. I already had
> a candy cane, and if I eat I'll have
> to go puke it up. I need to lose
> five pounds before winter break.
> We're going to Hawaii and I want
> to look good in my new bikini.

"You're kidding, right? If you
lose any more weight you'll dry
up and blow away. What are
you now? Size three?"

> Exactly. I don't think my bone
> structure will let me get down
> to size zero, but I'm trying.

"I think you're being ridiculous
but I can't force a cheeseburger
down your throat. I plan to eat one,
anyway. Fries, too. My modeling
career is on indefinite hold."

It's a Damn Fine Burger

And I take pleasure in eating
it slowly, watching Paige
salivate. She does swipe a few
of my fries. Hope she doesn't
feel the need to vomit them.

Fed, full, feeling pretty good,
I go throw my trash away and
when I get back, find Paige flirting
with a couple of guys who have
joined her at the table. Their faces
are vaguely familiar. I'd peg them
as seniors, and jocks. "That was quick."

> Paige laughs. *They're stalkers.*
> *Actually, this is Gary and James.*
> *You guys remember Whitney?*
> *She just moved back from Vegas.*

Gary seems to be connected
to Paige. So much so, in fact,
that I suspect she made sure to let
him know we'd be here tonight.
James, who's sandy-haired and
obviously built, turns assessing
dark eyes toward me and grunts
something resembling a hello.

Next thing I know, we've become
a foursome, which is irritating, but
at least it keeps Paige off her phone.

Gary, who is much better-looking
than the guys I've seen Paige with
before, keeps an arm wrapped
around her shoulders as we head
back toward the arcade. James
measures my stride and adjusts
his accordingly. "You a senior?"
I ask because one of us should

> say something. *Yep. Five more*
> *months and I'm out of here. Not*
> *sure where I'm going yet, though.*
> *Did you like Vegas? I hear it's ugly.*

"Oh, baby, you have no idea.
I mean, if you like lots of neon
and phony facades, the strip is kind
of pretty. But underneath all that
it's filthy. And goddamn hot, too."

> *So, are you in school or what?*

"Right now, I'm homeschooled."
I give him a very short version
of the modeling/rehab story.
He's surprised when I tell him
I'm only a junior. "Why? I look older?"

> *Yeah. Drugs can do that to you.*
> *My sister got into that shit. Hope*
> *you can stay clean. She couldn't.*

His Concern Seems Genuine

Some people look at rehab
like it's for losers. Others,
like it's a badge of honor.
James sees it as a necessity
for someone who's chosen
to play with fire. His sister
got scorched. She OD'd.
"I'm really sorry to hear that."

> *Thanks. It sucked. What a waste.*
> *She was special, too. And it*
> *was all because of some dude.*

"Usually is." I don't elaborate.
It's been a long time since I felt
this comfortable around a guy.
He's different somehow. Sweet.
That's the word. At least, on
the surface. Which makes me
wonder what, exactly, he's hiding.

Gary, however, is obnoxiously
obvious. The arm that was
around Paige's shoulders now
circles her waist, and once in
a while his hand falls to test
the muscle mass of her butt.
Doesn't bother her at all.
Not sure why it's bothering me.

Finally, the Two of Them

Brake to a stop in front of
the laser tag entrance. Damn.
I was hoping to avoid it, but
Paige and Gary are hot to play.
I shake my head. "I'll wait for you."

> *Come on. It'll be fun. We used
> to do this all the time, remember?*

I'm not brain-dead. Of course
I remember. She's right. We
did, and it was fun. Besides,
they're all looking at me like
I'm totally lame. "Okay," I
agree reluctantly. "I've just
been a little claustrophobic
lately, so I might quit early."

We pay, go inside. Strap on
vests, choose our weapons.
James and I play blue; Paige
and Gary go red. The game
begins and everything goes
dark and my stomach starts
to churn. Now neon streaks
the shadows and, as I feared,
I'm back in the black alleys
of Las Vegas, and there's
movement signifying faces
I can't see and don't want to.

And this is nothing like fun.

Now Someone Yells

Behind you!

I spin, heart stammering,
and a laser beam lights my chest.
Inhale. Exhale. I breathe in stutters.
"You're fine, you're fine," I chant.

It's a game.
No danger here.
Kids are playing.
Danger loves kids.
Danger seeks kids.
Danger leaves kids
to die in the desert.

Exit.
Where's the exit?
There. Over there.
I run for the door and feel
someone running behind me.
"No!" I scream. "Leave me alone!"

> *Whitney.* He's there. Right
> there. Reaching for me. His
> hand falls against my shoulder.
> *Whitney. It's James. It's okay.*

James? James! I turn into him,
sobbing, and he takes me gently
into his arms, guides me to the exit,
my pendulum swinging toward crazy.

A Poem by Andrew McCarran

Reaching for Me

Finally, Eden's found
the courage to tell me
where she's been hiding
these long, lonely weeks,
and today—today!—I'll see

                                 her

again. The mirror
reveals a different man
than the one who last held
her. It's not just that my hair
is longer, or that my

                                 face

has grown winter pale
beneath a full beard.
No. It's the deep
trepidation that

                                 haunts

my eyes, despite the surfacing
joy. What if we've moved
too far beyond the halcyon
days we share in

                                 my

recollection? What if
she isn't real at all, but only
something I imagined,
or the invention of overactive

                                 dreams.

Eden

It's Been a Nightmare Few Days

First, my mother informed me
that she has condemned my sister
to the dungeons at Tears of Zion.
She caught your disease, that's
what Mama said, as if falling

in love is a contagion—a virus
of the heart. I vowed to find a way
to get Eve out, and know transparency
is the only way to make that happen.
I have to confess before I can accuse.

But before I could take my story
public, we got the news about
Shayleece. No one stepped forward
to claim her body, so the counselors
here pooled enough money to bury

her properly. All the girls went to
the funeral, so at least she had people
there to say goodbye, whether or not
they wanted to. Most of us did. Most
of us realized it could have been one

of us lying in that coffin, which
remained closed. The speculation about
why turned into some interesting,
if macabre, gossip. Hard to think
about what the buzzards managed.

The Best Thing

To come out of all the bad
is I get to see Andrew today.
My decision to talk about Tears
of Zion freed me to let him know
where I am. He's catching the first

available flight. My stomach
is doing flip-flops. I'm scared
and happy and crazy excited,
all knotted up together. I wish
I had something nice to wear,

instead of the thrift-store clothes
in my drawers. When I told him
that, he said he couldn't care less,
he'd be looking at my face, not
my jeans. That's good, because

I've gained a few pounds since
the last time I saw him. Will
he look the same? It's been almost
eight months. Not a lot of time
in the scheme of things, but enough

to change our appearance. What
matters is what's left inside.
Right now, my heart is buoyant
with love. I just wish I knew for
sure that's how he feels, too.

Speaking of Feelings

Mine are in upheaval because
my parents cut me loose. That's
a relief because going home
is unthinkable. But what Mama
said is I'm no longer their daughter.

I've been orphaned, and that hurts
more than I could have guessed.
And what will I do about Boise?
Andrew still has solid ties there,
and it's not a very big city.

If I go back, I'm sure to run into
my ex-family, plus people from
church, where ugly rumors must be
circulating. Once I make a big stink
about Tears of Zion, that's bound

to get worse. Some pills are worth
swallowing, I guess. At least I'm
moving forward. I can't change
a single minute of yesterday.
But I can take charge of the future,

and at the top of my list is saving
my sister and hopefully playing
a role in the demise of Tears of Zion.
It's anyone's guess what will happen
once I report Father Samuel Ruenhaven.

I Wanted to Do It

Before I see Andrew, so
I can't change my mind.
Right now, I'm sitting
in the offices of the Nevada
Investigation Division.

Tears of Zion is in a different
county, and it will be up to
a detective here whether or
not to inform Elko County
that they might want to take

a look at this so-called religious
retreat center. Sarah is with
me, sensing I could still bolt
at any time. I'm relieved when
the detective who calls me in

> turns out to be a woman.
> It would be harder to look
> a man in the eyes and relate
> the horror stories I have to
> tell. *Come in,* she says. *I'm*
>
> *Detective Finnegan. But you
> can call me Marlene.* She must
> see the sudden rush of fear.
> *It's okay,* she soothes. *Don't
> be afraid. I'm on your side.*

A Half Hour Later

I almost believe she might,
in fact, be on my side.
She listens intently to every
word, and I find no disbelief
in her body language.

> First off, I want to thank
> you for bringing this to our
> attention. We take allegations
> of child abuse quite seriously
> in this office. I do have a couple
>
> of questions for you, though,
> as I'm sure the Elko County
> DA will be asking them, too.
> One: Why did you wait so long
> before coming forward?

"Humiliation, for one thing.
Before all this happened I'd
had exactly one boyfriend,
and we never did anything
like . . . that. I had no idea

people *ever* acted like that.
And then, what I did here
on the streets, just to eat . . ."
Emotion wells up, uninvited.
"I'm sorry. I didn't mean to cry."

Marlene leans forward,
hands me a box of tissues.
Please don't apologize.
Memories like that are hard
to relive. Any other reasons?

"I didn't want my mother
to know where I was, so I gave
Walk Straight a made-up name
and told them my parents were
dead. Eventually, though, I had

to come clean. I'm a horrible
liar and besides, the people
at Walk Straight are so good
to me, I couldn't risk them
getting in trouble on my account."

Okay. Two: I understand this
Jerome fellow assaulted you.
What about Ruenhaven himself?
I could make something up to
implicate him. If I don't, he might

just walk. Still, I can't lie. "Not
sexually, no. But he was completely
responsible for the isolation,
and lack of water, food, and
opportunity to use the bathroom."

When she asks how I know
that, I tell her, "Because he was
very clear that he had personally
written the Tears of Zion rule book,
and deviation meant punishment.

He straight-on informed me that
my parents sanctioned whatever
actions he saw fit to provide,
and let me know they didn't want
me to come home. They still don't."

> *Okay, then. I'll type this up
> into a formal complaint and
> have you sign it. One last
> question before I do. Why
> choose to come forward now?*

"Because they sent my little
sister there, too. She's only
fourteen, and doesn't deserve
to be hurt the way I was. I need
you to help me save her."

Marlene winces, and I know
she's thinking the same thing
I have over and over for the last
eight months: How could any
parent do this to their child?

I've No Clue

What the outcome will be,
but I leave reassured that,
at the very least, Nevada
law enforcement has Tears
of Zion on its radar. Marlene

swears that's the case. "Also,"
I add, "my counselor did some
independent research. Samuel
Ruenhaven has had charges
brought against him personally

in Idaho. That's Sarah, waiting
for me, in case you want to talk
to her. I mean, I know you'll be
thorough and all. . . ." Come on,
Eden. Don't irritate her now.

But she's not mad. In fact,
she laughs. *I promise our
investigators can dig deeper
than Sarah can, but thanks
for the heads-up. And, Eden?*

*I know you're worried about
your sister. We'll do everything
we can to make sure Eve's safe.
The Elko County DA is a good
friend of mine. Try not to worry.*

Worry? Me?

But that's all I can do at this
point. I despise feeling helpless,
can't stand spending every day
being reactive. How do I change
that? How can I become proactive?

On the ride back to Walk Straight,
I broach the subject with Sarah.
"I believe Marlene is on my side.
But how long will it take before
we hear something from Elko?"

> Sarah's sigh could sink a life
> preserver. Not a good sign. *Longer*
> *than you'll want it to, I'm afraid.*
> *Bureaucracy, you know. One*
> *hand has to wash the other.*
>
> *It's good that Marlene knows*
> *the DA personally. That will*
> *help speed up the process some.*
> *And any extra time between now*
> *and when this thing blows open*
>
> *will benefit your emancipation.*
> *Once your parents sign the papers*
> *and they're filed, it won't be easy*
> *for them to change their minds.*
> *Hopefully this stays quiet till then.*

We decided emancipation
is the best way to go, for
the very reason that once a judge
agrees, no one can decide otherwise
except the court itself. Walk

Straight is instrumental to my
qualifying, as they've "hired" me,
so I have a job that includes room
and board plus necessary transportation.
But Mama and Papa have to agree.

Riling them up now could be bad.
"You mean because my mother
might decide to get even."
That revenge trumps disowning
her demon-possessed daughter.

> She seems like the type, yes.
> I'm expecting the notarized
> papers any day now. Once I get
> them, we file the petition and
> secure a hearing date. Then
>
> we still have to serve notice
> on your parents, and that's before
> you even see a judge. It's not really
> complicated. It just takes time.
> But don't worry. We'll make it happen.

Don't Worry

Everyone keeps saying that,
but nobody tells me how
to make myself quit. Every
facet of my life is stressful.
Thank God I've got such great

support at Walk Straight.
Without this place and these
people, especially Sarah,
where would I be living today?
Would I even be alive,

let alone have a solid chance
at a decent future? Which
brings me back to Boise and
Tears of Zion. Because if
Elko County closes it down . . .

"Question. What happens
to Eve if Father packs up
his disciples and moves on?
She'd go home, right?" Yeah,
and if she does, then what?

> *I'm afraid that would be up
> to your parents. As I said before,
> usually parents are clueless
> about what actually
> goes on at these facilities.*

It would be very hard
to prove they knew what
went on at Tears of Zion,
and even if you could, it
wouldn't be enough to make

the state step in and take
custody of your sister. Not
unless they actually took part
in the activities, or somehow
inflicted physical abuse.

But let me ask you a question.
Are you absolutely certain
your mom and dad do know?
Did you talk to your mother
about it when she was here?

"She never gave me the chance.
You don't talk to my mother.
She tosses words at you,
or in my case, insults. Besides,
no way would she admit it."

Sarah shrugs. *Probably not.*
But you never know, and I'm
big on communication, if
for no other reason than to
let the bad thoughts escape.

Once We Get Back

I've got around an hour
to kill before Andrew
is supposed to arrive.
I spend it helping Sarah
file paperwork. Earning

my paycheck, and letting
the bad thoughts escape
through mindless office
activity. I can hardly believe,
after this long, I'll see

my Andrew in just a short
while, and I keep watching
the time. *Click. Click. Click.*
The hands of the old-fashioned
wall clock barely move at all,

then suddenly it's twelve
thirty, the appointed time.
But no Andrew. *Click. Click.*
Twelve forty-five. *Click.*
One o'clock. He's not coming.

I keep working, pushing
back tears. 1:10. 1:20.
And suddenly there's a male
voice outside the office.
The door opens, and . . .

We Stare

At each other for several long
seconds. Oh my God. It's him.
It's really him. "Andrew."
He opens his arms, and I'm in
them, and he picks me up,

> spins me round and round
> until my head is spinning, too.
> Now he stops, looks down
> into my eyes. *My beautiful
> Eden. I finally caught you.*

Our kiss is tentative at first,
and not just because he's wearing
a beard, but then it's like our lips
remember, and no amount of
facial hair can interfere with

this connection. It's sweet. And
passionate. And soaked in love.
It lasts for a very long time, until
finally I have to say, "Oh, Andrew,
I love you. Don't let go of me."

> He keeps his arms wrapped
> tightly around me. *I'll never
> let you go again. Can this
> really be you? I thought I'd lost
> you forever.* Tears fill his eyes.

And I'm Crying, Too

I can't bear to pull away.
I lay my ear against his chest,
listen to his heartbeat, which
sparks delicious memories of lying
together under the Boise sky.

That scene fades into another,
out on his ranch, inhaling alfalfa
green while we made love for
the first—and only—time.
And that makes me think of Mama.

I extract myself from his arms,
reach up to touch the hair curling
softly around his chin. "You
grew a beard. I like it. Makes
you look so Idaho rancher."

> He smiles and his eyes glisten.
> *That's what I am, ma'am. Or, I*
> *should say, miss. Have to remember*
> *polite talk. I spend an awful lot*
> *of time alone. Not anymore, though.*

"Oh, Andrew, there's so much
to talk about. Some of it's good,
some I'm scared to tell you. But
I'm strong enough with you here."
It's a three-hour conversation.

Some Conversations

Just don't happen, no
matter how important
they are.

                              You

keep putting them off—
let's talk tomorrow, Cody,
or next week or next year—
because, think as hard
as you're able, you

                              don't

have the right words
to launch them. Or,
you withhold pertinent
facts because you don't

                              know

how the person across
the table might react.
But sometimes,
despite everything,

                              what

must be conveyed erupts
from your mouth
like a geyser you dare
not cap, and once that
happens, there's nothing left

                              to say.

Cody
Been Practicing

Transferring myself from bed
to wheelchair and back into bed again.
The first few times were pretty damn

lame. Without Federico on my ass
to show me the ropes, I never
would have figured out the trick,

which has to do with weight shift
and lean, and compensating for what
my legs have lost with the strength

of my arms and core. Both were in
miserable shape until I decided I'm not
going to lie around grieving for the rest

of my life. Screw that. So I asked
for weights I could use in bed, and I'm
looking forward to time in the gym.

Tomorrow I move over to the rehab
hospital, where I'll work my butt off
every day, gaining what I can. If I wind

up back in Kansas, something I'm real
determined not to let happen, I want
to be the strongest wheelchair jockey

around, in case I need to kick some
farmer's ass for hitting on Mom or
something. I mean I could always use

a gun instead. But where's the challenge
in that? The game would be two viable
limbs conquering four. Not great odds,

but that's where the bluff—playing
the disabled card—comes in. Once
a gambler, always a gambler, I guess.

I'd probably be a better gambler
in the sticks, too, playing poker with
country boys. In Vegas, everyone knows

the rules of the game. Just, please God,
if there is a You, don't let me go back
to Kansas. "Hey, Jack. You up there?"

I hiss out loud. "Could you please put
in a good word for me? And if you
happen to be looking down, check this out."

I pull the wheelchair over, very close,
angle it so I don't have to push up
over the wheel. Lean forward, scoot

my butt back, which puts my weight
forward. Feet flat on the floor, arms
close to my sides. Grab the bed frame

with one hand, the chair with the other,
and lift . . . The wheelchair rolls back
and in one sudden motion, fuck! I find

> myself on the floor. *Did someone forget
> to put on the brakes?* Federico sweeps
> into the room. *How many times have*

> *I told you to do that first? It's the most
> important part. Oh, well. Why not
> work on floor-to-wheelchair transfers?*

"Really? That's the best you can do?
Aren't you even going to ask if I'm okay?"
I'm not really pissed, and he knows it.

> *Will that make you feel better? Okay,
> you okay, Cody? Now shut up and get
> to work. Pull the chair up behind you,*

> *and lock the wheels this time. Right
> hand on the chair frame, left flat on
> the floor. Remember, the farther*

> *forward your head goes, the higher
> your ass goes. One. Two. Three.
> That's it! First try. Now, the other way.*

He Makes Me Work Hard

For ten minutes. Floor to chair.
Chair to floor. When he says I
can quit, my arms are sore and

I'm winded. "Damn, man. I need
aerobic exercise. I feel like a smoker
on a bad air quality day in Beijing."

> *I hear that's every day in Beijing.*
> *Until you get there, you'll be able*
> *to work out your lungs at the new*

> *hospital. By the way, I went to school*
> *with one of the PTs there. Mandy's hot.*
> *I figured you'd appreciate it if I made*

> *sure you'll get to work with her.*
> *She doesn't take shit, either.*
> *You're a match made in heaven.*

"Are you saying I give you shit?
Okay, maybe I do sometimes.
But no more than you deserve."

> Federico tsks. *Listen to you. That's*
> *the thanks I get for the vast amount*
> *of hard work I've invested in you?*

"Dude. Who's doing the work here?"
Wow. Despite his grumbling,
I think I'm going to miss this guy.

After Lunch

Carolyn comes in dressed in zebra-
striped scrubs. "Interesting pattern
there. Enough to cross my eyes."

> *I thought it might distract you
> while I take out the Foley. You
> still want it removed, yes?*

I nod. Since I've been here,
a Foley catheter has resided
in my penis, automatically

draining urine into a bag beside
the bed. After an SCI, two things
can happen to your bladder. Either

it will empty itself, all on its own,
and whether or not you want it to
(jeez, just picture *that*, out on a date

or something!), or it doesn't know
when to go, and you've got to remind
it. After a thorough workup, my doctors

concluded my bladder is the second
kind, and I've got to encourage it to
empty several times a day. I want to be

mobile, which means I'll have to insert
a tube into my joystick (not that it's so
joyful anymore) so I can use a toilet

instead of wearing a piss bag on my leg.
At least, I'm going to give it a try.
Carolyn extracts the Foley. Not sure

if it would hurt if my urethra could
feel something, but it can't, so there's
zero pain. Once, the process would

have embarrassed me, but I've kind of
gotten used to health-care professionals
poking, prodding, manipulating,

and otherwise studying my not-so-
private parts. Once upon a time,
that might have turned me on.

Maybe it still does, not that I'd know
without looking, and that would be
perverted. Carolyn gives nothing

> away. *Okay. Now I'll show you*
> *the do-it-yourself routine. Always,*
> *always, wash your hands before you*
>
> *touch anything. That's good advice*
> *for everyone, but for you, it's imperative.*
> *Last thing you want is an infection.*
>
> As always, she is matter-of-fact, and
> that's exactly how she demonstrates
> intermittent catheterization.

So Much to Learn

So much to understand
about the myriad ways
my life has changed.

I'm still swinging between
denial and acceptance, but
the former comes less often.

Before the incident, I knew
a little about SCI—I watched
Superman movies when I was

a kid, and heard the guy
who played him fell off
his horse and wouldn't ever

go flying again. Now,
the Christopher & Dana
Reeve Foundation is a font

of information on SCI, not
to mention a funding stream
for nonprofits that provide

services to people like me.
So thank you, Superman,
for your personal sacrifice.

I've learned a lot from
the foundation's website
and others like it, and what

the best of them offer
is not only resources, but
the knowledge that I'm not

alone, and that other people
with injuries much worse
than mine have risen above

denial, and even acceptance,
all the way to proving common
wisdom about spinal cord injury

wrong. It was Ronnie who
introduced me to them. Ronnie
who brought me a laptop

to investigate them. I'd pawned
my own when things began
to cartwheel out of control.

I asked if she didn't need
her laptop for school.
She said not to worry, her dad

would get her another one.
Wonder if he'll get pissed.
Wonder if he knows what

happened to the old one.
Wonder if he knows
what happened to the old me.

Almost Time

To check on out of here—my hospital
home away from home for months.
Ronnie comes in with some clothes.

> *Got these from your mom. She'll be*
> *here in a while to sign you out.*
> *She would've brought them herself . . .*

"Is there a 'but' attached to the end
of that sentence?" Ronnie moves
closer, looks at me with concerned

eyes. Eyes the shade of . . . violets?
"Purple contacts? That's, um, unique."
Ronnie changes eye color regularly.

> She grins. *Yeah. They make me look*
> *exotic, don't you think?* Now she grows
> serious. *Anyway, I guess they're releasing*
>
> *your brother from detention. Your mom*
> *had to take care of some paperwork.*
> *Meanwhile, I can help you get dressed.*

Cory. Man. I've been so focused
on myself, I've hardly even thought
about him. "Jesus. Has it been that long?

Poor Mom. Like she deserves something
else to worry about." Hospitals. Lockup.
Paperwork. Bills. Her job. And now,

trying to keep Cory in school,
and out of the liquor cabinet.
"Mom's going to need my help."

> *Yep. And the best way to help
> her at the moment is for you to get
> dressed and check into the new*

> *facility. This is prime time for you
> to get stronger, and they are experts
> at that. By the way, Vince dropped*

> *your car off and Leon says he can
> have it finished in a couple of weeks.
> You'll be on the road again in no time.*

On the road. Freedom. A measure
of independence. Except . . . "Ronnie,
I don't know how we'll pay for it."

> *Don't worry. It won't be that much,
> and I've been looking into grants.
> If all else fails, we'll crowdsource it.*

"Have I mentioned you're an angel?
A stubborn, demanding, purple-eyed
angel? And have I told you lately

how very much I love you? More
and more every day. Kiss me. Please?"
My angel kisses like she's possessed.

By the Time

I'm out of the ridiculous hospital
gown and comfortably dressed,
Mom hustles in, worry evident

on her face. "Everything okay?
What's up with Cory?" Ronnie
excuses herself in case the conversation

should remain private. Mom waits
for her to go, then says, *He's out, in
an intensive supervision program,*

*meaning he has to wear a monitoring
device and submit to regular drug tests.
To qualify, he has to reside within*

*GPS range and attend school at
the detention center, plus there's
a community service requirement,*

*so it looks like you're safe from
Kansas, at least for the near future.
I don't know, Cody. Cory's distant.*

*Sullen. I'd hoped the experience would
make him appreciate what he has,
but I think it only made him colder.*

Yeah, lockup will do that to a kid.
"Give him time, Mom. He'll come
around." I hope. "Where is he now?"

Home with his ankle bracelet.
I asked if he wanted to visit you,
but he said no. He's scared to see

you, not that he'd admit it. Under
that tough exterior, he's a child,
and the idea of your disability

is hard for him to accept. In his
eyes, you've always been invincible.
If you're not, he isn't either.

"Makes sense, I guess." Little shit.
If I can put up with it, he'd better.
"You sure he's okay alone?"

Not really. But life has to go on,
doesn't it? Best I can do is support
him, and let him know I love him.

Man, she looks beat down.
I wish I knew how to help her.
"Hey, Mom? As soon as I get out

of the rehab hospital, I'll find
a job. We'll make this work, one
way or another, okay? I want you

to be able to rely on me, the way
I've relied on you." No pressure
there, Cody. None at all.

We Are Interrupted

By Carolyn, Federico, and Doctor
Harrison, who's taken time from
her busy schedule to say goodbye.

I demonstrate a bed-to-wheelchair
transfer, brakes on, and everyone
seems suitably impressed, including

Ronnie, who has joined the farewell
party. She helps Mom gather my few
belongings as Carolyn hands me

> a paper sack. *Disposable catheters
> and a cupcake.* I peek inside the bag.
> She isn't kidding. *I expect updates.*

> Federico hugs me. *I'll be stopping
> by to check up on you, not to mention
> Mandy. Did I tell you she's hot?*

"Hey, dude. My girlfriend's standing
right there, you know, and she's got
one hell of a temper." The mood is light,

but the implications of my leaving
are sobering. I've largely been taken
care of here, and while I'll still have

plenty of help in the coming months,
I have to stand up (figuratively, if nothing
else) and take responsibility for my future.

Tailed by Federico

Who's determined to show me
wheelchair-to-automobile transfers,
I maneuver said chair down the corridor

and through the door into the parking
lot. "Oh, man. It's bright out here!"
I've been under artificial illumination

for so long, my eyes fight accepting
the mild December sunlight. City
fumes hang heavily in the tepid air,

but beneath them is a the smell of
desert, much better than antiseptic.
Mom's cramped car won't accommodate

me comfortably. Ronnie's new SUV
is a better fit, not to mention a surprise.
"When did you get this? It's sick."

> *Three weeks ago. Daddy said*
> *my old car was an embarrassment.*
> *What was I going to do, argue?*

> Federico laughs. *I want a daddy*
> *like yours. Is he into adoption?*
> He oversees the transfer, watches

> me buckle myself in before
> shaking my hand. *You're gonna*
> *do great. Go kick some ass.*

Kick Ass

It's a phrase tossed around
thoughtlessly, but as we weave
through streets, familiar and not,

I ponder it. Cory kicked some
woman's ass for no real reason
other than he could. I doubt

getting his own ass kicked by
the system mitigated the wide
stripe of mean inside that boy.

That bastard Chris kicked my ass
before his bullet kicked it worse.
Kicked it forever numb. Ronnie

pulls up in front of a modern
stucco building, rolls my wheelchair
around the side of her new car.

I manage the transfer unaided
and we go inside, where it smells
like fresh fir thanks to the tall

Christmas tree in reception.
After Mom signs the admission
papers, a plain-Jane blond (not

hot, not Mandy) tours us around
the well-appointed facility,
where I'll learn to kick some ass.

A Poem by Alex Rialto

Christmas

Has no place in Vegas,
where Mr. Claus plays slots
and elfettes walk the streets
in Santa hats and crotch-short
skirts. You can count me

one

of them—just a sad, skinny
girl hustling a slender living.
Honestly, Christmas wasn't
a whole lot better in Barstow,
but then, for at least a month or

two

I thought I had a chance
at happiness with Ginger.
Stupid me. What I've learned
is yes, some people born into
shit holes can rise from
the cesspool and come to

enjoy

a decent existence, free
from the stink. The rest
of us surrender to sinking
back under, and I've embraced

the view

that it's all a matter of fate.

Ginger
Going Home Tomorrow

That's the plan. Gram's driving
over this afternoon and will stay
the night, then pick me up in
the morning. So I've got today

to find Alex. I wake early, despite
the silence in my room. They
moved Miranda last night—both
because they knew she was primed

to run, and also for the safety of all
the House of Hope girls. Security
has been tightened, just in case,
which will make getting out of here

kind of tricky. We're not exactly
on lockdown, but I'll need a good
excuse. At breakfast, I sit beside
Brielle, listening to the buzz,

which is louder than usual this
morning, everyone speculating
about Miranda and why she walked
out of here with her caseworker.

Brielle nudges me. *What happened?*
After I explain, she says, *Why don't
they just make an announcement?
The gossip is getting crazy.*

Good Point

Girls and gossip!
They're thinking:

> *She must be pregnant.*
> *Yeah, but how? In here?*
>
> *Who could it be? One*
> *of the teachers? A janitor?*
> *Someone she sneaked in?*
> *Hey! Pastor Martin!*

"Crazy barely covers it.
Do they really believe
we'd have a security guard
at the front door because

Miranda got pregnant?"
Not like the guy isn't obvious.
He's about the size of a grizzly
bear, and almost as hairy.

"Listen." Under the table,
I slide my hand into Brielle's.
"You have to help me figure
a way to get out of here after

prayer. I got a text from Alex
last night. She's back on the street.
This will be my last chance to—"
Brielle pushes my hand away.

> *That's right. Last chance,*
> *and today is our last chance*
> *to be together. Instead, you want*
> *to find your old girlfriend?*

Wow. I think this is called
jealousy, something I've never
experienced, at least on
the receiving end. Is love always

jealous? The noise level around
us has dropped. People tuning in.
"Shhh. Listen, Brielle. I'm afraid
for Alex. She's headstrong, and

impulsive, and pretty much lacks
common sense. But she's good
inside. I don't want her to end
up like the girl in the paper.

This takes nothing away from
what I feel for you. I'll always
love Alex as a friend, but there's
nothing left of what we were."

> Brielle softens immediately,
> reaches for my hand again.
> *I'm sorry. I don't mean to be*
> *selfish. It's just . . . Let's go.*

Ten Minutes

To morning prayer, Brielle
and I come up with a plan
for my escape. It's brilliant.
But first we have to suffer

> through Pastor Martin's usual
> badgering. That's what it is,
> and today it's directed toward
> me. *I understand one of you*

> *left House of Hope last night,*
> *and that another of you will*
> *be leaving us tomorrow.* His
> gaze falls on me. *I pray both*

> *of you girls will continue to*
> *walk in God's light. Go forth*
> *and sin no more, that's what*
> *Jesus would have you do.*

I wish circumstances would
allow me to kiss Brielle right
here. But that would cause
a stir and I don't need that kind

of attention right now. Still,
since I won't have to deal with
his condescension anymore,
I feel the need to say something.

I Raise My Hand

But don't wait for him to call
on me. "Excuse me, but I was
wondering if you understand
the reasons why most of us are

here. Because sin implies will,
and if you cared enough
to know our stories, you'd quit
accusing us of it. I appreciate

you worrying about our immortal
souls or whatever, but if there
is an all-knowing God, he must
be aware that we were coerced

into the life. That word is even
written into the definition of child
trafficking, and is why every one
of us has to listen to you remind

us of a past we're struggling
to forget. I doubt any of us wants
to return there. Maybe, through
considered prayer, the Lord would

grant you a bit of compassion
for girls whose childhoods have
been stolen and whose futures
are in doubt. Think about it."

Lecture Over

I stand up to leave,
surrounded by gasps,
yeahs, and one *Holy
shit,* not to mention

an outbreak of laughter.
"I'm sorry," I mutter,
heading toward the door.
"I didn't mean to interrupt."

I wink at Brielle, letting
her know it's almost time
to put things in motion.
She'll have to stay until

the good minister invokes
his benediction, but I'll be
ready as soon as the room
clears. I chance a glance at

Pastor Martin, expecting
the evil eye back. Instead,
he looks confused, as if I
was speaking in tongues

        or something. And as I
        take my leave, I think
        I might hear him say,
        You're right. Forgive me.

Probably My Imagination

The only thing more surprising
would be if the sky opened up
and belted out thunder, as if
someone-on-high was yelling, "Amen!"

Brielle finds me in my room,
reaches for my hand and slips
a twenty-dollar bill into it.
Cab fare, she explains. *Unless*

you can cover it, and I know
you can't. That there is from
Sonya, by the way. I'll be doing
her algebra for a week.

I don't ask for details. A few
of the girls have managed to
stash a little cash, but most of us
are flat broke. "Thank you. I'll get

it back to you when I can. Kiss
for luck?" Her lips are sticky
with maple-flavored syrup.
Delicious. "Okay. You ready?"

She nods and picks up the thick
government textbook from
my desk. *Be careful. And . . . go!*
We decided she'd count to ten

as soon as I'm out of the room.
I'm halfway to the front door
when there's an awful crash of
glass, followed immediately by

Brielle's scream. The security
guy, who's half dozing, jumps
to his feet and hauls balls right
past me. With all the commotion

behind me, no one notices when
I slip out across the threshold,
into the morning. Just in case,
though, I run up the block, smiling

at the scene unfolding inside,
where Brielle is explaining there
was a black spider the size of a
golf ball on the window, at least

till she smashed the book through
it. No sign of Los Sureños outside,
Grizzly Bear Dude will relax
and the on-duty house parents

will be so busy with glass repair
they won't even notice I'm gone
until my English teacher lets them
know I wasn't in class today.

And to Think

It only took ten minutes
to come up with the plot.
Maybe Brielle should be
an author, too. We could

cocreate amazing books
and live a life of luxury.
Okay, there's a novel.
Lovely fiction. Will I ever

be able to write my own
future? On one hand, it's been
good at House of Hope, where
everything is regimented.

Boring, but safe, because I
wasn't allowed to make
decisions for myself. As of
tomorrow, I'm free to screw

everything up again. How
do I chisel a better path?
Guess I'll figure it out later.
Meanwhile, I need to focus

on Alex. The first thing I do is call
Lydia. Makes sense she'd go back
to her. But when I dial the familiar
number, a generic woman's voice

tells me it's been disconnected.
Huh. I try the Have Ur Cake
business line next. This one
asks me to leave a message. I don't.

I walk a decent distance toward
what looks like a main road.
House of Hope isn't anywhere
near the heart of the city. Not sure

twenty will get me that far in
a cab, but this looks like a bus
route. It is. There's a stop. While
I wait, I consider my next move.

I could call Alex, but I'm sure
she'd just hang up on me. In
fact, I have no idea what to say
if I do find her. All I know is

I have to try. Not sure why,
but I scroll through my contacts,
and when I get to the L's, my
eyes settle on a name. Lenny—

Alex's and my favorite cabbie,
when we were working for Lydia.
Lenny. Yeah. The bus squeals
to a stop, and I board. The trip

downtown costs me four eighty
and takes twenty-five minutes,
plenty of time to give Lenny
a call. His hello sounds sleepy,

and it hits me he used to work
nights. "Uh, sorry to wake you.
It's Ginger. I know it's been a while,
but you used to drive Alex and me—"

> *Yeah, yeah. I remember you.*
> *I don't have dementia. And it*
> *has been a while. So now I'm*
> *awake, what can I do for you?*

"I'm looking for Alex, actually.
I'm leaving town tomorrow, and
have some of her stuff. Would you
know how I can get hold of her?"

> *What makes you think I might?*
> *And if you don't know, there's*
> *probably a reason. Now if you'll*
> *excuse me, I'm going back to bed.*

Now what? I get off the bus near
the Stratosphere, not far from
the strip club where Alex and I
got busted. This area is ripe for guys

on the hunt, and despite it being
just approaching noon, working
girls in all colors and shapes decorate
the sidewalks. All of them look tired,

and this time of day is the easiest.
Fewer creepers prowl before dark.
Still, as I show some of the ladies
a photo of Alex, ask if they've seen

her, a couple of men inquire about
my rates. One actually dares to touch
me. I wheel and push him backward.
"Fuck off. Do I look like a hooker?"

I'm dressed in jeans, a long-sleeved
crew-necked tee, and my face
is scrubbed. Hardly the wardrobe
of a girl working the sidewalks.

> *Uh, no . . .* he sputters, *sorry.*
> *I just thought . . . well, looks like*
> *you know these ladies. Happen to*
> *know any younger ones?* Sicko.

"You do realize that paying
for sex with an underage girl
is not only illegal, but also feeds
child sex trafficking operations?"

He Looks Confused

Eighteen is okay by me. He thinks
again. *Hey, wait. You a cop?*
Then he reconsiders one more time
and laughs. *No, you're too young.*

"Yeah, and you're a fucking
pervert. Why don't you go whack
off and call your fist Sweet Little
Miss, you disgusting piece of crap."

Too far? Usually I can tell how much
is too much, but this guy seemed
like a mouse until he turned into
a badger. I've seen it before, but not

often. He bottles his anger, stuffs
it inside. You can see it in the way
his face blooms red, and his fists
begin a slow clench-unclench.

Now the crazy billows in his eyes.
As he starts walking toward me, people
scatter in a wide circle. *No goddamn
whore's gonna talk to me like that.*

This one will. The voice I know so
well falls over my shoulder. *It's two
on one, in case your math isn't good.*
I don't dare turn away from the guy

to confirm who it is, but I don't have
to. Alex moves up beside me, locks
my arm, elbow to elbow, plants
her feet. The badger stops, assesses.

"You don't want to mess with her. I
hear she keeps a razor blade 'up
there.' I know she's got Mace
in easy reach. Better back off."

> *It's pepper spray, actually, and
> it's evil.* She points a small canister
> at the man, who flees. *How'd you
> know I had this?* she asks, laughing.

"Good guess?" I turn to hug her.
"God, it's so great to see you."
I want her to melt, but she freezes.
"How'd you know I was here?"

> She pulls out of my arms. *Lenny.
> I figured you'd return to the scene
> of our crime and was on my way
> to the club when I noticed trouble.*

I smile. "Funny. It's usually you
attracting trouble. You look good.
You okay? I'm sorry about the baby."
I am. It was her ticket out of the life.

That Realization Strikes

And suddenly I understand that
this mission will fail. "Gram's picking
me up tomorrow. You can still change
your mind and come with us. Please?"

> She avoids looking into my eyes.
> *Ginger, listen. There's nothing for*
> *me in Barstow but painful memories,*
> *and you are among them. We have no*
>
> *future together, not even as friends.*
> *You deserve love. I can't give it.*
> *Sex work is the best I can do, and*
> *not only am I good at it, I like it,*
>
> *at least most of the time. Some of us*
> *are meant to live this way. It's the world's*
> *oldest profession for a reason—there's*
> *a demand. Someone has to supply it.*

"It's not the best you can do, Alex.
You're brilliant. Please come home
with me. Don't you get it? You gave
me a reason to live. You saved me."

> *Maybe. But you can't save everyone,*
> *and that includes me. Come on. People*
> *are staring. Let's find some coffee, then*
> *get you a cab back to House of Hope.*

A Poem by Kate Carville
You Can't Save Everyone

But not every loss is weighted
equally. When it's someone
you respect, you examine
your own achievements, or

                                      lack

of them. What if it was your
time? What would you leave
behind? Conversely, if you
don't really care for the one
who's given an early out,

                                        perspective

argues maybe he deserved
to go. But when it's a person
you care deeply for,
hovering so close to

                                        death

you can hear the flicker
of the harbinger's wings,
knowing he'll leave this earth
weighted with regret and there

                                        is

nothing you can do
to lighten his burden,
it's hard to accept
that all your attempts
at reconciliation are

                                        meaningless.

Sad that Bud never even
gave poor Seth the chance.

Seth
Drowning

In dreams—some violent, some worse,
because in them, I'm sinking into a slime

of sadness—I come up for air midmorning.
A fist is thumping my face, just above

my left eyebrow, and that eye is swollen
most of the way shut, and now the details

spring from the ether. Shit. Pippa. I have
to go see her. And then, I need a big helping

of Micah. Something beautiful to mitigate
my overdose of hideousness last night.

The world teems with hatred and I think
it gestates in fear of what is different.

But if that's true, how do you explain
the human fascination with the freakish—

sideshows and circuses and even porn,
to some extent, capitalize on and monetize

it. Is it only when you stumble across
the unusual, free, and obviously happy

(maybe even happier than you) that it's
threatening? Is the difference chains?

A Long Steamy Shower

Makes my body feel better, but it
can't do anything for my face,

the left side of which has swollen up
to the approximate size of a grapefruit.

Ugh. Lovely. No way to disguise it,
I go find David, who is poolside on

a lounge chair beside a hard-bodied
young guy, both wearing nothing

but Speedos and a thick sheen of
suntan oil. The implications are crystal

clear, and what can I do? The word
"celebrate" comes to mind. "Morning."

> David lowers his sunglasses. *Holy*
> *shit. What the hell happened to you?*

I have a story, mostly true, prepared.
"Last night was movie night at the center.

We were most of the way through
The Birdcage when we got a call

from one of the kids that two guys
were following her, and she was afraid

they were going to rape her. By the time
I got there, they were mid-assault,

and when I tried to stop them . . ."
It's a good story, and I expect sympathy.

> Instead, David attacks. *Are you stupid
> or what? Who do you think you are,*
>
> *the cavalry? Why didn't you just call
> 911? In fact, why didn't she? Why*
>
> *would she expect you to rescue her?
> You're lucky they didn't kill both of you.*

His companion nods agreement,
which is the most he's moved

since I got here. David reaches over,
settles a hand on the guy's chest.

> *This is Marco, by the way. I'd thought
> maybe we could enjoy a game of tag*
>
> *team. We waited up for you, but when
> you didn't come in by midnight, I was*
>
> *afraid Marco's magic spell might wear
> off. And now . . . I'd try ice if I were you.*

Dismissed

And though he didn't say forever,
it sure seems that way. I should be

scared, or at least, torn. But I feel
infused with hope, even if I've no clue

where I'll be tomorrow. One thing I do
know is I won't accept playing tag

team anymore, at least not unless I
initiate the game. David, bless him,

has just unshackled me. I watch him,
fingers combing Marco's chest hair.

Once, that might have turned me on,
made me want to jump in. But now,

it kind of sickens me. "I think icing
my face sounds like a good plan.

And then, if it's okay with you,
I'd like to visit Pippa in the hospital."

> David's free hand waves me away.
> *Go play Good Samaritan. I've got*
>
> *other plans.* He leans over to find
> his stash, hidden beneath a towel

under his chair. He takes a huge
whiff, offers the small plastic bag

to Marco, ignoring me, which is
totally fine. I'm sick of that shit,

too. Time to make some positive
changes. Resolved, I start toward

the house, then turn back to offer
David two words, well deserved.

"Thank you." I'm sure he has no
clue why I say them. If he'd bother

to ask, I'd explain: Thank you for
taking me in, for seeing something

in me worthy of rescue. Thank you
for helping me grow closer to being

a man. Thank you for teaching me
that independence is more valuable

than a cocaine-and-caviar lifestyle.
Thank you for allowing me the time

to understand that sex is undervalued
as barter, and that I am worthy of love.

Back inside, I take a few minutes
to absorb the magnificence of the house,

something I've taken for granted
for quite a while, and I know David

must have forgotten what attracted
him to this place originally. Sad, and

what a waste—all these gargantuan
rooms boasting lavish furnishings

and art, yet emptied of the emotions
that make those things truly valuable.

Wonder if all palaces feel this way,
if royals throughout time have always

favored hedonism and narcissism
over love, or if there have, in fact,

been epic romances among the chosen
few. I wander from room to room,

my footsteps the only sounds disturbing
silence so thick it seems to breathe.

Yes, I admire this place. But it embodies
loneliness, and could never truly be home.

I Leave David's

Marginally better off than when I
arrived. I stuff an upscale wardrobe

and four pairs of pricey shoes into
my old duffel, along with a nice

electric razor, a decent supply
of expensive toiletries, and the finest

plaque-removing toothbrush money
can buy. My only real valuables—

my phone and laptop—go into
a leather satchel I bought David for

Christmas. Glad this happened now,
before I got the chance to wrap it.

I've got a bank account, and a lot
of cash in my pocket, thanks to last

night's lucrative play. Better make
a deposit, in fact, and I will on the way

to see Pippa. I call for a cab; no more
limos and drivers in my near future.

Then I text Micah to let him know
I'll be stopping by this afternoon.

The thought elicits shivers,
anticipation threading my veins.

We have a chance at a normal
relationship now, but I don't say

so in my message. Don't dare jinx it.
Scares me enough just to think about

it. I consider writing a goodbye note
to David, but ultimately don't. What

if I change my mind? Is it already too
late? Endings are daunting, but every

irrevocable bridge burning initiates
a beginning, and a new direction.

I light the figurative fuse, prepare
to torch this chapter of my life, move

forward, build momentum. As I get
into the cab, carrying all my earthly

possessions in two bags, a strange
word pops into my brain, "strange"

as it applies to me, that is: purify.
That's it. I'll work on purifying Seth.

After a Quick Stop

To make my bank deposit, the cab drops
me off at University Medical Center.

UMC is the go-to hospital in Vegas for
ER patients who look like they might

be uninsured and/or on Medicaid.
At reception, I ask for Pippa Young.

> The silver-haired woman studies
> her computer. *Pippa? No record*
>
> *of a Pippa here. Are you sure you have*
> *the right hospital?* She peers at me

over the wire rims of her glasses.
"Maybe it's under Philippa? Or Philip?"

> Now she looks annoyed. *You don't know*
> *if it's Philippa or Philip . . . oh. I see.*
>
> She tries again. *Oh, yes. Philip. And*
> *what is your name, young man?*

She's awfully nosy, isn't she? Still,
I'll be polite. "Seth Parnell."

> Her head bobs up and down. *Very well.*
> *Since Philip named you as his liaison,*

you may visit him anytime. If I
might just see some identification?

Apparently, Pippa told them I'm
her partner, something they sanction

as a legitimate spokesperson for
a patient. How progressive! I find

her in a regular room, no ICU, despite
a whole lot of damage, mostly repaired

by some talented emergency room
doctors. If I tried not to look horrified,

I'd fail, so I embrace what I see. "Holy
shit, those fucks did a number on you!"

> She wheezes through a rib-shrapnel-
> punctured lung. *You don't look so hot,*
>
> *either, big boy.* Her tiny smile reveals
> a missing front tooth. *Except to me.*
>
> *Thank you. I mean . . . If not for you . . .*
> Resilience isn't always easy. She reaches
>
> deep inside and finds a little. *I'm afraid*
> *it might be a while before I can dance.*

Oh Man

"Yeah, well, about that. I might have
just cut off ties with my choreographer

friend." I pull a chair over to the side
of the bed, tell her why I've brought

two bags with me. "My mom used to
tell me things happen for a reason.

I'm sorry it had to be something like
this to open my eyes. I'm worth more

than this, Pippa, and so are you, no matter
how bad our families make us feel about

ourselves. Perhaps we're approaching the true
Age of Enlightenment. Maybe not everywhere,

but in more and more places, including
here. Excluding assholes like the ones last

night, people are starting to understand
that gender is something you're born with.

We can be who we are, follow our dreams,
succeed on our talents, celebrate falling

in love. But if we buy into the bullshit, believe
our only option is submission, we're doomed."

Pippa has listened quietly, sponging
the words, but now she says, *I wish*

*I could believe that, but people are
basically mean. Survival of the fittest*

*or whatever. Hurting others gives
them a small sense of power, and*

*that includes verbal abuse. And
men like the ones who did this . . .*

She lifts her hand, not quite touching
her pulped face. *Want people like you*

*and me to disappear completely. They
want us on the endangered species list.*

"Yeah, but they'll be extinct someday.
Until then, we can't cave in to fear."

The tears, expected, begin to fall.
How do I keep from being afraid?

"You have to stop living in isolation.
Find an accepting community. Jump in."

She thinks it over. *And where is your
community, Seth?* Excellent question.

I Chew on It

All the way to Micah's. Other than
the YouCenter kids, I belong to no real

community. I don't fraternize with other
escorts, and even if I did, I plan to quit

the business ASAP, because now I'm
free to move in with Micah and living

with someone you love negates having
for-pay sex with others, at least in my mind.

Who knew I had any moral sense left?
What little I have totally disintegrates

the minute Micah opens the door,
wearing nothing but a pair of blue

silk boxers. It's been a few days
since we've seen each other, and lust

attacks fiercely, at least for me. Micah,
however, jerks backward as if looking

> at a monster. *Jesus. What happened
> to you?* My face. Forgot about that.

I set down my luggage, close the door.
"Is that any way to talk to a superhero?"

I repeat the grisly details, hoping
my manliness will impress him.

Unfortunately, it seems to have
the opposite effect. *Seriously, Seth.*

*You should have called 911, then run.
Those guys might have killed you.*

"You sound like David. I couldn't
let them annihilate Pippa, could I?"

His shoulders relax. *I guess not.
So, you really* are *a superhero.*

"Nah. Just a regular hero. Now,
where's my reward?" I push him into

the bedroom, kiss him hard as I lay
him down, all the right muscles tensing

between us. He looks up at me with
those amber eyes, and a confession

spills from my lips. "I love you, and
I want you." I show him how much,

and what we share isn't sex, it's making
love. Micah becomes my community.

Somewhere Mid-Event

My cell phone rings. I ignore it, though
the thought briefly crosses my mind

that it could be important. No way
as important as this, though, and

when we finish I'm in no hurry to get
up. We lie tangled together in mute

satisfaction. Finally, I ask, "What do
you think about me moving in here?"

It's the first time I mention leaving David.
Micah's muscles (all the wrong ones) tense.

> *You can stay for a while, of course.*
> *My main concern is David. If he finds*
>
> *out, what would that mean for me?*
> Sucker punch. I'd hike hot coals for Micah.

I roll out of bed, go to find my clothes
and check to see if that call was critical.

> There's a voice mail from Aunt Kate.
> *Thank God I found you, Seth. You have*
>
> *to come home right now. Your father's*
> *in the hospital. He doesn't have much time.*

A Poem by James Buckman

Coming Home

To judgment is a concept
I'm familiar with—
being that person

                                  everyone's

analyzing, without
ever once asking straight
up where you've been
or why you were gone.
I understand self-medicating,
playing hide-and-seek with

                                  a

personal monster. In my case
(not to mention my sister's),
our father, who returned
from the Middle East
conflicts tweaked. So, yeah,
I indulged in more than a

                                  little

booze and pills and powders.
Anything to shut out
the noise of his waking
nightmares. Until I, too,
went most of the way

                                  crazy.

It was a long, hard
journey back, but if I
could do it, Whitney can, too.

Whitney
Getting Used To

Flipping out at random
intervals, for reasons sometimes
obvious, and other times
anyone's guess. I knew
laser tag was a poor choice,
all that neon cutting through
the darkness too reminiscent
of my time with Bryn and the Lady.

If not for James, don't know
how deep into memory-
driven insanity I might've sunk,
clutching shallow breath
as I went under. He saved me
that night, and I still can't figure
out why, let alone the reason
he wants to see me again.

Today, I was scratching for a way
out of the house to escape
the dual energy of my mom
and Kyra, who's home on winter
break. So when James called
and asked if I wanted to see
a movie, I jumped at the chance.

He's picking me up at one.
As long as I can talk Mom into
letting me out of the house.

Mom's in Her Office

With Kyra, looking at plum
pudding recipes online.
They're planning to cook
Christmas dinner, too.
But seriously. Plum pudding?
Better play nice.

"What's wrong with gingerbread,
or maybe chocolate cream pie?"

> Kyra cocks her head, points
> her chin in my direction.
> *I happen to like plum pudding.*
> *You got a problem with that?*

"Nope. Whatever you want
is fine by me. But can we please
have gingerbread, too? Maybe
Dad can pick it up from the bakery
if you don't want to make it."

> *Why should I make it? You can*
> *follow a recipe, can't you?*

Why is she always such a bitch?
Back away, Whitney, back
away. "I'm happy to give it a try,
but it probably won't turn out
very well. Baking is not my thing."
Change the subject . . . now.
"Hey, Mom. Can I go to the movies?"

Well, we're kind of busy here,
and I thought we might go out
to dinner later. Finally, she pulls
her eyes away from the computer
long enough to notice I'm dressed
to go somewhere. *Oh. Did you*
already make plans with someone?

"Well, yeah. See, I met this kind
of amazing guy at the arcade
the other night." I never told her
about the incident. No need to
mention it now. "You'll like him.
He'll be here any second."

You told him you'd go without
asking Mom first? blasts Kyra.

"I know I shouldn't have,
but I really like him a lot,
and when he called I was so
surprised, I just blurted out okay."
Okay, Whitney, make it good,
or Mom will never say you can go.
"Is it okay, Mom? He'll come
in and you can meet him.
You don't have to worry,
by the way. He's straight edge."
I won't mention it's because his
sister OD'd. Mom might worry
about the genetic factor.

When the Doorbell Rings

Mom's still considering. I let
James in. "Come meet my mother.
She's all worried about me going
out with you, so put on your best
perfect gentleman disguise."

> He grins. *What disguise? Mom
> says I was the perfect gentleman
> at conception. No morning sickness,
> short labor. And I've only gotten
> better with practice.* Sweet. Yep.

Sweet enough, that in less
than five minutes, he's got Mom
wrapped around his little finger.
Kyra is tougher, but even she mellows
and I'm allowed freedom.

James drives a new-model
Camaro, burnt orange and spotless.
He opens the passenger door
for me, and as I slide into the seat,
I wonder again what he's hiding.
No guy is quite this perfect.
He's probably a serial killer
or something. Wonder if he's ever
raped someone. Wonder if
he's ever hired a whore.

Wonder if I'll ever quit
thinking like a whore.

He Takes Me

To the Del Mar, an amazing
old Art Deco–style theater
downtown that plays a lot of
off-the-wall indie films.
The one today isn't new,
but it is really good. It follows
a boy from kindergarten
through high school, and is
really about relationships—
how they change with time.

I don't freak out when the lights
go down, so that's good.
I like sitting next to sweet James,
who totally acts the gentleman
role quite naturally. I'm surprised
he doesn't come on to me—don't
all guys use a dark theater as
an excuse to run a hand along
your thigh? James doesn't,
sensing, I guess, my need
for trust. Is it that obvious?

After the credits, there's still
light left outside. "Want to take
a walk? I'm not ready to go home
yet. My sister's making me crazy."

> The words are barely out of my
> mouth. *Wish my sister was still
> around making me crazy.*

"Jeez, man, I'm sorry. I'm an
idiot." Without even thinking,
I reach for his hand and our
fingers lace. It's the first skin-
on-skin contact I've had with
a man in months, and my initial
instinct is to pull away. Instead,
I force myself to hold on, even

> when he takes my other hand,
> too, and coaxes me nearer. *It's
> okay. No need to apologize.
> It was an observation, nothing
> more. Besides . . .* He smiles.
> *It brought us closer together.
> I didn't want to rush you.*

I study his eyes, seeking hints
of serial killer, but find none.
"Why did you call me? I mean,
after what happened the other
night, most guys would run
screaming in the other direction."

> *Let's take that walk.* He lets go
> of one hand, keeps hold of the other.
> After a few steps, he says, *This will
> sound weird, but from the moment
> we started talking, I wanted to reach
> inside you, grab hold of whatever
> is haunting you and smash it to pieces.*

Haunting

Funny verb to use in that
sentence, but accurate enough.
"Is it because of your sister?
Do I remind you of her?"

> *To a point. You're tough like*
> *her, on the outside. But she turned*
> *tough inside, too. There's more*
> *vulnerability in you, despite*
> *what you show the world. Besides . . .*
> He stops, turns to face me again.
> *I never wanted to do this to my sister.*

He leans toward me, but stops,
and his eyes ask permission,
which my eyes grant. His lips
are soft for a guy, and this kiss
is gentle, as if he's afraid to chase
me away. His instinct is good.
As nice as the kiss is, it's all
I can do not to yank back and run.

> This he senses, too. *It isn't me,*
> *though, is it? What happened*
> *to you in Vegas, Whitney?*

Before I can manufacture a word,
at the end of the block, a pickup
screeches around the corner. I cower
at the noise, and that's when the man

riding shotgun sticks his head
out the window. *Hey, lovebirds.*
Want a beer? A bottle comes flying,
smashes into the building beside me,
as the truck vanishes down the street.

It all happens so fast, I don't feel
myself go down until I land, hard,
in a pile of brown glass. I do hear
myself scream. The sound echoes
along the walls of an invisible tunnel.

   Whitney. The voice finds me
   in the tunnel. *Let me help you up.*
   James reaches out, and the hand
   that finds mine is familiar. I was
   just . . . holding it? Yes, that's right.

He pulls me up and into his arms,
and I let myself stay there until
the trembling stops. "I'm sorry.
I'm a fucking freak." Passersby
stop to see what's going on, and
someone comes out of the store
we're in front of to investigate
the crashing noise. James handles
everything, but refuses to let go
of me. Eventually, explanations
made, we walk back to his car.

Again, James opens the door
for me and I fold into the soft
leather seat. He comes around,
settles in beneath the steering
wheel, where he rests his hands.
I have to tell him something.
Just not the whole truth.
"I . . . I . . . what happened
in Vegas is that I was sexually
assaulted, and more than once.
You can take me home now."

He doesn't move. *Thank you
for telling me. I know that's hard
to admit. It wasn't your fault,
Whitney. Stop blaming yourself.
And you're not a fucking freak.
If I were to guess, I'd say you
have PTSD—post-traumatic
stress disorder. My dad has it,
too, though it was war-induced,
and it manifests differently.*

*Dad's disorder-fueled rages
drove my sister to the boyfriend
who destroyed her, and pushed
me toward self-medication. Yeah,
I get addiction because I was right
there, too. I fought my way through
rehab two years ago. It does get
easier, but only with support.*

I Thank Him

For understanding. For offering
his support. Still, the fact remains
that, PTSD or whatever you call
it, I'm abnormal. Freakish. Crazy.

He drives me home, walks me to
the door. It's comforting to know
he does these things, despite
understanding enough of what
I experienced to drive most guys
far, far away. I could never tell
him the rest. Never admit it to
anyone, ever. Not even my parents.

Under the yellowish porch light,
we say goodbye, and I accept
his kiss, knowing in my heart
he'll never call again. Why would
he? Why would anyone as sweet
as James want to spend a single
second more with disgusting me?

I go inside to find everyone gone.
A note informs me they went out
to dinner and will be home by nine.
That gives me two hours alone
to find a way to fill the hollow space
inside my shell. Music, yes, but
I don't want to think. I want to fly,
and I find my magic carpet inside
a bottle in Dad's medicine cabinet.

Ambien

As if someone taking it needs
to know, the label says to take
one tablet immediately before
bed, but only if you have a firm
seven to eight hours to sleep,
and to expect dizziness in
the morning. It comes with
a stiff warning: *Do not exceed
recommended dose.* I've never

been real good at following
directions. Let's see. I have nowhere to be tomorrow but here.
It will be eight o'clock before it
kicks in, and I can sleep till noon
if I want to. That gives me sixteen
hours. So yeah, I'll take two. I do,
then replace the bottle exactly
where I found it before going

to my room. Screw it. What good
is staying clean? Your brain has
too much time to work. Mine
needs a vacation, especially from
these lilac walls. What was Mom
thinking? I strip off my clothes,
and the air hits my skin, cool.
I dig through my drawers for
some warm, comfy clothes,
choose some soft PJ pants and
an old favorite sweatshirt.

About the time I slip beneath
the covers, plug headphones
into my phone and turn on
my music, the Ambien kicks
in, and hard. My head spins,
hopefully quickly toward sleep
because I'm also feeling a bit
nauseous. Don't want to throw
them back up. I close my eyes,

lie back, thinking about many
trips to the bathroom in that
stinking Vegas apartment,
happily puking and crapping
right before crawling back
to the other room to nod off
into the land of oblivion. Talk
about a love/hate relationship.

As I turn onto my side, there's
a crinkling noise. Something in
my sweatshirt pocket. I reach
in and my hand closes around
a small piece of heavy paper.
A business card? Through thick,
drooping eyes, I read: *Perfect
Poses Photography.* Bryn.
Remembering the day he gave
me this makes me smile. How
quickly I fell in love with him.
He was the only one who ever

made me feel beautiful. Those
days, shooting gorgeous photos
on the beach. Photos of me. Me!
This amazing warmth creeps up
my spine, and on a total whim I dial
his number. Will he answer? Will—

> *Hello? Is this really you, Whitney?*
> *Oh, girl, I'm so happy you called.*

He remembers me. "Hey, Bryn?
I can't talk very long . . . kinda messed
up. Gonna sleep soon. Jus' wan' you
to know I miss you. It's crazy, cuz,
I mean, you fucked me up good.
But I do miss you. 'Member the beach?"

> Sliding in and out now, still I hear,
> *I'll never forget the beach, Whit.*
> *God, you were stunning, all long*
> *brown legs in that white skirt.*

"Hey, Bryn? I don' wan' back
in the life. But could you maybe
bring me a li'l taste of the Lady?
Jus' a li'l. I could meet you. . . ."
Jus' wanna see his face
one more time.

It's Early Afternoon

By the time I ascend from
a deep pit of sleep, head
pounding and disoriented.
What did I do again? Guys.
Right. The movie. James.
Thump-thump. Agh! Make
it stop. Thinking hurts. Why?

Now it all whirls back.
The truck. The beer bottle.
A nice kiss or two. Ambien.
Bryn. Bryn? Oh my God, did
I talk to Bryn? Did I ask him
to score some H for me, or
was that only a dream? No.
Not a dream. We're supposed
to meet up tomorrow. What
the fuck have I done? I pull

myself from bed. As soon as I
stand, the room somersaults.
I barely make it to the bathroom
on time and as I empty bile
into the toilet, stink sweating
and skull beating pain, a trill
of excitement trembles through
my veins. I'm going to see
Bryn again! And visit the Lady.
I just have to fake my way
through this day first.

A Couple of Days Before Christmas

Gives me the perfect excuse
to do two things—go shopping
alone, and take money out of
my bank account. Do I feel
guilty? Yeah, a little. But I'll
be careful with the H, no needles
or pipes, just a whiff now and then,
when the crazy shit takes over.

Mom drops me at the mall
midmorning, promises to pick
me up in three hours. As I watch
her drive away, regret plucks.
Still, I go inside, and the moment
I see Bryn, smiling exactly the way
he did the first day we met, every
last bit of guilt vanishes. He doesn't
wait for me to reach him, but rushes
straight toward me and for one
ridiculous instant, I'm scared.

> But his hug is friendly. Loving.
> *Wow. You look great. So happy*
> *you called. I never thought*
> *I'd see you again. Hey, I've got*
> *the stuff. Let's take a drive.*
> When I start to protest, he kisses
> me silent. *We can't do this here.*
> *Just a quick stop at the beach?*

How can I say no?

A Poem by Joan Streit

How Can I Say No

To my child—tell her
she can't come home,
she doesn't belong
here—my flesh and

blood

daughter? When you
give your full measure
of love to the Lord, it

isn't

permissible to sidestep
his laws, no matter what
your heart whispers. Eden has

always

been willful, and when she met
her punishments with stonewall
stares, I wondered if she was

thicker

than most. Spare the rod,
spoil the child, as God would
have. That's how I was raised,
and I knew no better way

than

that to bring my girls up right.
Some might think I could have
been kinder, a cool drink of

water

to soothe their thirsting souls.
I say it takes a scalding tap
to scrub sin away.

Eden
Forgiveness

Is the most precious thing
in the world. God's forgiveness
tends to be expected by believers.
Taken for granted, really.
I knew God had forgiven me

the moment I heard him speak
through the priest who'd heard
of this place and sent me here.
A Bible story is embedded in
my brain: A woman, caught

in the act of adultery, was brought
before Jesus by the Pharisees,
who told him Moses would have
had her stoned to death. What
would he do? This was a test,

of course, but rather than interfere
with their laws, Jesus said, *He that
is without sin among you, let him
first cast a stone at her.* Instead,
they left, one by one, leaving her

there alone with Jesus, who told
her he did not condemn her, only
she was to *go and sin no more.*
I never feared God's condemnation.
It was Andrew's that terrified me.

I Told Him Everything

I've had a long time to think
about a partial confession.
But keeping secrets from Andrew
would be the same as lying
to him, and that I can never do.

Some of what I said stung.
A powerful hurt reflected in
his eyes. He listened without
comment until the very end,
hanging his head once in a while.

But I didn't stop until every
ugly truth gurgled out, bubbles
in a cauldron, and I really thought
he'd tell me, "Sorry for your trouble.
Been nice knowing you." But no.

> Instead, he kneeled in front
> of me, laid his chin on my knees,
> and I understood his pain was
> for himself. *Oh, Eden. If I'd had
> any idea your mother was capable*
>
> *of such cruelty, I would've risked
> prison and taken you away
> in a heartbeat. Now all I can do
> is try and make it up to you.
> Can you ever forgive me?*

He Asked Me

To forgive him. I was stunned.
Still am. His heart is huge, and
he swears it belongs to me forever,
no matter what. We just have to
figure out where we go from here.

The notarized, signed emancipation
papers arrived. We filed them
right away and got a court date
after the first of the year. Now the
hearing notice has to be served

on my parents. Shouldn't be hard.
Papa—no, Pastor Streit—is well
known in Boise. I haven't heard
back from Marlene about Elko
County. Sarah warned me that

the wheels of bureaucracy turn
slowly, but tomorrow is Christmas.
I can't imagine spending it locked
up at Tears of Zion. Oh, and Eve
must be so cold! Those rooms

were like ovens in the summer.
They must be like freezers when snow's
on the ground. Thinking about
it makes me so angry! I wish
there was something I could do.

I Never Would Have Imagined

Spending Christmas at a place
like Walk Straight, either. Much
like Thanksgiving, most of the girls
don't have wonderful holiday
memories, but I do have a few.

With Papa being a pastor,
Christmas took on even deeper
meaning, and we did it in style
when I was little. Not that we had
a lot of gifts. My parents didn't

believe in them. *This is Jesus's
birthday, not yours,* Mama told
us. Still, we always had a lovely
tree, and the carols filled me
with happiness. The presents

we did receive were usually
clothes, and something new
to wear was a rare thing. Right
now, I'd love a sweater or pair
of jeans that no one else wore first.

There will be a Christmas party
here, with excellent food and
communion. But one day, I will
celebrate the holidays with Andrew,
in a home of our own. What a dream!

Another Tradition

My family adhered to—
because as pastor, Papa
pretty much had to—was
Christmas Eve church
services. I asked Sarah

for permission to attend
a local service tonight,
and not only did she agree,
but she also said it was okay
for Andrew to come along.

He's been at a nearby motel
for several days, but will
have to go back to Boise soon,
to start the new semester.
He picks me up in a rented

car—a small sedan, very unlike
anything he drives back home.
It's not much to look at, he
apologizes, *but it's comfortable.
Where to, beautiful lady?*

"I thought it would be proper
to say thank you to the priest
at Guardian Angel Cathedral.
He's the one who helped me.
I don't know much about

Catholic protocol, though,
so you'll have to help me
out." I give him directions
and he starts the car, after
a Christmas Eve kiss.

> *I haven't been to Mass in*
> *a very long time, you know.*
> *But I'm grateful to the priest*
> *who helped you, and I'm happy*
> *to thank him personally.*

It's about a fifteen-minute
drive, plenty of time to talk.
Andrew's been thinking,
he says, and he wants me
to consider something carefully.

> *I know your emancipation*
> *is underway. But I don't want*
> *us to be apart for another year.*
> *I looked into transferring*
> *to the university here, but*
>
> *the logistics are a nightmare.*
> *Besides, my mom still needs*
> *my help at the ranch, and to tell*
> *you the truth, I can't imagine*
> *living in this city. I'd do it for you.*

*But I'm wondering if there
isn't a better way.* We've been
driving along Charleston Blvd,
and make a right turn down
the strip. I haven't been anywhere

near this part of the city since
I moved into Walk Straight,
and my discomfort grows as we
approach the big casinos. My voice
is thick when I ask, "Like what?"

*Please don't think I'm crazy,
because I've thought and thought
about this, especially as it regards
your sister. What if we approach
your parents directly? Sarah's right.*

*It's possible they don't realize
exactly what's going on at Tears
of Zion. Your mother is a harpy,
for sure, but that doesn't mean
she can't be reasoned with.*

"You can't be serious! When she
was here, she wouldn't even talk
to me except to tell me, yet again,
how I'm damned to eternal hell.
She doesn't know what reason is."

The Cathedral

Is only a block off the strip,
behind the Encore. Andrew
pulls into the parking lot
a few minutes before the four p.m.
Mass is scheduled to begin.

> I start to open the car door,
> but he stops me. *Wait. I want*
> *to give you your Christmas*
> *present before we go inside.*
> He reaches into his jacket
>
> pocket. *Sorry I didn't wrap*
> *it, but I figured you wouldn't*
> *care.* Out comes his closed fist,
> which he opens slowly. Centered
> in his palm is a gold ring with
>
> three square diamonds, two
> small stones flanking a larger
> one in the middle. *It's my mom's,*
> *but she wants you to have it.*
> *Will you marry me, Eden?*

"I . . . uh . . ." The air is being
sucked from the car. Either that,
or I've forgotten how to breathe.
"Are . . . are you sure?" He erases
the space between us, kisses me

gently. *I'm one hundred percent
positive. There is no one in the world
but you for me. We're young, I know.
But if our love has survived the past
eight months, eight years or eighty*

*can't possibly destroy it. I want you
to be my wife, and I want us to live
together out in the country, far, far
away from this city and its memories.
You don't belong here any more*

*than I do. You can have a career
if you want one. In fact, I'll help you
through college. Or you can stay
home and raise a bunch of kids.
Or colts. Or puppies. So . . . ?*

I can't comprehend how we'll work
it out, but I know we've got to try.
The idea of him leaving me behind
scares me more than the thought
of facing my mother. "Yes. Yes!"

This kiss leaves me panting,
probably not the right way to go
to church. I take a deep breath.
"Let's go inside or we'll be late.
I've got something to thank God for."

A Catholic Mass

Is like no church I've ever
experienced. Compared
to Papa's boisterous call
to stand up, confess, and
speak in tongues, the priest's

soft liturgical repetition
is soothing, the music—
both traditional carols and
melodies familiar to most
parishioners, but not me—

more lullaby than praise
song. Christmas trees and
tall poinsettias surround
the altar, sentries guarding
Baby Jesus, who smiles

at us all from his crèche.
My left hand wriggles into
Andrew's right, which plays
with his mother's ring,
circling that telltale finger.

I haven't really spoken to
God very much in the time
since I left Tears of Zion.
I talk to him now, in my heart.
"Forgive me for losing faith

in you. Forgive me for
blaming you for the actions
of people who hurt me in
your name. Forgive the things
I've done and help me to walk

forward in your light. Give
me the strength I need to fight
for love and Eve's safety.
Thank you for speaking to
Andrew's heart and bringing

him back into my life. I will
never take him for granted,
will always cherish and honor
him. Please guide my way
in the future. In your name."

Amen. Around me, others
are chanting an entreaty for
peace, and an overwhelming
sense of serenity washes over
me. This is how God should

feel. Not like a punishment.
Not like something to fear.
I don't want to live afraid
anymore. Not of God. Not
of Tears of Zion. Not of Mama.

Andrew Is Right

The only way to move past
the things that scare me most
is to confront them head-on.
I won't have to do it alone.
Not with Andrew at my side.

As everyone bows their heads
for the benediction, it strikes
me that the things I've regretted
have been the wrong ones—things
beyond my ability to control

then, or change now. If I could
wish for anything, it would be
to go back and be just a regular
high school kid again. I swear
I'd find a way to have more fun.

Join clubs. Go to dances. Maybe
try out for musicals or sing in
the choir. Of course, I'd have to
convince my parents, but since
this is all fantasy, anyway, I can

make them be open to everything,
including Andrew. Because he'd
have to be there, too. Okay, that
kind of wish can't come true.
But Andrew is here with me now.

Post-Mass

I seek out Father Gregory,
whose expression says
I look familiar, but he's not
sure why. I could pretend
we met under different

circumstances, but that
would negate the reason
I'm here. "Hello, Father.
I'm not sure you remember,
but you helped me find

my way into a safe haven,
and I wanted to thank you
for that." Recognition flickers
in his eyes and, looking at
Andrew, a hint of surprise.

> *You are most welcome.*
> *It's good to see how well*
> *you're doing. Our heavenly*
> *father is merciful, yes?*
> *Merry Christmas to you.*

"He is, indeed, Father, and
Merry Christmas to you as
well." We shake hands all
around, and Andrew and I
are on our way, blessed.

The Plan

Is for Andrew to take me out
to a nice dinner. I had no idea
it would be to celebrate our
engagement. Can this really
be happening? He reserved

a table at Hugo's Cellar, a cool
old mafia-themed steakhouse on
Fremont, well away from the strip.
On the way in, the hostess hands
me a rose. (Every lady gets one,

but still I feel special.) We
Idahoans are skeptical about
seafood, but all about the beef.
Andrew and I both order steaks
and are waiting for our tableside

salad to appear before I even try
to talk. "Andrew, I've been thinking. . . ."
He looks concerned, so I hurry,
"Don't worry. I haven't changed
my mind. In fact, what I want

to say is, you're right. I don't know
if the direct route will turn out
to be the best route, but I do
believe it's the only way to deal
with Mama, and not only her,

but Samuel Ruenhaven, too.
I want to go to Elko and talk
to the district attorney. But I
should confront my parents first.
Boise is my home—our home.

I won't be afraid to walk down
the street or bump into people
I happen to know. If you don't care
about ugly gossip, how can I?
As for my family, I don't need

a relationship, except with Eve.
The support of your mom and
sister is more than enough. We'll
have to work out some logistics.
But I'm sure Sarah will help us."

> Andrew sneaks his hand under
> the table, rests it on my knee.
> Not long ago, I would've flinched.
> *You're a brave girl, Eden, but you*
> *don't have to do this alone. I love you.*

"I know. And I love you, too."
Our waiter interrupts, wheeling
a salad cart to the table. It's the start
of an excellent meal, capping off
a memorable Christmas Eve.

A Poem by Cody Bennett

A Memorable Christmas Eve Eve

Never thought about
the holidays with regard
to hospitals and patients.
I always assumed a shopping
mall was the only place to see

                                    Santa

and sit on his lap for a pic.
Who knew the Jolly Old Elf
straps on his gear,
hops in his sleigh, and

                                    comes

calling on the bedridden,
wheelchair jockeys, and
caregivers who draw short
straws, condemning them

                                    to

spend their holiday
emptying bedpans and
collection bags, inserting
catheters, and going to

                                    town

on overcooked turkey,
soggy stuffing, weepy
cranberry sauce, and some
pretty damn good pumpkin pie?

Cody
Santa Did Come to Call

On us patients here at Mojave Palms Rehab
Hospital. He dropped by yesterday, Christmas
Eve Eve. Guess that's the best he could do

during this busy holiday season. Hey, not
complaining. The dude brought gifts—
comfy plaid flannel pajamas and matching

robes, the key word being "matching." This
morning, we were a matched set of patients.
Last night, we had an okay not-quite-Christmas

dinner, with Santa carving the turkey, which
was dry, and in need of gravy. Yeah, so the food
here isn't exactly like Mom's home cooking.

It might be marginally better than at the last
hospital, but that's a narrow margin. Still, I like
it here. My roommate, Craig, is pretty cool.

He's a T4 complete, much further into his rehab
than I, and quite the cheerleader. He got to go
home for Christmas, and without his rather large

presence, the room feels empty. He's given me
all kinds of advice, and actual interaction with
someone who's worked through the initial stages

of mobility grief and come out swinging has been
a blessing. As for the staff, they've been great.
The caregivers are kind. Well, except for the PTs,

who give the requisite amount of physical therapist
crap. They're drill sergeants, forcing us to be the best
we can be with our limited skills. I've only been here

a week, with one day off to detour muscle strain,
but I already feel stronger. Mandy is, in fact, hot,
and she's not above flaunting her assets (just a small

tease) to encourage correct behaviors like on-time
arrival for scheduled workouts and giving one
hundred and ten percent every time we meet.

Right now, the work is all about balance, core and
upper-body strength. One day at a time, one skill set
at a time. But this place has the latest, greatest

equipment, and before I leave here, I'll be on
my feet again. Not without help. Not without
braces or crutches or a walker. But I will stand

upright, and once that happens, losing those aids
will be totally up to me. I'll never be what I was,
but come to think of it, that Cody wasn't such

a great guy anyway. What I've lost physically
to injury I've gained in strength of will. At least
on good days, and not every day is one of those.

404

Last Night

My brain vacationed in Dreamland.
At first it is a nice place to be. I am
home for Christmas, and Jack is there,

too, and we are drinking eggnog in front
of the fireplace. Christmas stockings,
embroidered with our names, hang from

the mantel, which is a little strange,
because our fireplace is gas and doesn't
have a mantel, but you know how dreams

go. Now Mom turns on her personal
iTunes Christmas playlist, which is
traditional carols jazzed up by a trio

of greats—Frank Sinatra, Elvis, and
John Lennon, backed by Mötley Crüe—
and yeah, absolutely that's weird, but

dreams often are. From weird to
completely whacked, for no real
reason Cory starts shouting at Jack,

> *Why the fuck didn't you tell me*
> *you're dead? Dead people drink*
> *eggnog. You're totally messed up.*

> That makes Jack laugh like a crazy
> man. *Well duh. Dead is shorthand*
> *for messed up. You'll know all about*

that soon enough. You're halfway
to hell already. In fact, I'll take you
back there with me right now.

Jack reaches out with a rotting
zombie hand and shuffles forward
in slo-mo, singing "So This Is

Christmas" in decent harmony
with John Lennon. Cory screams
and the next thing we know, he throws

his ankle monitor bracelet at Jack
and goes running out the door.
"Come back, Cory!" I yell, and

I'm on my feet, running after him,
trying to catch him before the cops
do. The little shit is fast, but I'm

faster. I always have been. Cory
could never beat me in a footrace
and I'm starting to catch up, when *BAM* . . .

My legs worked fine in my dream,
but when I woke up and tried to jump
out of bed, they didn't remember how.

Bad Start to the Day

And it hasn't improved since. Fall
out of bed before breakfast, your appetite
vanishes along with the nightmare.

PT on an empty stomach might work
fine as a weight-loss gimmick, but
halfway through rolling forward and

back over a medicine ball, gravity
trumps form. Abuse your body
long enough, despite lack of feeling,

pain takes center stage. Hard to get,
unless the experience belongs to you.
It belongs to me, and I still don't get it.

So when Mom and Ronnie both show
up midafternoon to visit, I'm not
in the best of moods. At least now

I don't have to be prone and pissed off.
I'd rather be in my chair for Mom's news,
which her scowl tells me isn't good.

> Ronnie asks if she should leave, but
> Mom says, *No. You're practically
> family, aren't you? You might as well*
>
> *hear this. Cory had a huge meltdown
> last night. He found out about the house,
> so he went on a tear and started smashing*

furniture against the walls, screaming,
"They want our house? How will they
like it now?" He actually threw a chair

at the sliding glass door. Luckily, it
didn't break. It would be hugely expensive
to replace. I called a handyman about

patching the holes and repainting. His
estimate is eight hundred dollars.
If I could, I'd make Cory do it, but . . .

"What the hell is wrong with him?
That kid needs serious help.
He hasn't been drinking, has he?"

Mom shakes her head. There's no
alcohol in the cupboards, except maybe
in cold medicine or something.

Actually, I never thought about that.
No, I think he's just scared, Cody.
But he won't even talk about it.

I'm frustrated. She needs me at home,
at least as long as we have one,
but I can't even get in and out of

the doors in my chair. "Tell Cory
either he comes here to see me or I'm
coming to him, one way or another."

I'll do my best to convince him,
but I don't think he'll visit. I'd better
get home before he burns it down.

I watch her go, hunched over as if
she's sixty instead of forty-two.
When I'm positive she's out of earshot,

I tell Ronnie, "Every time I see her
she looks older. I don't know what I
can do to help her. I'm not even sure

which one of us is the most responsible.
Probably me, but maybe not. She has
to deal with Cory the most, and what

he did last night . . . How could he?"
Ronnie looks every bit as confused
as I feel, and almost afraid to say

anything. Finally, she hugs me. *I'm*
so, so sorry. Your mom's definitely
been through a lot. But she's strong.

"Staying strong takes a toll, doesn't
it? First Cory. Then Jack. Then me.
And now, the house. It fucking sucks."

She's quiet for a minute, but now
she asks, *Why didn't you mention*
there was a problem with your house?

"Ah, you know. It wasn't like I was
trying to hide it from you or anything.
It just didn't seem like something

you needed to worry about. You've
done enough stressing over me
without tossing that into the mix."

Cody, I love you. Even if things
were one hundred percent okay,
I'd worry about you, just because.

So, why don't you tell me what's up
with your house? Other than
the newly decorated walls, that is.

I give her the lowdown. "If not
for Cory's intensive supervision
program, we'd probably be on our

way back to Kansas by now. Uncle
Vern said we could stay with him
for a while. Scared the crap out of me.

But if Mom has to sell on a short sale,
she won't have money to invest, and
her income won't qualify her for a loan.

So we'd be renting, and in this city
pretty sure whatever she could afford
wouldn't be in the best neighborhood."

I'm Actually Very Sure

About that. Mom's done some
scouting, without much success.
And as far as anything accessible,

just, no. "Don't suppose we could
crowdsource enough money for
a house suitable for the disabled,

could we? Yeah, probably a long shot."
I rotate my chair until I'm facing
Ronnie straight on, knees touching

knees. Today she's wearing bright
green contacts and her eyes remind
me of emeralds. "You are incredible,

know that? Hey, think you could flirt
a little with Cory and maybe convince
him to visit me for Christmas?"

> She smiles. *Persuasion is my middle
> name. I'll stop by your house on
> my way home. But first, let's make out.*

Ronnie takes control, and ten
seconds into this very hot kiss,
my day begins to improve.

When she lifts my hands to
the luscious, full rounds of her
breasts, encourages me to explore

the suede skin beneath her sweater,
the bad of this day sizzles away
like water dripped on a hot skillet.

If it wasn't for the float of voices
somewhere beyond the door,
I'd be tempted to see how far

my messed-up body would let me
take her, and just how far it might
follow. I rest my forehead against

the taut muscles of her abdomen.
"I have no clue why you're still
here, after the god-awful shit

I've done, and I'm pretty sure
you'll get sick of me eventually,
but I'm damn sure going to cherish

every single minute together with
you. By the way, you smell amazing."
She wears her perfume like she wears

her hair—in gentle wisps. The thought
initiates a rush of pleasure, static.
Ronnie lowers her hand and though

> I can't feel it, I believe her when
> she whispers, *Look what woke up.*
> *Is that what's called muscle memory?*

Tomorrow Is Christmas

And that is the best gift I can imagine—
the knowledge that I might actually
be able to give Ronnie pleasure, and not

just with my hands and mouth, but
the way an intact man does, and maybe
even come myself. "Thank you, baby."

> *Baby,* she purrs. *I like that. But what
> are you thanking me for?* Those
> gemstone eyes lock onto mine.

"For keeping my hope alive. Seriously,
Ronnie, without you, I would have
given up already. You make me want

to get better. I want to be strong for you.
Will you come see me tomorrow?
It's Christmas, so if you can't, it's okay."

> *Baby,* she repeats, redirecting the word.
> *Would I miss spending Christmas with
> you? Anyway, don't you want your present?*

We agree that I do, of course I do,
and she kisses me goodbye, flits
from the room, a beautiful hummingbird.

A Poem by Ginger Cordell
Brielle Kisses Me Goodbye

And though our hearts
say this isn't forever,
our brains insist that's
a misrepresentation, as

                    time

will keep shuffling
forward, wearing us on
its shoulders. Our love

                    is

young, and perhaps
that's good, because
well-seasoned connection
would sever more

                    painfully,

scar deeper. We promise
to keep in touch, knowing
our separate journeys
make it unlikely, that the

                    impatient

erosion of affection
is hurried with distance.

Ginger
Saying Goodbye Sucks

I'm not sure which was harder,
kissing Brielle goodbye, promising
it wasn't the end of us, but knowing
it probably was; or finally, completely

giving up on the hope of Alex and
me together again and happy.
There's a lesson here, and that is
I have to find happiness inside

myself before I try to partner again.
But knowing there's a lesson and
learning it are two different things.
Right now I am torn between the need

to leave and the desire to stay where
I've come to feel safe for the first
time in my life, and where seedling
love took root in my heart, though

I didn't believe it was possible.
It isn't fair. But then, I should
be used to that by now, shouldn't
I? Does life ever get fair, though?

These thoughts tumble around in
my head as Gram steers her new used
minivan onto Interstate 15 South.
We'll be home in less than three

hours, as long as the vehicle
cooperates. "Thank you for coming
to get me. I never thought I'd
make it home for Christmas."

> *Christmas Eve, she corrects.*
> *The kids are so excited to see*
> *you. They even made you some*
> *special presents. Can't say what!*

I'd forgotten how cheerful
she always is, or at least pretends
to be. "Gram, I'm so sorry for all
the worry I put you through,

and for not being there to help
when you needed me. I never told
you what happened, but meant
to, and then I got sucked into—"

> *We don't have to talk about it*
> *now. Or ever, if you don't want*
> *to. I know you wouldn't have*
> *run off like that without a reason.*

"No, I wouldn't have. But I do want
to talk about it. It's important to me
that you know." I tell her everything,
start to finish, going back all the way

to Walt, the first of my so-called
mother's men who paid to have
a little fun with her daughter or,
as Iris put it, "to make me a real

girl" by ripping me apart. I don't
try to remember all the others
I've invested so much effort into
trying to forget. I just tell Gram

Walt wasn't the only one, finishing
the bulk of my confession with
the man who forced my hand that
day, convinced me running away

was my only option. "Also, so you
know, not that it matters I guess,
Alex and I did strip for money
in Vegas, but I never let a man

touch me, and I probably never
will in the future." I keep the part
about sleeping with girls to myself
for the time being. What I just shared

is more than enough. She gives
it some time to sink in, and I keep
my mouth shut while she does,
staring out the window at desert.

It isn't a beautiful landscape,
and it won't improve by the time
we reach Barstow. Someday I'll live
in the forest or near the ocean, or

maybe find a place where I can have
both. Northern California or Maine.
West Coast or East, makes no difference,
as long as there are trees and water.

> Finally, Gram takes a deep breath,
> releases it in a low whistle. *I never
> even suspected anything like that,
> Ginger. Why didn't you tell me?*

"I'm not sure," I admit. "I was
hurt. Embarrassed. Scared. But
mostly I was pissed at Iris. I couldn't
stand to look at her. Couldn't take

a chance on her doing something
like that again, and she would have.
I'll never forgive her. I hate her."
My voice has risen in volume and

pitch, building toward a wail before
total breakdown. "I'm s-sor-ry." It
escapes as huge sobs. "But I don't care
that she's dying. Is that wrong?"

Gram Stays Silent

For a very, very long time.
Is she angry? Disappointed?
Have I managed to smother
every hint of good cheer?

> Finally, she opens her mouth.
> *I'm going to tell you something*
> *I haven't talked about in many*
> *years. I never thought it was*
>
> *proper to share this, but now*
> *I think you should know. I told*
> *you Iris's childhood was no walk*
> *in the park. Military brats never*
>
> *have it easy, but what happened*
> *to her at Fort Irwin was beyond*
> *terrible.* She falls quiet again,
> gathering her thoughts. *I believed*
>
> *the neighborhood was safe, and*
> *I let her outside to ride her bike*
> *all the time. Turned out I was naive.*
> *Not every soldier is a good guy,*
>
> *and one evening as she rode home*
> *one of the not-good ones got hold*
> *of her. She was only seven. That*
> *man raped her, almost killed her,*

and would have, except Mark—your
grandfather—heard Iris screaming.
He beat that bastard within an inch
of his life, but the damage to your

mother was already irreversible.
I will forever carry a heap of guilt.
It's why I've continued to support
her, and even apologized for her

behavior, despite the awful choices
she's made, including how she earns
a living. Now I'm not claiming
the incident in any way pardons

the things she allowed done to you,
but it does explain, to some extent,
why she went the direction she did.
I can't tell you it's best to forgive her,

but what I can say with certainty is
holding on to resentment won't make
you any happier, and banking hatred
inside will eat your soul alive.

No! I don't want there to be a reason
for what she did. I want to hate her.
Forgive her? I've never forgiven anyone.
I have no clue what the word even means.

Sobering

That's what it is,
like having a bucket
of ice water splashed
into my face, and as

chilling. I have never
offered forgiveness
to a single living person.
Or to a dead one, either.

Even after his death,
I never pardoned my father
for deserting Mary Ann
and me, leaving us at

the mercy of Iris's whims.
Instead, I've choked back
a giant grudge, held it in.
Pointless, really. As for

people still breathing,
the men whose scars
I'll always wear aren't
worthy of clemency.

But Gram is totally right.
Stowing hatred for them
does nothing but deny me
any chance at happiness.

The problem, of course,
is how to free myself of
the rage, welded into
the iron jaws of memory.

And then, there's Alex.
In some ways, she hurt
me more than the others
because I gifted her with

trust, something I don't
own much of. And while
she claimed to love me,
slowly, slowly, she excised

me from her life, declared
my devotion dependency.
Unnecessary, when in my
eyes it was affirmation that

I could, in fact, experience
such depth of emotion.
That wound still bleeds.
Will forgiveness suture it?

Finally, Iris. Mother. Traitor.
How do I reach beyond my own
pain, tap into hers, and find
a measure of sympathy?

Gram's Stooped Stucco House

Has never looked so welcoming,
and that's before we go inside,
where my family is waiting.
Gram pulls the minivan into

the driveway. *Welcome home,*
Ginger. It hasn't changed much,
I'm afraid. Maybe one day I'll
hit the lotto and we can remodel.

I like the sound of "we," and yet,
a sudden attack of nerves makes
me hesitate. The kids have always
looked up to me, and I am so not

a role model. Doesn't matter.
The front door opens, and out
spills the pack of my siblings,
running toward me, to a rousing

chorus: *Ginger! Ginger! Ginger!*
Missed you. Where you been?
Wait till you see the Christmas tree!
Wait till you see your presents!

Now four pairs of arms wrap
around me—all except Mary Ann,
who stands back slightly, observing.
"Okay, okay, let me look at you.

Wow. I can't believe how big
you all are!" I barely recognize
them. How can so little time apart
make such a difference, or did I

somehow forget the way they
looked before? No, they've changed.
Honey and Pepper have grown
their hair to below their shoulders.

Porter is two inches taller at least,
and his cheeks have lost baby fat.
Sandy looks more boy than toddler
now, and that has everything to do

with the scars the accident left on
his face. Mary Ann has changed
the most. Not only does she look
older, but she also seems more . . .

worldly, I guess. Is it her makeup,
something she never wore before
I left here? Or is it something
else? Something more sinister?

Whatever it is, I wade through
the kids clamoring at my feet, go
straight to her side and open my
arms, inviting her hug. "Hey."

She rewards my effort with
a reluctant embrace, pulls back
immediately. Everything is not
okay, but I refuse to believe

the worst until I hear it from
her mouth. "We've got a lot
to talk about, yeah? I know
I've got plenty to tell you."

> She nods, and her shoulders
> relax a notch or two. *Just so
> you know, I'm glad you're home,
> but I'm still mad at you for leaving.*

"I don't blame you," I say, but
she's already walking away.
Honey and Pepper scramble
inside behind her, followed by

> Gram and Porter, who carries
> my small suitcase. Sandy slides
> his little hand into mine, tugs gently.
> *Hey, Ginguh. Where ya been?*

I reach down, scoop him up—
he's not too big for me to manage
that yet. "That's a very long story.
Think I'll save it for another day."

A Poem by Seth Parnell

Another Day

We always believe
we'll have another day
to make things right,
but the concept of future

reconciliation

is a pencil sketch.
Erasable by circumstances
beyond our power to foresee,
and what remains

isn't

predictable. The longer
you wait, the wider
the rift becomes,
and it isn't

always

possible to manage
the crossing before
continental drift carries
you too far apart. It's

a

sad fact of life
that distance weakens
bonds, and reconnection
is simply not a

given.

Seth
Finding a Christmas Eve Flight

On such short notice was a nightmare.
I finally managed to book one into

Evansville, but the layover in Detroit
is impossible, and the price tag was

out of sight. Still, I'm going, and
I'm scared as hell, and not just because

I've only ever flown one other time—
when I left Louisville with Carl—and

the weather looks to be an ugly mess
of blizzarding snow. No, I'm terrified

that Dad will turn me away, even as
weak as I hear he is, tell me he can't

bear to look at me, his blood-born
abomination. It's almost enough

to make me forget the whole idea,
stay here where I feel safe, though

that right there is a ridiculous notion.
Look at me. "That right there." "Notion."

I'm thinking in Indiana vernacular,
something I've tried to culture away

for close to a year now, ever since
I first hooked up with Loren back

in Louisville, escaping field work
for cultivation of a whole different

kind. Loren. Wonder what he's up
to now. Preaching? Partnered?

Partnered and preaching? Funny,
though they look nothing alike,

Micah's soft-spoken determination
reminds me of Loren. Both, in fact,

are a bit too determined to succeed
in their chosen careers, no matter

what it takes, even if that means
love taking a backseat to their dreams.

Even if that means me, unfortunately,
taking a backseat to their dreams.

I think I can still convince Micah
to move in with me, but not until

I return from this trip. This sad, lonely
journey to say a final goodbye to Dad.

When I Called

Aunt Kate, she gave it to me straight.
Despite decades of hard work, all that

sausage and gravy was not good for
Dad's heart. By the time he actually

decided something was wrong and
went in to see a doctor, hard-core

> measures were necessary. *They sent
> him by ambulance straight to St. Mary's*
>
> *in Evansville,* she told me. *They performed
> a quadruple bypass, but apparently there*
>
> *was also extensive damage to the heart
> itself. He was terribly sick already, and*
>
> *has had complications. He's in intensive
> care and the prognosis isn't good. Try*
>
> *your best to get here right away. Sorry
> to do this to you at Christmastime.*

She never asked where I've been,
or what happened to make me go.

Dad must have told her something,
but it was not part of the discussion.

I suppose at some point it needs to
be. I won't hide who I am anymore.

Micah drops me off at the airport,
and I kiss him goodbye in full view

of a throng of Christmas Eve travelers.
"I wish you could come with me.

Hey, maybe you could fly out next
week. I've got enough cash for a ticket,

and I'd love for you to see where I
come from. Even if it is covered in snow."

> He smiles wistfully. *Maybe one day.*
> *But I have to work next week. Besides,*
>
> *if I go back there, it won't be in winter.*
> *I had the chance to relocate in the Midwest,*
>
> *but this California boy hates deep-freeze*
> *cold. Why do you think I moved to Vegas?*

I shrug. "So you could find a cute
boy, fall in love, and settle down?"

> *You sound like Mom. Hey, better go.*
> *Those cabbies are giving me dirty looks.*

One More

Long kiss goodbye, dirty looks
from cabbies be damned. One

more promise to see him in
a few days. One more plea for

him to consider sharing a place
when I get back. One very large

stab of pain when he drives off
without looking back, just a small

wave over his shoulder. I wander
over to curbside check-in, get in line,

and suddenly it hits me that I could
go home and never return to Vegas.

Would Micah even miss me?
Would he ask me to return?

> Someone behind me taps my
> shoulder. *Line's moving, dude.*

"Sorry," I mutter, shuffling
forward and digging in my pocket

for my wallet and ID. As I approach
the counter, I notice the sign:

TIPS APPRECIATED. The baggage
guy is an older man, grizzled and slightly

bent, but he lifts my duffel easily,
assures me it will reach my flight in

plenty of time, and when I slip him
a ten, his eyes go wide. "Merry Christmas."

Kind is as kind does, my mom used to say,
and that seems to be the case because

when I make a few missteps at security,
the TSA people calmly remind me

to remove *everything* from my pockets.
I reach the correct gate in plenty of

time, only to find my flight's delayed
due to the Midwest weather. While

I wait I should charge my phone,
and that reminds me I need to make

a couple of calls—one to YouCenter
to let them know I won't be in, and

the other to Pippa. "Hey. I'm heading
home for a couple of days. You okay?"

Never better, she jokes. *But are you
really going back to Indiana?*

"As long as the weather gods allow
it. My dad's in the hospital." I omit

the deathbed part, but Pippa intuits
it anyway. *Oh, wow. Sorry. The Grim*

*Reaper does love the holidays. Seth?
I was thinking about community.*

*It's the next best thing to family,
isn't it? Will you help me find mine?*

"I'll do the best I can. Meanwhile,
you heal up and get out of there."

*And find a cheap plastic surgeon.
Can't go around looking like this.*

"You'll always be beautiful, Pippa.
Oh. Just called my flight. See you soon."

*Hey. One thing before you go. Try
to forgive your dad. Easy to say,*

*hard to do, I know. But if you don't,
you'll beat yourself up forever. Be safe.*

"You, too. Have a happy Christmas."
Who the hell made her so wise?

Squished into a Middle Seat

At the very back of the plane, not
much to do for three and a half hours,

I entertain myself with my laptop
for a while, but after the drink service

and two Jack Daniel's, I put it away
and sink into an alcohol-enhanced stupor.

I close my eyes, wishing back-row
seats reclined and wondering if

someone might be joining the Mile
High Club in the lavatory behind me,

or if people ever pay random strangers
for the experience. I will myself to nap.

Floating. Floating. Someone taps
my arm and I straighten, ready to let

my seatmate out to go to the bathroom.
Except he's sleeping, and the seat on

the aisle is empty. So why does it seem
occupied? I extend my hand into

the space, and for just a second, I feel
him there. "Dad?" The barest hint

of fingertips brush my cheek
before vanishing, and I know.

He's Gone

He didn't wait for me. Was that by
design, or did he try to hang on?

"No." It's not even a whisper. "Why?"
Why did you leave without saying

goodbye? Except, you did, didn't you?
Does this mean you've forgiven me?

"I forgive you, too." It's important
I say those words out loud, to steep

them in meaning. The man beside me
stirs, and I swallow the sound of my tears.

Maybe I'm wrong. Maybe it was only
a by-product of my buzz. Yeah, that's it.

So why do I shiver at the skin pluck
of goose bumps? I close my eyes again,

am vaguely aware when the aisle seat
refills with a flesh-and-blood human.

Window-seat man begins to snore.
I want another drink. But now the captain

informs us we're on our final descent
into Detroit, where the temperature

is five degrees Fahrenheit, under
a light snowfall. The flight attendant

adds an apology for our late start,
reminds us many connections have

also been delayed. Mine was hours
away and even if the Evansville

flight is on time, I'll have to wait
at least an hour to board it, which

proves to be the case. When we touch
down, out come the cell phones. That

includes mine. The expected message
from Aunt Kate has not yet appeared,

so I text her first. DAD DIDN'T MAKE IT.
The forty-one rows in front of me

deplane first, and I am most of the way
to my connecting gate before the bell

> on my phone sounds, signaling her
> response: *I'M SO SORRY, SETH. HIS*
>
> *PASSING WAS PEACEFUL. BUT HOW*
> *DID YOU KNOW?* How did I know, indeed?

If I tell her, she'll think I'm crazy.
"Gay" is probably bad enough.

One Word

Keeps surfacing on the ninety-
minute flight to Evansville: lost.

So many things lost to me, and
much too soon. My mother, claimed

by cancer before I could ever even
try to make her understand the "me"

of me. My identity, through the early
years of my childhood, not because

I couldn't see it, but because of what
was expected of me. My faith, stolen

by one who claimed to stand fast
representing it. One deviated priest,

and my God was taken from me.
And Dad, who deserted this world

in favor of the next where, he believed,
the love of his life awaits him in

eternity. But where lies the key
to heaven's gate? In dogma or ancient

scripture? Or might it be found within
the creeds of love and forgiveness?

A Poem by Whitney Lang
Deserting This World

Would be easy. The Lady
would make it a gentle ride.
So why has it taken me this
long to recognize that fact?
What's the point of

                                fighting

to hold on to solid
footing, when slipping
toward darkness
requires almost no
effort and the struggle

                                to live

a routine existence
is an uphill battle?
Anyway, how can "average"
be a goal for someone
like me, who is

                                tempted

by the extraordinary
and drawn toward
the unexpected?
It must be better

                                to die

a quick death
than to stare at the clock,
as the hours drag you toward
the very same inevitable
conclusion.

Whitney
What Have I Done?

After everything I managed
to live through—barely—before,
eking out a slender escape
from the hands of death, knotted
around my throat, how can
I invite the demon king
back into my life?

I. Am. An. Addict.
There is zero doubt of that,
and not only am I addicted to
the sensuous dance with the poppy,
but I am one hundred percent hooked
on the son of a bitch sleeping
beside me. Why did I call Bryn?

In less than five minutes,
he convinced me to leave
the relative safety of the mall
and take a drive to the beach,
despite the fact I understood
there was treachery in his motive.
I'd asked for the heroin,
that wasn't his fault, and he didn't
need to twist my arm to make me
take a whiff. Oh, I wanted to visit
the Lady, and she was everything
I remembered. One tiny taste,
every drop of fear melted like candle
wax tongued by flame.

Then Bryn kissed me. Things
are a little hazy this morning,
but I think I asked him to.
I haven't wanted a man near
me in a very long time,
but Bryn is the man who taught
me what it means to be a woman
(if not a lady), and his practiced
touch rekindled the passion
I'd truly believed died in Vegas.

He laid me back on a pillow
of sand, and though it was cool,
the billowing heat of my body
warmed it soon enough. I closed
my eyes, and didn't move,
just let him take me all the way
there, listening to the serenade
of surf beneath the steady,
building beat of my heart.

And when he said he loved me,
I stupidly confessed, "Oh God,
I love you, too." And that was all
I needed for him to convince me
to leave Santa Cruz behind again.

He is a masterful player.
And I have been played.
And I know I've been played.
And I invited the game.

The Question Is

Do I really want to keep playing,
knowing this game allows no
winners? I slip out from under
the covers, tiptoe into the little
bathroom, sit on the cracked
toilet seat, pee into the rust-stained
porcelain bowl. The experience
carries me straight back to Vegas,
a place I vowed never to return to.

We're halfway there now, in
a seedy motel, all Bryn could find
off the freeway, two nights
before Christmas. Or maybe all
he could afford. I go to the sink
to wash my hands and can't avoid
looking at the girl in the mirror.

> She stares back at me with mascara-
> stained eyes, still holding vestiges
> of the H inside them, and she insists,
> *You're better than this. He says*
> *he won't lock you back in his stable,*
> *that when you were taken from him*
> *he realized that you were the only*
> *girl he loved. But you know it's a lie.*

She's right. He lies, and the Lady
is a liar, too, but last night, held
in her arms, I finally felt right.

It Would Be So Easy

To go back into the other
room for that little plastic
bag of powdered courage.

Snort myself brave.
Chase the dragon, and
smoke myself fearless.
Send Bryn into a drug-
store for clean needles.
Shoot myself heroic.
How many heroes require
such encouragement
to face their enemies,
conquer them—or not?

> *Dope or no, you'll never
> be a hero,* says Girl-in-
> the-Mirror, *and your past
> is the enemy. Tomorrow
> embraces hope. Yesterday
> holds despair. It's not too
> late to turn back around.*

"Shut up," I tell her, then
turn the shower faucet
as hot as I can get it, do
my best to steam away
the lingering tendrils of H,
and scrub the scent
of Bryn from my skin.

No Clean Clothes

I put on yesterday's, then
reach into my purse, past
the plastic bag, to find my
hairbrush. On its way out,
it bumps my cell, which
I've tried to avoid, knowing
there'll be messages from Mom.

I go ahead and check them
as I wrangle the snarls from
my hair. As expected,
she's left quite a few.

> I'M HERE TO PICK YOU UP.
> WHERE ARE YOU?
> WHITNEY? I'M HERE.
> WHERE ARE YOU?
> WHITNEY, ARE YOU OKAY?
> WHERE ARE YOU?
> WHITNEY?
> WHERE ARE YOU?

There are voice mails, too,
including one from Dad:
Whitney, your mother called.
She's worried sick. Where are you?
There's even one from James.
Hey, Whitney. I was hoping
to see you today. Where are you?

Good question.
Where the fuck am I?

All Sense

Of feeling right dissolves
completely. James. Damn.
I might have had an actual
shot at something like a normal
relationship. That's gone now.

> Bryn stirs in bed, rolls
> over and into awareness.
> It takes him a minute to
> realize where he is and who
> he's with. *Whitney. Right.*
> *Morning, babe.* He smiles,
> lifts back the covers.
> *How about a little lovin'?*

Once upon a time, I would
have been tempted. Instead,
I'm sort of creeped out, and
shake my head. "Not right
now. I already showered."

> *Hey, that's okay. I've got*
> *nothing against a clean*
> *woman, although raunchy*
> *is usually better.* He laughs
> at his own stupid joke,
> very much resembling a hyena.

I've a made a huge mistake.
But how do I rectify that?

The Direct Approach

Is the only way. "Hey, Bryn.
I've been thinking. As much
as I've missed you, I can't go
back to Vegas. I really don't
want to be in the life again
and I know that's where I'll
end up. I'm so, so sorry, but
will you please take me home?"

> All signs of humor vanish
> from his face. He sits up,
> swings his feet over the side
> of the bed to the floor. *Home?*
> *I do hope you're kidding, bitch.*
> His voice drips menace like
> venom. *Surely you wouldn't*
> *have asked me to drive all*
> *the way to Santa Cruz just to*
> *deliver some dope, would you?*

Every nerve in my body
jumps to attention. This
is a royal fuckup. "I . . .
uh . . . okay, listen. You
don't have to take me back.
I'll call my parents to come
pick me up or I'll take a bus
or something. Look. I was
in a bad place, and you came
to mind, and I just wanted
to hear your voice, and—"

*And you called and begged
me to come to you.* He stands,
starts toward me. *Because
you can't forget how good
I was to you, and you know
you'll never find anyone else
who'll love you the way I do.*

I watch his approach, half
hypnotized by his confident
motion, not to mention
the way he can make me
believe that he really does
love me. But now that he's
close enough to look into
his eyes, the predator rises,
and I understand that I'm
in major trouble unless I
play this hand well. "I know
you love me, Bryn, and I
love you, too. I always will."

I take a small backward
step, and Bryn counters,
reaching out for me. "Stop."

*Stop? Oh, I can't stop now,
pretty Whitney. You're mine,
and that means I can do whatever
I please with you, whore.*

He Lunges at Me

I manage to sidestep, but
he's between me and the door,
no way out but past him.
"Please, Bryn. I won't bother
you again." I try to circle
him, but he lunges for me
again. This time he catches

> hold of my shirt, jerks and
> I am in his grasp. *I'll never*
> *let you go again. The first*
> *thing I'm going to do is fuck*
> *you dirty. I actually hate clean.*

He pushes me facedown
on the bed, ignoring my weak
plea to leave me alone. Just
as he starts to rip at my clothes,
there's pounding on the door.

> *What the fuck? Who is it?*
> Bryn yells, then he hisses
> at me, *Keep your mouth shut*
> *or I'll kick your ass, hear?*

> *Police. Open the door.*

"Help me!" I scream, ready
for Bryn's blows. Unbelievably,
he chooses defeat, backs away,
and I have, once again, been rescued.

I'll Never Forget

This Christmas Eve—the one
I spend in custody of the Kern
County Sheriff's Office
waiting for my parents to come
pick me up. Bryn was arrested,
charged with rape and kidnapping
with the intent of trafficking
a child under the age of seventeen.

With all the crazy commotion,
I managed to sneak the heroin
out of my purse and toss it
under a car in the parking lot
without being spotted. I swear
I will never touch that shit
again. This time I'll work
the programs, choose a sponsor,
quit relying on substances
to see me through tough times.

Probably. I hope. I have to.

The cops are nice. After all,
it's Christmas Eve and I'm a heisted
teenager who was on her way
to market. I don't confess
that I called the alleged broker,
invited his advances, though
surely my mom and dad suspect
that's the way it went down.
Neither do I ask how they found me.

My Parents Pick Me Up

The two, together, as if they
actually need each other to lean on.
So weird. After wading through
the paperwork, it's late afternoon
by the time we start the four-hour
drive home. The first sixty or
so miles are mostly silent. Finally,
I say, "I know you're pissed, and
I don't blame you. I'm really, truly
sorry. Guess I'm not fixed yet, but
I want to be, and I need your help."

> Now comes the barrage:
> *Who is he? Where did you meet*
> *him? When?* And most of all, *Why?*

I answer them fairly honestly,
right up until the last one
because I don't know why.
"I was really scared I'd never
see you again. I tried to get
away, but he was too strong.
Please, Mom. Please, Dad.
I want to get well, I want
to be normal, or something
close to it. I swear I'll work
hard to get there. But I can't
do it without your support."
Down drops the curtain
of silence again. We all
have some thinking to do.

A Poem by Eden Streit
I Don't Know Why

God smiled on me,
and sent him my way,
this uncomplicated
gentle man whose

love

threads my veins, pulses
within my heart, and
fortifies me, sustenance
for my hungry soul. Hope

flickers

within me, when not so
very long ago I was lost,
wandering the shadows,

a

weary traveler on a winding
track to nowhere.
But then, like the Magi,
I caught sight of a

star

to guide my way out
of the wintry desert,
toward meadows green
with spring, and planted

in

them, countless possibilities.
The sun rose within me,
light blossoming from

the darkness.

Eden
The Sun Rises

On this Christmas morning,
and the spirit of the day blooms
inside of me. I'm up at first light,
and waiting for Andrew, who
will pick me up at seven for

the very long drive—nine hours,
with luck—to Boise. I didn't want
to wait, once determination set
in. That and the message I truly
believe God delivered through

Andrew. I have to go home. Today.
With the proper paperwork already
in place, I'm safe enough from
my parents' grasp to risk an in-person
dialogue. I don't belong to them

anymore. When I called Sarah last
night to let her know I'm leaving
Walk Straight, she counseled me
to return, at least long enough to
appear in court on my scheduled date.

I promised I would, and asked
for sanctioned leave from my job
here until I can make it back.
A deal is a deal, and Andrew says
he can live with whatever it takes

to move us one step closer to
spending the rest of our lives
together. I glance down at my
left hand, as I've done dozens
of times in the few hours since

Andrew gave me his mother's
ring. The diamonds glimmer in
the muted early light. Can there
be a luckier girl in the whole
universe? Lucky. The word

makes me think about the girls
here, safely off the streets
this Christmas. A wave of sadness
splashes into me, for Shayleece,
forever sleeping in the ground,

and for the walking dead who
must spend today in backseats
and alleys and cheap motels,
servicing customers. If I could
help them, I would. Wait . . .

Maybe I can't do much to help
them now, but with the right
focus, I can one day. And with
sudden clarity I understand
what God is calling me to do.

Andrew Is Right on Time

It being Christmas, the girls
are allowed to sleep in, and
few are stirring as I pick up
my small bag and slip out
the door. He greets me with

> the sweetest kiss and his eyes
> shine with love when he says,
> *Merry Christmas, my lady.*
> *Ready to go?* Since I'm seated
> shotgun and belted in, the answer

should be obvious, but I agree,
"Ready as I'll ever be." I suffer
a bit of déjà vu riding in his
Tundra. It starts to fade several
miles in, but I expect it to resurface

in full force as we get closer to
Boise. The highway is mostly
deserted, and we make excellent
time, stopping only to eat and use
the restroom. We listen to music

and talk about the scenery, or lack
of it, and I tell Andrew that I've
decided to go into social work,
without mentioning the God factor.
That's between me and him.

At one point, Andrew starts
to look a little road weary.
"I wish I could help you
drive, but I don't know how.
Promise you'll teach me?"

He smiles. *I think you're old
enough, and out on the ranch
is the perfect place to learn.
Dad taught me to drive his
pickup when I was eleven.*

*Speaking of the ranch, Mom
and Mariah are expecting us
to stop by for dinner before
we go to your parents' house.
Hope that's okay with you.*

"I'll need fortification, and
I can't think of a better place
to find it. Thank you for sharing
your family with me. I wish
I had presents for them."

*Don't worry. I did a little Vegas
souvenir shopping. Fuzzy dice
for Mariah, who will probably burn
them, and for Mom, a photo of Elvis,
signed by the King himself, they said.*

That Makes Me Laugh

But when we get to the ranch,
I discover he wasn't kidding.
I'm pretty sure Elvis's signature
is a fake, especially since Andrew
tells me the picture only cost

five dollars. We bump up the long
dirt driveway, and now the déjà vu
slams into me like a semi. This
time of year, there's no alfalfa
to smell. The fields are winter-

bare and shimmer beneath a thin
layer of ice. But the memory of
that afternoon carries the green
scent with it, and nerves attack
in the same way—what will happen

next? I remember the feeling—
like standing at the very edge
of a cliff, the wind in my face—
knowing Andrew and I were about
to make love, each of us gifting

the other with our virginity.
I carried the beauty of that with
me through all the ugliness that
soon followed, and it's entrenched
in me now. "I love you, Andrew."

The words slip out so easily
and his reply comes as quickly.
*And I love you. But what was
that for?* He puts the Tundra
into park in front of the house.

"Nothing. Everything. Just
thinking about the last time
I was here. It's all I thought
about at Tears of Zion, and it's
the only reason I'm halfway sane."

Before he can respond, the front
door opens, and out bounds
a bluetick hound. "You're right.
She's not a puppy anymore."
Sheila sniffs around the truck,

looking for Andrew, who jumps
out to scratch her head hello.
When I exit the cab, her attention
shifts to me, and she comes over,
tail stump wagging recognition.

Now Andrew's mom and Mariah
materialize on the porch, signaling
to come inside, out of the cold.
Andrew takes my hand, and Sheila
leads the way into my soon-to-be home.

The Sense of Family

Is almost overwhelming,
everyone yammering happily
and simply expecting I will
join in because they accept
me as one of them already.

The house is as I remember
it—hardwood and leather,
refurbished antiques—only
prettified with the season's
decorations, including a tree

that touches the ceiling. We
gather in the kitchen, basking
in the oven's warmth, not to
mention its perfumes—prime
rib, sweet potatoes, and apple

pie. Andrew's mom comes
over, lifts my left hand. *I knew
it would fit you, don't ask me
how. It looks beautiful, too.
I'm so happy for you and Andrew.*

"I love it. Thank you. And thank
you for encouraging Andrew's faith
in me. I promise to make you proud
of me." Somehow, I believe her
when she says I already have.

I assume Andrew has told
everyone why I'm here, so I
don't go into it. In fact, I try
hard to avoid thinking about it
mid-celebration. Dinner is even

better than last night's five-star
Vegas experience, and that much
I do relate, along with the details
of my coming emancipation.
"My counselor is looking into

transferring jurisdiction to Idaho.
The requirements are similar—
school, the ability to support myself,
a place to live. I've got those in Vegas.
What I don't have there is Andrew."

> *Between the three of us, we've
> got plenty of connections here,*
> says Andrew's mom, who now
> insists I call her Victoria. *We'll
> work it out. Andrew needs you.*

> *She's right,* agrees Andrew.
> *I absolutely need you here
> close to me.* He takes my hand,
> infusing me with his strength.
> Good. I'm going to need it.

There Is Discussion

About whether to wait until
tomorrow to go to my parents',
but by the time we finish our
pie, I feel bolstered by the love
I've absorbed for the past three

hours. "Hopefully they'll have
a little Christmas spirit left
and will let me come in," I tell
Andrew on the way over.
He parks on the street in front

of the house that will never be
my home again, but when he starts
to get out, I stop him. "I know they
won't let *you* in. Last thing you
need is a trespassing charge."

> *Are you sure you want to do*
> *this alone?* There are lights on
> inside, and movement beyond
> the windows, and it would be
> easy, in this moment, to change

my mind. But then I think about
Eve, alone in the cold on this
Christmas night, and I discover
my courage again. "Just don't go
anywhere, in case I come running."

I Toss a Prayer

Toward heaven as I approach
the door, ring the bell. The weight
of the footsteps tells me Mama
will answer, and she does. "Hello,
Mama. Merry Christmas."

> She startles. *What are you doing
> here?* Then she notices Andrew's
> truck beneath the streetlight. *Of
> course. I should have guessed.*
> Papa moves into place behind her.

"May I come inside for a few
minutes, Mama? When I saw you
in Las Vegas, you never gave me
the chance to tell you about Tears
of Zion. There's stuff you should know."

> She starts to say no, but Papa
> rests his hand on her shoulder.
> *It's Christmas, Joan. Show some
> compassion. Maybe what she has
> to say is important.* Papa as the voice

of reason? Maybe Somebody's
whispering into his ear. For
whatever reason, my parents
step back, let me inside, where
it's even more sterile than I recall.

I start the conversation as if
they're totally ignorant of Samuel
Ruenhaven's tactics. "I'm not sure
how much of this you're aware of,
but . . ." I tell them everything,

watching their expressions change
from haughty to something like
horrified. I wait for Mama to call
me a liar. Instead, she shakes
her head slowly, disbelieving.

> *No. Samuel wouldn't approve*
> *of such things. He's a man of God.*
> *I've known him for years, or I'd*
> *never have sent you girls to him.*
> *You're wrong. You must be.*

"Mama. I was there." I let that
sink in. "And now Eve's there."
I start to tell her I'm planning to
talk to the Elko DA, but change
my mind. One call from Mama

to Tears of Zion, the place might
fold up and vanish into oblivion.
"Will you help me get her out
of there? Please?" They can't
possibly say no. Can they?

A Poem by Cody Bennett
Can't Say No

To my angel.
I'd give her the universe
if it was in my power,
and it would be

                                        nothing

compared to what
she's given me.
Whenever she's close
she makes me feel

                                        like

I can accomplish
anything, all she has
to do is offer a word
of encouragement.
The thought of losing

                                        her

sears hotter than
phantom bolts of pain,
those unappreciated
interruptions

                                        in

almost every one of
my days. But she swears
she'll stay, and that someday we'll travel

                                        the world

together, damn
the disability, and she
makes me believe it's true.

Cody
I Wonder How Many People

Take Christmas for granted.
Family. Friends. Decorations.
Gifts. Food. A little alcohol.

Always in the past I figured
there would be another Christmas.
Maybe even a better Christmas

than the one I was celebrating.
Mom was central to every holiday
gathering, and for most of my life,

my brother was there, too. In recent
memory, Jack looms large, singing
carols in his brilliant baritone,

and cracking ridiculous jokes that
never failed to make us laugh.
If someone would have told me last

year that Jack wouldn't be here today,
or that Cory would be fresh out of
lockup, while Mom toiled her butt

off at a miserable job just to make
ends meet, I would've called him a liar.
And if he'd insisted I'd soon gamble

away most of our money, then
try to earn it back by turning
tricks, often with men, I would

have spit in his face. And if he
somehow could have convinced
me the choices I'd make would

result in my becoming a T12
incomplete paraplegic, and
wheelchair-bound for the rest

of my life, I would've spiked
my eggnog with a lethal dose
of strychnine and happily taken

that long, dark walk into eternity
before having to witness any
of that, let alone accept the facts

of my future. Yet, here I am, alive
if not exactly kicking, and holding
my own in a staring match with

tomorrow. So, yeah, it's Christmas.
And if I can't have my legs back,
all I really want for it is Ronnie.

I Did Not Expect Her Early

Christmas is a day for family,
and I told her I'd be grateful
for any time she could spare.

She'll be here after dinner.
Mom shows up right before,
and she brings me a present.

Cory shuffles into the room,
eyes on the ground, and I know
he must be struggling with more

than the hospital stink. No, he
can't quite bring himself to look
at me. Fuck that. Get used to it.

"Cory! Dude! Jesus, you look like
shit. But I don't care. Come over
here and give me a hug, man."

I'm chilling in bed, on top of
the blankets because they keep
the temp hovering well over seventy

and I'm dressed to go to dinner.
As I use my hands to help my legs
swing over the bed, Cory chances

a glance, wincing as he watches
my well-rehearsed protocol. "What?
It took work to figure this out.

Now, if you don't come give me
a hug, I swear I'll flop out of bed,
onto the floor and crawl over to you."

> *No! Holy shit. I don't want to*
> *see that.* He looks ready to bolt.
> Instead, he takes a deep breath,

forces himself to cross the room.
His hug, however, is lukewarm.
"Hope you're not worried about

hurting me. In case you haven't
noticed, I'm almost bulletproof.
In fact, I'm immune to anything

except a real bullet." It's lame,
and Cory doesn't find it funny.
He backs away like I'm on fire.

> *Shut the fuck up. How can*
> *you joke about being so messed*
> *up?* He looks over at our mom

for support, but she just shrugs.
"Hey, Mom, can you let us talk
privately for a couple of minutes?"

I wait for her to clear the door
before I jump all over my little
brother. "Listen. What happened

to me sucks. But I'm mostly to blame
for the hand I was dealt, and now
I have no choice but to play it.

Actually, that's wrong. I could choose
to lie here feeling sorry for myself,
and I've done a fair amount of that already,

but it won't help Mom dig out of this
mess. She needs me, and she needs
you, so grow the fuck up now."

> He bristles, pulls himself straight
> and tall as he's able. But what comes
> out of his mouth is, *I'm scared.*

"*You're* scared? I'm scared, dude,
and pissed, too. I want to fuck
my girlfriend. I want to go skating.

Hell, I just want to stand up and
walk but that won't happen without
commitment. Will you help me try?"

> His expression morphs to horrified.
> *Me? Now? Don't you need, like,*
> *crutches or something?* That busts

me up. "No. In the future. Like maybe
after dinner? I'm kidding, Cory. I just
want to be able to count on you."

He Agrees

But it's hardly a foregone conclusion.
Still, it's a step (so to speak) in
the right direction. He and Mom walk

me to the dining room. "Sure you
won't stay? I hear it's turkey potpie,
and probably good. Cook's a genius."

> Mom shakes her head. *I promised*
> *Cory we'd go to Red Lobster.*
> *Saved up two paychecks, even.*

> > Cory responds to my "really?"
> > look. *Hey, they don't serve seafood*
> > *in jail, you know, except for some*

> > *fried supposed-to-be-shrimp.*
> > *So many times I got a craving*
> > *for that damn Ultimate Feast.*

> *It's the only thing he wanted for*
> *Christmas. But don't worry. He*
> *got socks and underwear, too.*

That makes us all laugh. Mom,
being a practical woman, always
put such necessities under the tree

so there were more gifts to unwrap
than the few toys she could afford.
I guess some things never change.

The Potpie Rocks

The leftover turkey finally got
the gravy it needed. The company
is fine, but I find myself wishing

I was at Red Lobster with Mom
and Cory. How long it will take her
to feel comfortable including me?

Oh, well. After dinner, some guys
are playing cards and invite me to join
them. I decline gently. Not only do

I need to leave any form of gambling
deep in my wake, but my girl will
be here any time, and nothing

is as important as being with her.
I wheel back to my room, anxious
to share time with her tonight.

It's a short wait, and she's a vision,
in a short red skirt and white angora
sweater. "Mm. You look yummy."

> I expect her to go gooey. Instead,
> she's all business, and excited.
> *We'll get to the kissing and stuff*
>
> *in a minute. But first, don't you
> want your present? Oh, almost
> forgot. Merry Christmas, Cody.*

Her Hands Are Empty

"Merry Christmas to you, but
I don't see any presents. Wait.
Are they under your clothes?"

> *Stop. No. Listen. You've never
> really asked about my parents.
> Like, who my dad is or anything.*

Hm. I guess I haven't. "Is he a serial
killer or president or a lion tamer?"
Oops. She's irritated. "Sorry. I'll shut up."

> *Good. You should. My father happens
> to be the CEO of a big gaming tech
> company. He also deals in investment*
>
> *properties, and has purchased quite
> a few short sales. I asked if he'd be
> interested in buying your mom's house*
>
> *and renting it back to her. He said
> he'd look into it, and as you know,
> I can be very persuasive.* She winks.

"You're serious." She is a bottomless
well of surprises. Emotions—relief,
joy, disbelief, and most of all, love—

upwell inside me. How can I possibly
be this lucky? I reach for her, thinking
Santa Claus must be real after all.

A Poem by Ginger Cordell
Santa Must Be Real

That's what my little
brother said when he saw
the tree this Christmas

morning.

How did Gram manage
it? Two presents for each
of us, not extravagant,
but for the love they came
wrapped in. The memory
of little Sandy's face

brings

joy, hours later.
I've forgotten the concept
of finding happiness
in little things. Coming
home makes everything

new

and I never want to leave,
though I know one day
I'll have to find a more
positive way out into
the bigger world, enticed by

possibilities.

Ginger
Home

The concept is still foreign,
though Gram's is the closest
I've come to a place I can always
return to. One thing's for sure.

I'll never go back to Las Vegas,
not even for "fun" because, though
most Sin City tourists either
don't know, or don't care, Vegas

fun is carried on the backs of people
who clean toilets or sweep streets
or turn tricks, not to get rich, but to
squeeze some semblance of living

from the fight to exist. Only CEOs
and pimps prosper, and sometimes
they are one and the same. No,
people go to Vegas in search

of dreams, but rarely notice
the living, breathing nightmares
right under their noses. Unless,
of course, that's what their dreams

consist of. It hurts to think about
the girls I've left behind there—Alex,
who'll probably never leave. And
Brielle, who'll move on without me.

Hard to Leave Love Behind

But there's plenty here,
surrounding me like a force
field. The kids love in the way
children do, with pure devotion.

When they asked where
I've been, I detoured around
everything prior to House
of Hope, and told them

I've been living with some
girls who were in need of
help, which was one hundred
percent accurate. I failed

to mention the fact that
I was one of those girls,
or exactly what kind of
help we needed. Only

Mary Ann is old enough
to understand there were
words to be read between
the lines. Before, I would

have believed she was too
young to hear my story.
But now I see the importance
of telling her everything,

so she'll understand what's
at stake within the realm
of choices—those we make,
and those others try to take

from us, especially as young
women. I want her to be
informed, so she can make
smart decisions. I also want

her to be afraid, or at least
cautious. There are predators
everywhere, and sometimes
they look totally harmless.

And there are people who
offer up prey to feed those
carnivores—people like
Miranda's brother, Ricardo,

who traded in his sister on
his dope debt. People like our
mother, who I'm struggling
to find compassion for.

When I got home yesterday,
my prodigal return caused
way too much commotion
to even consider attempting

some sort of conversation
with Iris. She was in the living
room, sitting in the old recliner,
specter-pale and quivering

as she watched an old black-
and-white holiday movie on TV.
She squinted at me when I came
in, managed a little wave,

and I acknowledged that with
a curt nod before taking my stuff
into the bedroom I'll share again
with the girls. Nothing has changed

while I was gone except the art,
hung with Scotch tape, proof
of Honey's and Pepper's slight
improvement as watercolorists.

The kids swirled around me,
then jumped on the beds,
chattering like monkeys, and
the noise and sharp motion

was almost too much. I flopped
down anyway, absorbing
their energy, and tried to remember
being that young, if I ever was.

Yesterday's Homecoming

Is something I'll always remember.
Dinner was Gram's enchiladas,
and afterward the kids brought out
their surprises—tie-dyed T-shirts,

one short-sleeved, in orange, yellow,
and red, the other long, in turquoise
and purple. "Wow! These are amazing,"
I gushed, and though I'd never in a million

years pick them out in a store, I'll wear
them and make them look good.
Then we watched *A Christmas Story*
and *Elf* on TV, until Gram finally said

enough and insisted the young ones go
to bed or Santa wouldn't come. Iris sat
in the same chair, droopy-eyed, sharing
space but not the experience, and I couldn't

help but steal glances. She is dying.
I've never been this close to death.
I can feel it, hovering near, waiting
to tap her on the shoulder. She'll

survive this Christmas Day, probably
even see the New Year, but not
a lot of it. She deserves pity.
But is she worthy of forgiveness?

The Kids Are All in the Kitchen

Baking and decorating Christmas
cookies with Gram. Iris is in her
usual place, quietly drinking wine.
I sit on the corner of the sofa

> closest to her, and she looks at
> me with inquisitive eyes. *Glad*
> *you came home. We missed you*
> *around here. 'Specially Mary Ann.*

> *An' now I can't work, would*
> *be good for you to. Your gram*
> *could use some help paying*
> *the bills. Lots of bills. Too many.*

How much do I say? Is now
even the right time? Screw it.
"Do you know why I left, Iris?"
Something changes in her eyes,

> which seem to shroud black.
> *I think I know,* she snarls. *What*
> *do you want from me? An apology?*
> At least she doesn't deny it. *Because . . .*

> Now the dark veil lifts and tears
> trickle. *Goddamn it, I'm sorry.*
> *So fucking sorry. I'm a crap mother*
> *and always have been, and now*

it's too late to fix it. I really wish
I could, but I can't take any of it
back, and I'm just so goddamn sorry.
I wasted my life. I could've been

somebody. But here's the thing. . . .
She wipes the snot dripping from
her nose with the back of her hand.
You can still be somebody. I won't

be here to see it, and that makes
me sad. Listen to me, Ginger girl.
The past will influence your future,
but it doesn't have to destroy it.

Holy shit. Iris as philosopher?
I hand her a box of tissues, refill
her glass from the bottle on the end
table. "Merry Christmas, Iris. I need

a cookie." I don't know if that was
enough to help me forgive her. Maybe,
with time, and that's more than I could
have said only five minutes ago.

A Poem by Seth Parnell
With Time

He'll forgive me,
that's what I kept telling
myself, repeating it in
my head like a mantra. With

                          time

he'll come to accept
me for who I am,
the way I was born,
how the good Lord
exactly created me. Dad

                          was

only forty-eight, not old
enough for his heart
to fail in such spectacular
fashion. This event was

                          not

in my game plan. How
on God's good green earth
could he just up and die

                          on

me? Why couldn't
he hold on a couple more
hours? I was almost there,
Dad, and we could have said

                          our

goodbyes. My Christmas
dinner: a heaping plate
of sadness with a giant bowl
of regret on the

                          side.

Seth
Empty

The fields are empty. Dad managed
to harvest the corn before he got sick.

Aunt Kate says it was a good crop
this year, and that gives me a lick

of pride. Lick. Yeah. I figure I'll go
ahead and indulge the Indiana farm

boy in me by de-culturing his voice
for a while. It's damn cold today,

Christmas Day, but I'm walking
the Parnell land in a big old down

jacket, stocking cap, and winter-weight
gloves, all of them Dad's. I inhale

the scent of him clinging to his clothes,
exhale streams of warm breath into

the snow-frosted air. Our hunting
hound, Ralph, stays close by my side.

Aunt Kate brought him to her place
when Dad went into the hospital,

and when we got there last night,
Ralph practically knocked me over,

he was so happy to see me. I reach
down and stroke his head now.

"At least someone around here missed
me. What are we going to do with you

when I go back to Vegas?" It won't
be for a while. The funeral is set

for next week, and then there's legal
stuff to deal with. Dad didn't have

a whole lot, just the farm and equipment,
a decent Ford truck, and a small bank

account. Aunt Kate says she hasn't seen
Dad's will, but she's sure he left everything

to me. Ralph and I circle around to
the barn. Dad kept a few chickens

and they're all inside, along with
Matilda and Jane, the goats who manage

weed control. Aunt Kate's been feeding
them, but she lives in town, fifteen minutes

away, so I told her I'd care for the critters
while I'm here. I toss hay to the goats

and scratch to the chickens, just like
when I was a kid. Nostalgia hits hard,

carried in the perfume of oats and seed,
motor oil and manure; and in the cluck

of hens and the munching of the nannies
and the creak of old rafters in the wind.

It presses me down to the ground, where
I sit, surrounded by ghosts. "Why?"

It escapes, a wail of mourning. "How
could you die and leave me without

a friendly word between us? Damn
you, Dad!" Ralph creeps over, lays

his head in my lap, telling me I'm not
totally alone, here in the barn, here on

my farm, here where I worked and played
and hid from myself. Here at home.

All the fear and rage I've kept bottled
inside spills out of me now in a flood

of tears. "Why, Ralph? Why did I wait
so long to come home? I could have

made him listen. Could have made him
change his mind, and now I'll never

get the chance. I should have tried
harder!" I give myself permission

to cry for a good, long time. Once
I'm mostly finished, I get to my feet.

"Come on, Ralph, let's go." He follows
me to the house, and that is empty,

too. Not of furnishings—those are all
here, exactly the way they were the day

Dad sent me away. I'm slightly gratified
to see he didn't change my room.

There are dishes in the sink. I wash them,
put them away in their proper place in

the cupboard. After Mom died, Dad and I
made sure to keep her kitchen organized

the way she liked it, in her honor. I pay
tribute in the same way now, neatening

the house and making Dad's bed,
which I've never seen tousled before.

Dirty Dishes and an Unmade Bed

Dad must have been feeling really
bad to leave the place like this.

And what will I do with it now?
I click the heat lower. I'll be back

later, but I'm supposed to share
Christmas dinner with Aunt Kate

and the clan. I load Ralph into Dad's
Ford, drive slowly along the vacant

road, the route to town so familiar
I can drive it with my eyes closed,

as Dad used to say. Damn. I miss it,
and I also miss the family gathered

at Aunt Kate's—cousins and in-laws,
and little kids, laughing and arguing

and jostling around. Everyone seems
welcoming, either because they don't

know or care I'm gay, or maybe they
just feel sorry for me. Doesn't matter.

They suck me right into the midst
of them, and today that is necessary.

In Honor of Dad

Aunt Kate chose to roast a huge prime
rib. It was his absolute favorite. She's even

fixed it just the way he liked, with a rock
salt and cracked peppercorn coating. As it

finishes, filling the house with its heavenly
scent, the men find a game to watch while

the women play a rousing game of euchre
and the kids entertain themselves. When Kate

goes to check the meat's progress, I follow
her into the oven warmth and quiet.

"Can I help with anything?" I ask, watching
her set the roasting pan on the granite

> countertop. *I think I've got things under
> control, thanks.* She turns toward me,

> grinning. *You know, considering how much
> you always liked to cook with your dad,*

> *I kind of thought you might wind up a chef
> in some fancy restaurant or something.*

"I've actually been considering culinary
school. But now . . ." I think about the farm—

about the sparring emotions coming home
initiated. Home. I'm here. But can I stay?

"Aunt Kate? Did Dad tell you why I left?
I mean, did he tell you . . . about me?"

> She inserts a digital thermometer into
> the heart of the prime rib. *About you?*

Not sure if she's distracted or acting
coy. But I have to know. "Did Dad tell

you he kicked me out because I quote-
unquote chose the path to damnation?"

I thought I was cried out, but I was wrong.
The room sways slightly. "Did he tell you

he wouldn't talk to me or let me come
home until I decided I'm not . . . not . . ."

> *Gay?* She turns to face me. *No, Seth.*
> *Bud didn't tell me. He was a private*
>
> *man and held everything close. But I*
> *knew. I've known for a very long time.*

I want to talk more, but now we hear
a volley of rapid-fire questions beyond

the door: *How's that meat coming?*
Are we going to eat soon? Should

someone set the table? Did Kate
make eggnog? Hey. Where did Seth go?

I'll finish the conversation with
a question of my own. "If you can

accept me, why couldn't Dad?
Now we'll never get the chance—"

Oh, there you are! Uncle Dan comes
looking for us. *Everything okay?*

Just fine, says Aunt Kate. *The meat's*
resting for ten, then I'll ask you to carve.

Sure thing. Smells mighty fine. I'll go
let everyone know it's almost time.

Kate waits till he's gone. *Try not to fret.*
I've got something for you later. Now, here.

She hands me a platter of baked potatoes,
and I carry them to the dining room table.

I don't care if I look like I've been crying.
A dead dad at Christmas gives me the right.

After Dinner

Aunt Kate pulls me down the hall,
into her room. She lifts an envelope

*off her dresser. I picked up Bud's stuff
from the hospital, and this was in it.*

*I'm not sure when he found the time
or energy. I'll leave you alone with it.*

It's a note to me from Dad, written
in a shaky hand, barely legible.

*Dear Seth, I wish I could say this face-to-face,
but I don't think I'm gonna make it. I wouldn't*

*mind dying so much except for a couple of things.
One is the farm. Without you there, I'm scared*

*of what will become of it. I don't want it to fall
into bad hands. See to it that doesn't happen.*

*The other is you, son. I'm a stubborn fool, and
I let my pride get in the way of loving you without*

*conditions, as God would have me do. Please forgive
me, and I pray the Lord forgives me, too. Just know,*

*despite the harsh words, I never stopped loving you,
though it took this to see it. I promise, if God allows,*

*I'll always stay close to you. All my worldly
possessions belong to you now, including this:*

It's the Recipe for Venison Sausage

Guess Dad approves of my culinary
ambitions. I reread the note ten or twelve

times, etching his words into my heart.
I need time to think. I call for Ralph,

bid adieu to the family. Snowflakes dance
in the headlights as we maneuver the icy

road to the farm. Home. Suddenly, I understand
I can't go back to Vegas. Not sure I'm cut

out to be a full-time farmer. But maybe
I can hire outside help, keep the old place

in good hands. I still want to go to school,
but I bet I can find a good program in

Louisville and commute. Memories, good
and bad, linger in that city, but that's where

I first found my community, and I can always
tap into that there. Community leads me to

Pippa, who I adore, and Micah, whom I love.
Neither belongs in rural Indiana, but maybe

I can convince them to give Louisville a try.
If not, I'll weather the loss and move on.

A Poem by Whitney Lang
Move On

I want to. I really do want
to turn my back on yesterday,
leapfrog today, into

tomorrow,

but how is that possible,
tethered by fear? People keep
asking what I'm frightened
of. The real question

is

what doesn't trouble me?
I'm scared I can't escape
the legacy of turning tricks,
that too much filth and

too

little affection will forever
define my relationships.
I'm afraid I've deviated so

far

from decency that I'll never
again deserve respect,
let alone a full measure
of love, and keep pushing it

away.

I'm terrified that faces
will float from the past,
into the present, and there
will be no place to hide.

Whitney
Top to Bottom

Left to right, the Lang family
totally defines dysfunction. I mean,
after everything that happened
yesterday, the sun rises and everyone
pretends it's just another Christmas.

Mom wanted to drive me straight
back to rehab, but I managed to persuade
her to bring me home, and let me mend
my mind via outpatient therapy.
I built a strong three-pronged argument.
One: I need to rely on my family
to follow through with treatment.
Two: Inpatient care costs a whole
lot more. And three: They'd be closed
for Christmas anyway.

Okay, the last one is weak, but
the other two swayed her, or maybe
it was her feeling guilty about Kyra
unwrapping presents while I was locked
away. So home we came, and with a stop
for dinner, we arrived before Santa.
Lang tradition dictates no presents go
under the tree until Christmas Eve,
which made sense when Kyra and
I were little. Not so much after
we knew what was what, but Mom
has always insisted on it anyway.

So this morning we wake up,
grab coffee, and collect ourselves
at the tree, where someone-not-Santa
has deposited presents sometime
between midnight and dawn.
Quaint tradition, but it put a strange
slant to the big picture. Whatever.
I'll just try to embrace the weirdness.

I don't have presents for anyone,
and truthfully, I am surprised to
find gifts for me. As usual, Mom
gives Kyra and me clothes. She loves
to shop, and building our wardrobes
gives her pleasure. I don't think she realizes
how much weight I've lost. She's bought
me last year's size six, and everything
from jeans to sweaters will be baggy.
That's fine. I'm not into "tight" at
the moment, and won't be for a while.

From Dad, an iPad for each of us,
and a Mac Air for Mom. He's all
about Apple, from his phone to
his computer, and probably gets
volume discounts. Kyra gives me
a purse. Coach, of course, maroon
leather, and way too big. It will
swallow the few things I carry.

After the Whole Gifting Thing

The four of us, yes, including Dad,
go to work on dinner. I can't
remember *ever* doing something
as family-wholesome as that.
Mom assigns jobs. Kyra, of course,
is responsible for the plum pudding.
Dad volunteers to do the pumpkin
pie, which only scares me a little.
And, no surprise, I get to do
the gingerbread while Mom takes
charge of everything else.

The kitchen feels claustrophobic,
and a few seconds of panic set
in. But when I try to explain,
rather than let me get some fresh
air, Mom is adamant that I stay.

> Sit at the table and take deep
> breaths. We're doing this as
> a cohesive unit. I realize that's
> new for us all, but I can't see
> another way to keep us together,
> and I refuse to let us fall apart.

I have no idea what's gotten into
her, except maybe it has everything
to do with almost losing me, not
once, but twice. Turns out, she had
GPS tracking installed on my phone.
Just in case. And that proved provident.

That Information

Was passed down on our trip
home last night, when I asked
how the cops knew where to find me.

> *You didn't think we'd take*
> *a chance on you disappearing*
> *again, did you?* Mom asked.

> *You do realize technology*
> *makes tracking people relatively*
> *easy these days?* interjected Dad.

So then they gave me the lowdown
on GPS tracking, and made it very
clear that if they are paying my cell phone
bill, I can expect they will know
where I am anytime they need to.

But there's more to this story,
the surprising plot twist if this were
a novel. Mom shared this part on the way
home, too. I haven't as yet approached
Kyra, asked about motive. I'll wait until
her plum pudding is steaming.

Who knew that's how you make plum
pudding? Who knew the absolute best
plum pudding begins a year in advance?
She only started a couple of days ago,
so tonight's will be decent. Then, I bet,
she'll go straight to work on next
Christmas's, and it will be perfect.

Of Course It Will

Because Kyra will make damn
sure to improve. That's my sister.
As this part of the story goes,
she was putting together the fruits,
spices, and cognac that went into
her plum pudding when Mom
dropped me off at the mall,
where Bryn lay in waiting
like the predator he is.

She was missing an ingredient
and wanted to call Mom to pick
it up, but her phone was dead,
and she'd left her charger back
at school, so she went into my
room to look for mine.

I guess I'd dropped Bryn's business
card on the floor the night I found
it in my pocket. Kyra discovered
it, and something about the Perfect
Poses Photography logo sparked.
When Mom couldn't find me at
the mall, it clicked into place and
was an important piece of the puzzle
when Mom reported me missing.

With the pudding steaming nicely,
she excuses herself and goes into
the other room. I follow. "Kyra?
Can I talk to you for a minute?"

She flops on the sofa, signals
for me to join her. *Guess so.*

"Why did you show Mom Bryn's
card? You didn't have to, and I'd
be back in Vegas, out of your hair."

*She squints, and her forehead
creases. What? Like I wouldn't
show it to her? Whitney, you piss
me off regularly, and there are
things about you I don't get at
all. This last little "adventure,"
for instance. Just . . . why? You've
got so much potential. Why are
you so intent on throwing it away?*

"I . . . I don't know. I guess
I never thought anyone cared."

*We all care! Look, just because
none of us is the huggy-kissy type
doesn't mean we don't love you.
Do you really believe I'd rather
you were back in Las Vegas?*

I can only respond with a shrug.

*Kyra is quiet for a moment.
Looks like we've got to work
on some relationship building.*

It's an Acknowledgment

And it's a start. I'm thinking long
and hard about the roles I've played
within my failed relationships.
My family has been fractured
for a while. The support I've received
lately is the most I've had from Mom
and Dad since I was a little kid,
before their partnership ruptured.
That they're trying to repair it now
is largely because of me, so maybe
I can be a catalyst for good there.
Or maybe they'll fail at it again.

Kyra? When we were little, I looked
up to her, but she outshone me in
every way, and after a while it got
old taking the backseat to her well-
earned accomplishments. I chose
silent resentment in favor of expressing
my feelings, and that was a mistake.

Lucas was never a real relationship
at all. I clung to the idea that he cared
about me, though he was nothing but
all out for himself. Good riddance.

And now, James. If there's the slimmest
chance for us, it will be rooted in honesty.
I want to try if he does. I need someone
wonderful in my life, and guess what.
He's calling me right this minute.

A Poem by Eden Streit

Someone Wonderful

Is in love with me.
He's my light, my warmth,
my bread and water.
How did I make it
through even one day

                                without

him? Someone wonderful
promises to spend the rest
of his days by my side.
People will say we're too
young to experience undying

                                love

that time will agree.
But the bond between
our hearts is steel, unbreakable,
and with proper care, won't rust.
One day he and I will explore

                                the world

hand in hand, and maybe
little hands will join ours.
Someone wonderful
gives me hope for the future
and without him my life

                                is colorless.

Eden
Mama and Papa Listen

To my Tears of Zion exposé.
I'm not sure they really believe
me, but at least they don't send
me away. They haven't as yet
agreed to remove Eve from

Ruenhaven's grasp. What else
can I say to convince them
she's in evil hands? "May I ask
you something? What did Father
tell you about how I left?"

> As always, it's Mama who
> answers. *He said, like your sister's*
> *namesake, you listened to*
> *the serpent. That you seduced*
> *that man, who was weak of spirit.*

"No. He seduced me, with food
and soap. And I wasn't the first
girl he'd coerced in that way.
When you're starving, you'll do
anything for a piece of fruit.

Eve is hungry right now, Mama.
I don't know if Jerome is back,
or if there are others like him,
but whatever she did, this is not
a proper punishment for it."

She jumps on the defensive.
What she did *was emulate* you.
You ought to be ashamed of
yourself for encouraging her
immodest behavior. Just look

at you now, in fact. I knew
you'd figure a way to get back
together with that person
out there. Why . . . why . . .
It's a regular abomination.

It's no wonder you ended up
on the streets in that hideous
city. It was God's chastisement.
You can't circumvent his laws
and expect anything less.

Slapped down. I remember
this feeling so well, like I
could never deserve God's
mercy. I look her straight in
the eye. "Return to the scriptures,

Mama. 'If we confess our sins,
he is faithful and just to forgive
us our sins, and to cleanse us
from all unrighteousness.' God
has forgiven me. Why can't you?"

Tough Question

One she's having a hard time
answering. While she thinks
about it, I go to the door,
wave to Andrew for him to
join me. Might as well get

> to the meat of things. When
> Mama starts to sputter, Papa
> actually quiets her. Curiosity?
> Guilt? Some tiny hint of love?
> *Leave her be. She deserves to*
> *have her say, and so does the boy.*

As Andrew speeds up the walk,
no doubt worried that I'm knee-
deep in trouble, it occurs to me
that Papa rarely dared to disagree
with Mama in the past. Has he

grown tired of her domineering
attitude? Has my command of
scripture swayed him? Does he
hear the truth of my words?
Does he, maybe, miss having

his children in his household,
and sincerely regret he didn't
stand up for us sooner? I'd like
to think all of the above hold true.
I'd like to believe my papa loves me.

Whoa

Sobering thought, because
it doesn't include Mama. Would
I like to believe my mama loves
me, too? On some deep personal
level, I really don't care anymore.

>Andrew crosses the threshold,
>and as he does, I vow my children
>will never doubt their mother's
>love. *Are you okay?* he asks,
>concern obvious in his voice.

"Absolutely. I just don't want
to break our news to them without
you beside me." I twine my fingers
into his, squeeze hard, and tug
him toward the living room.

Mama's hackles rise noticeably,
and I try to lower them first.
"Do you know what thought
just crossed my mind, Mama?
That I don't believe you love me,

and to be honest, I wonder if you
ever did. I think you're afraid
of love, and that makes me sad.
Because love is *of* God, not in
spite of him. And you're wrong.

My love for Andrew is not
an abomination. It's real, and
beautiful, and so, of God. Look . . ."
I extend my left hand. "Despite
all that's happened, and Andrew

knows everything, he wants to
marry me. Yes, we're young, but
you were only a couple of years
older when you married Papa.
I wish . . ." A giant knot forms

in my throat, and I can't finish,
so Andrew tries. *I know it's hard
for you to believe this, but when
I first met Eden, I'd never been
in love before. And do you know*

*what made me love her almost
immediately? First, her incredible
spirit, which could only be born
of God. And second, her respect
for Creation, which had to come*

*from you. I'm sorry ego came
into play last year—both mine
and yours. Mine, because yes,
I wanted her to love me. And
yours, for much the same reason.*

Double Whoa

Forward momentum at full
throttle, I do my best to swallow
the lump in my throat. "Without
your permission, we can't get
married until I turn eighteen,

despite the emancipation.
It's only a year, and we don't
mind a long engagement, but
I don't want to spend it in Las
Vegas. Andrew and I plan to

live here in Boise. This is our
home. I hope we can maintain
a civil relationship with you, and
I'd very much like to stay in close
contact with Eve. I really wish

you can find room in your hearts
for me, but if not, I'll work through
it. Either way, please, please find
room there for Eve. She deserves
parents who will show her love."

Mama sits, speechless, eyes cast
toward the floor. Papa looks a bit
shell-shocked. "Come on, Andrew,
we should go. Merry Christmas,
Mama. Merry Christmas, Papa."

It's a Picture-Perfect Christmas Night

Crisp and clear, with myriad
stars sequinning the black velvet
sky. I beam a silent thank-you
in that direction. I'm not sure
how much we accomplished,

> but it could have gone worse,
> and as we left Papa said,
> *You've given us a lot to think
> about.* At least one of them
> heard us. I hope we used all

the right words. Andrew slides
his arm around my shoulders,
snugs me tightly against him
as we walk to the Tundra.
"I'll still need to go to Elko."

> *I figured as much. I'm on semester
> break for another week. We'll go
> in a day or two. Everything will
> be okay, Eden. I promise. Hey,
> have I told you lately I love you?*

"Andrew, you just told my parents
you love me." We stop beneath
a streetlight, where anyone can see.
And this time when he kisses me,
I know without a doubt I'm home.

Author's Note

I first became interested in the subject of Domestic Minor Sex Trafficking (DMST) when I came across the statistic that the average age of young women introduced into prostitution is twelve. This was in 2007, just as the widespread problem of child sex trafficking was becoming news. I spent the next year researching and writing *Tricks*, which introduces five teen characters from different parts of the country, all of whom, for very different reasons, end up turning tricks in Las Vegas.

All five lived on in the minds of readers, and eventually a sequel was called for, as the characters' fates were still undecided at the end of the book. While *Traffick* provides those answers, it also introduces readers to other DMST victims, some of whom become survivors, and others who don't. All these characters are inspired by very real people, living very real lives as DMST victims. We have become much more aware of the problem in the last decade, and awareness is the beginning of change.

With new federal guidelines in place, the penalties for DMST pandering have greatly increased. Trafficking children under the age of fourteen now carries a mandatory life sentence in many states, including Nevada. However, DMST will continue as long as there is a market. Education is paramount, as is intervention by law enforcement and great organizations like Children of the Night, GEMS: Girls Educational and Mentoring Services, and other rescue services. Help is available.

You can find a service provider in your area by calling the National Human Trafficking and Smuggling Center at 888-373-7888.

Or, report suspected child prostitution activity to the National Center for Missing & Exploited Children at 800-THE-LOST or cybertipline.com.

According to the National Human Trafficking and Smuggling Center:

- Human trafficking is the exploitation of a person for the purposes of forced labor or commercial sex, regardless of citizenship or nationality. Despite the connotation of the word, "trafficking" doesn't always indicate movement between cities.
- Sex trafficking is when a commercial sex act is induced by force, fraud, or coercion, or whenever the person induced to perform such an act has not attained eighteen years of age.
- Trafficking happens to US citizens, within the borders of this country, and in every state.
- The average age of a child introduced to DMST is twelve.
- Daily in the United States between 150,000 and 300,000 children under eighteen are trafficked.
- Up to 30 percent of DMST victims are boys, including straight, gay, and transgendered youth.
- More than 70 percent of homeless youth living on the streets turn tricks to survive.
- Victims of DMST don't always self-identify as victims. Often they believe they don't deserve a better life, or that their pimps truly love them and this is a small price to pay for that love.